Greg Weston lives in the sleepy little town of Felixstowe, on the East Anglian coast. He lives with his wife Julie and with Emily and Jack. He works as an accountant (which means he counts other people's money for them) rather than a children's author, but he does hope this won't be an isolated adventure into the world of writing... it has been fun.

This is Greg's second children's book. The first, Ocean View Terrace, was published in 2005 and was written about Emily and based in his home town of Felixstowe.

Of course, this book is based in a place somewhat further away! He does hope you enjoy this rather unusual story.

Greg Weston

The Man Upstairs

Have you ever looked up at the stars at night and wondered
just what's out there, far beyond space?...

First published in 2007 by

Lulu

www.lulu.com

ISBN: 978-1-84799-957-3

Cover design by Emily Weston and Greg Weston

For more information: lulu.com/gregweston

Chapter 1
The Gift...

Downstairs
Galaxy ref: P5763EARTH
Grid: UK729~Ami16

The table was strewn with leftovers. It looked like a bomb had hit it. But I was more interested in the last piece of Christmas pudding. What were my chances, I wondered? Gramps looked stuffed, Mum and Agnes's mum were ladies so they would never be seen dead scoffing the last piece, and Agnes... well she was just plain ugly. The odds were definitely in my favour. I glanced down the table at Dad, with the wonky paper hat, just filling the brandy glass again.

"Of course, when you were in the army, paps..."

Oh no, this was a very bad sign. Gramps was about to launch into another war story. This is where things got tricky. Was the last piece of Christmas pudding really worth enduring a war story? It was a tough one. Question was, how long would it last? Gramps had been known to settle in for the night. Many a perfectly good evening had been thrown away with the stories of crawling through swamps in distant lands or hacking through the jungles of Burma. It was OK I guess, but it got a bit tedious on the hundredth telling. I glanced around the table again. It was one of those typical Christmas day lunches which started on time but seemed to drift past three o'clock and then, before you know it, the evening has come and gone. The food had defeated everyone. It could have been a flock of beached whales sitting round the table by the look of it... Flock? Not sure whales flock. All except Missus Agnes that is (that's what I call ugly girl's mum)... she's so wafer thin she makes the coat stand look obese. It was no use; I abandoned the pudding idea and climbed down from the table.

It's not that Gramps couldn't tell 'em. He was the best. It was just... well... my dad. Everything he talked about was the army. No, that was an understatement; he was obsessed.

"Never make anything out of you at school, Monty! You just ain't got the brains boy! No, it's the army for you, me lad. Put some discipline into yah." That's what he always said. Charming isn't it? Those words, often repeated, haunted me. My future all planned out with depressing finality. I was even named after a war hero... Montgomery. I ask you, who names there kid Montgomery? Come off it, you just don't do that sort of thing if you want them to survive high school.

With these depressing thoughts I wandered through to the Christmas tree room to make a closer examination of my presents. It had to be said, it was an impressive looking pile.

Dad was never actually in the army himself. He's a double glazing salesman. It was a bit of a sad story but he went off to join the army once, a couple of years back, in a fit of misguided madness. He rolled back in again that evening rather more sober and, after much cajoling, whispered that they had said he was too old. He had mopped around upset for days, until he had bagged his next big double glazing order, and won the salesman of the month award, which meant he got to wear a rather large plastic badge in the shape of a sunflower with a smile on the front. No, I don't see the attraction either.

I always thought Christmas was a bit of an anticlimax after dinner. All the presents you've wondered about for months are open and the mystery's gone. The grownups are sleeping off lunch and what do you do now?

Agnes wandered in behind me, worst luck. There was just nowhere in this house you could get any peace!

"Shove off ugly," I said. OK, I know what you're thinking. I'm not the most subtle kid on the block. And I guess she ain't that ugly, if you squint a bit when you look at her. She has very curly ginger hair... almost frizzy... a tonne of freckles and thick glasses, not to mention the monster teeth. But then every girl looks ugly when you're eleven. She was just annoying me. Ugly and Missus Agnes lived next door and Mum had invited them for Christmas. What was even worse, they had slept over at ours the last three nights. I mean, seriously, what is the point when you live next door? And who has to vacate their room? Muggins here... me! What really worried me was school. If anyone caught on that she had been staying at mine, I'd have hell to pay.

Ugly was giving me a hard stare.

"At least I'm not named after a fish!" she retorted rather tartly, hands on hips, and stormed out of the room.

She had a point. If Montgomery wasn't bad enough, Montgomery Pilchard really had to be classed as a bad start in life. I hated my name. To my mates I was just called, Fish.

Our front room in Cornhill Rise was not a large one and had been invaded by the most enormous Christmas tree (Mum insisted on the largest real one, which Dad could stagger through the door with). Opening presents had proved interesting since we had all squeezed into the front room, which would have strained to hold us all anyway, and we then had to fight through the undergrowth to find the presents. It was nice to be alone for a few minutes in the cramped little house. Away from war stories, invading neighbours and Dad commenting on my poor school record. I dived for my present pile. It was a combination of playstation games, chocolate and socks. And of course, most importantly a rather large pile of football card packets. I hadn't opened them yet, so I started ripping them open. I knew all the remaining ones I needed off by heart. There were a few useful ones, which I crossed off my mental list. I still didn't have Ferdinand, but I had it on good authority that Charlie's brother had a mate who had a spare. But more concerning was Alan Smith. He was the rare card which no-one seemed to have. There was always one.

It was then that I noticed it. One last present hidden under the branches of the tree. I reached in and pulled it out.

"What's that?" asked Agnes, obviously still hanging around the door frame.

"I don't know," I replied.

It was a flat box like present, wrapped in sparkling emerald green paper. I could have sworn it hadn't been there before lunch.

"What does the gift tag say," Agnes pushed.

I pulled the tag towards me and turned it over. *"To Fish. Happy Christmas! Hope you enjoy the enclosed (but do be careful with it). From the man upstairs."*

"What?" said Agnes, screwing up her face. "Who's the man upstairs?"

Strange. Very strange. No-one called me Fish except my mates at school. And we certainly didn't have any strange men living upstairs. My eyes narrowed. This was some sort of joke. I pulled off the ribbon and paper. It was a box of chocolates. I was a bit disappointed. I liked chocolate; it was just that I had already eaten enough chocolate before dinner to sink a small aircraft carrier. But a closer inspection showed that this was no ordinary box of chocolates. It was one of those large flat gift boxes with a lift off lid which had a rather sickly nice picture of a view from a mountain on it. Agnes pointed and my eyes noticed the sticker on the corner of the picture. It said...

"PUBLIC HEALTH WARNING!

These chocolates may seriously damage your health. Used at owner's risk. The manufacturer takes no responsibility for adverse side effects."

"That's stupid," protested Agnes. "It's a box of chocolates!"

But I already had my suspicions. This was my mate Charlie having a laugh. He had probably injected poison or laxative into each of the chocolates. I toyed with the idea of feeding one to Agnes first but thought better of it. I pulled the lid off to have a closer inspection. There really was something weird here. The chocolates were not the normal brown blobs you get in most boxes, no, they were all strange shapes and sizes, and had intricate patterns on. It almost looked like writing. A rich cocoa smell rose from the open box, almost inviting you to eat one, and the surface of the sweets seemed to sparkle. This was no ordinary box of chocolates. A piece of gold paper had fallen out as I opened the box. I picked it up and unfolded it. It was the standard insert explaining all the chocolate fillings. The name of each chocolate was written in fine gold lettering below each picture. I glanced at the box. There was one shaped in a large Celtic style cross. *"The Queen's hero,"* announced the gold lettering. Well what use was that to tell you what it tasted like? More and more I was getting the eerie feeling this wasn't one of Charlie's jokes. I had never seen chocolates like it... the strange shapes and patterns. And the smell was so luscious; it tempted you to dive in. Charlie wouldn't have been able to come up with this. He would have had to make each chocolate himself. It really was a very strange present.

"What's that one?" asked Agnes. Stretching all along the top of the box was one long thin wavy chocolate. It was white chocolate with light brown truffly bits in it. I located it on the insert.

"Dream warrior."

"I don't get it?"

I looked again at the box. On the bottom right was a perfectly formed replica of an elephant, in dark, almost black chocolate. I glanced at the gold insert. *"African rescue."*

"You gonna eat one?" Agnes asked.

"Er... No. You want one?" I asked.

Agnes frowned. "I don't think so," she said uncertainty.

I wandered upstairs with my box of strange chocolates. Looking back, there's no doubt I should have binned them there and then. I could never have imagined then all the problems they were gonna cause me. But I didn't, and so my story begins. It is a very strange tale I'm going to tell you, and you have to believe me, totally true, every word. And it must be said, a lot more interesting than Burma year two on the fifth telling!

Chapter 2
The Old Codger...

Downstairs
Galaxy ref: P5763EARTH
Grid: UK729~Ami16

T he rest of Christmas day was uneventful. Gramps settled into his second year in Burma tales. I'd heard it so many times before I could have probably done a good job of telling it myself. Dad was well into it, laughing in all the right places and banging the table in delight. Mum and Missus Agnes were asleep by nine, still in their chairs at the dinner table, awoken every now and again as Dad slammed his hand down on the table.

The next day was Boxing Day, but also a Sunday, worst luck. Mum packed us all off to church before Gramps could launch into Burma, year three. My parents had always been a strange combination. Dad dreamed about being a war hero and shooting up everyone in sight (he lived in another world!) whilst my mum was a strict church goer and marched us off to church each Sunday morning. Dad undertook a miraculous transformation for about an hour and then returned to being a wild make belief war hero over Sunday lunch.

Church was totally ridiculous. I was in a small youth group which met in the upstairs corridor as all the other rooms in the building were being used.

"Right! Morning everyone," said Rupert. "Today we're going to..." I switched off. My group was led by Rupert. That wasn't his real name but he had once turned up in a yellow check scarf, someone called him Rupert and it sort of stuck. He was middle aged over enthusiastic, fat and definitely beginning to go bald, but he was desperately pretending he was still a teenager. He was a sad case. He was a total idiot. Tried to get us to do the most stupid things.

"Right," Rupert went on enthusiastically. "I want everyone to close there eyes and concentrate on Africa." There we murmur of... "Africa?"... "Why Africa?" around the room.

Why Africa? It was a good point.

"We'll join hands and make a low Ummmm, as we concentrate. It'll help."

Oh good grief. This got worse every week. I dutifully held hands, joined in with the collective "Ummmm," and set my thoughts on Africa. Nothing. The only thought which wandered through my mind was Mowgli from Jungle Book.

I lent across to Donny. "He'll have us doing monkey impressions next," I whispered.

"No, this is really cool, Monty," Donny whispered back. "My cousin's converted the whole of Argentina through prayer."

"But they're not all Christians in Argentina," I retorted.

"Yes they are. It's just they don't all realise it yet."

"Shhh," Rupert opened one eye and cautioned us.

I liked Donny. He was my only real mate at church. Hanging round with Donny made me feel good since he had an even sadder name than me. His mum was Trisha Osmond and she'd been a wild fan of The Osmonds, some 1970's pop group that were made up of a family of brothers. I'd seen a picture of them once, all wearing sparkly silver suits... a really sad bunch. Anyway, she named her kid after their lead singer, Donny Osmond. I mean, how cruel could parents get? Donny was a total head case. Believed in everything... converting Argentina, miracles, meditation, Father Christmas and the tooth fairy... You name it, he'd be hooked on it. Spending an hour saying, "Ummm," for Africa was his idea of heaven. He even reckoned Burnley'd win the FA cup one day. Be serious! I, on the other hand, was much more thought out in my approach to life. I believed in nothing. Survive today alive, hope your luck improves tomorrow, and run away from home before you're forced to join the army, that was my motto. I mean... all this God stuff? I definitely didn't believe in God! I heard all the arguments. The God squad always said God must exist; just look at the world around you, how it all worked and fitted together... Someone must have made it. Are you serious?!! They ought to open their eyes... come and live in our house for a bit. Looking at the world just proved to me that there was absolutely no way God existed. I mean... if he was up there he'd design it a bit better than this, wouldn't he? Or maybe this was just the first attempt? Or perhaps he was just havin' a laugh? Or he was just not that good at being God.

I opened my right eye. Everyone was deep in "Ummm" land.

After Sunday lunch, which was the traditional Christmas leftovers for Boxing Day, I wandered down to Jacob's. Jacob was a nice old codger who lived in a little wooden house on Mill Hill towards the hospital. I walked the long slog up the hill with a Tesco carrier bag of gardening tools. Mum was rather strict on Sundays, to the point of the ridiculous! Church, prayer and good deeds, that's all we were allowed to do! I wouldn't mind but you have five days of torture at school and only two days off. And then for one of those two days you spend half of it in "Ummm" land and the other half digging over the old codger's garden. There had to be something more interesting to life. And in December! Mum either only had half a brain or she didn't know much about gardening.

I knocked on the door of the wooden shack. I could hear the floor boards creaking inside and then the door was opened by a tall, skinny and slightly stooped elderly man. The face was suddenly split as a wide grin spread across the old wrinkled face.

"In ya come Monty." Jacob took the carrier bag off me as I walked back in time through the doorway... back to the 1950's maybe... or back to the ark! Jacob hadn't heard about modern technology. He still minced his own beef and even washed up without a dishwasher!! (I'm not sure I'd know how... and I was sure it must be illegal by now).

Jacob stared into the bag, a perplexed look on his face.

"Your mother's barmy, Monty! You won' be needin' this lot." He rescued a Madera cake Mum had put in the bag and then abandoned the garden tools in the entrance hall. That's what I liked about Jacob, he had his priorities right. Who cared about gardening anyway? I'd always wished I'd had an older brother, a partner in crime and someone to share the joke with, of all the silly things that went on in my house. But I didn't. I think I had been too much of a challenge to my parents, for them to have any more kids. Jacob was like an older brother. He had a sense of wickedness about him which most grownups seemed to have abandoned somewhere through puberty.

"'ave a seat Monty. I'll get ya a nice bottle a stout." Jacob gave me a wink and left the room. See what I mean? What would Mum think if she knew I put my feet up, drank beer and played cards with Jacob every Sunday afternoon? Hope she never comes to inspect the garden!

I sank into a rather comfy if ugly brown leather armchair. Jacob's wooden shack house was all a bit drab and looked like it hadn't changed in twenty years. He had china ducks hanging on the wall. No-one born this side of the dinosaurs has china ducks! The house was kept nice and warm by a gas fire and Jacob's smile which seemed to radiate warmth and always made me relax. He reappeared with two bottles of stout and a deck of cards.

"Whist," he said.

"Nah! Rummy. You always beat me at Whist."

"But you always beat me at Rummy!" he protested. I just grinned. I told him about church and chanting "Ummm" for Africa. He almost wet himself laughing, and I got a peek at his cards.

"So what's with the ducks?" I asked as I munched on a rather large piece of Madera cake.

Jacob frowned at the china ducks on the wall. "What's wrong with 'em?"

"They're a disaster!"

"Wife bought 'em for me in sixty-two."

I would have felt embarrassed with anyone else but I'd been a long way with Jacob. He talked about anything and everything. His wife had died before I was even born.

"Do you miss her?" I asked.

"Sometimes, yeah." There was a long pause as we both stared at the ducks. Jacob's eyes looked very deep, as if a million thoughts and memories were clamouring for attention.

"RUMMY!" he announced laying his cards on the table.

"What!" This wasn't good. He never beat me at Rummy. I tossed my cards on the table. Then I remembered. The chocolates! I rummaged in my rucksack and produced the long oblong box. I showed Jacob the "man upstairs" gift tag, pointed out the health warning sticker on the top, and then opened up the box. Again I stared at the intricate shaped and designed chocolates. They looked perfect, like a work of art. I showed Jacob the gold leaf with the description of the chocolates on.

Jacob read and I waited with baited breath. Jacob was as old as the hills. I had come to realise there was nothing he didn't know, and no subject he lacked an opinion on.

"Monty... Monty..." he murmured.

Yes... I waited. The suspense was killing me. "Well?" I prompted.

"This is something very special."

Well I knew that much! I could see it wasn't a bag of toffees, for goodness sake.

"And..?" I prompted again.

Jacob carefully read out the gift tag again...

"To Fish. Happy Christmas! Hope you enjoy the enclosed (but do be careful with it). From the man upstairs."

I could see that sparkle of excitement in his eyes.

"You know, Monty. I've seen a lot of different things in my life. Nothing much surprises me anymore." His eyes were wandering into dream land again. "Life is what 'appens to you when ya least expect it. Remember that. Be careful what ya do with this, Monty. You've been given a very special gift 'ere."

What was that supposed to mean?!

It was dark outside and the house was quiet and peaceful. I sat on my bed in the cramped spare room, which doubled up as a cupboard. I thought enviously of Ugly and her mum sleeping soundly in MY room! Why couldn't they push off next door to their place!?

I finished off going through my football cards, collected them up and put the elastic band back round them. Then I grabbed my bible and stared at it. It was so thick. If God was really up there he wouldn't have made it all so complicated. Why couldn't he just have given us one sheet of A4? Something like... *"Hi guys, God here. Just wanted to let you know I'm here and I exist... you know, just in case you wondered. Any problems just give me a call. Or better still, e-mail me... God@heaven.co.eternity."*

That would be cool. I closed my eyes, flicked open my bible, pointed randomly and opened my eyes and glanced down. *"He tore his clothes, sprinkled ashes on his head and cried."* Right... OK... useful. Oh well, at least I could tell Rupert I had read my bible every day. I tossed it to one side and reached for the chocolates. Time to take the plunge. I read the health warning sticker once more. It made me feel slightly uncomfortable. I pulled the lid off and my eyes wandered over the luscious contents. The cocoa aroma rose to my nostrils once again. I settled on the large Celtic style cross. *"The Queen's hero,"* announced the gold lettering on the leaflet. I picked the chocolate cross up. It was large, more like a whole bar of chocolate. The surface sparkled, and the strange intricate patterned writing covered the surface. I examined it closely but it certainly wasn't any language I knew. I turned it over. There on the back, on a slightly raised area, was a small section I could read. It said, *"In the heart of everyone is a hero."*

This was so weird. Oh well, here goes. What harm could it do? I took a bite. Wow! That was lovely. It tasted deep and rich with a slight tingling sensation... almost spicy and exotic. I couldn't resist finishing it off. And with that I went to sleep.

Chapter 3

The Man Upstairs...

Upstairs
Realm 1... Map Room

G od sat on a red satin armchair watching the world. It was tiring work being the creator of the universe. His eyes were sharp and alert, darting this way and that as they watched all that was going on. He had a pointy nose, and wrinkly skin from smiling and frowning so much (well, running the world gave you a lot to smile and frown about.) He also had a very short haircut - a crew-cut. It sort of hid the fact that his hairline was receding a bit.

Well, he thought, a busy schedule for today. The world was always active. While half the world slept, the other half would be waking up and yawning. Whilst half was in cold mid-winter the other half was in the heat of summer. It was a very interesting place to watch. It was by far the best of all his creations. He had created many worlds, of course. The dinosaurs had been a disaster. They just wanted to eat each other all the time. And the world of green splodgy aliens with antennae was a bit boring. And then one day whilst he was in the loo they had gone and flown off in their spaceships and landed on earth. Ever since then the humans liked nothing more than making TV programmes about green splodgy aliens with antennae, however much he discouraged it.

But a busy schedule, today. He had the building works to supervise later, at ten am there was a welcome party arriving from Australia and court was in session in the afternoon. Not to mention the three hundred and fifty seven thousand invites to tea he had received for this evening. He really did enjoy being invited places. He was particularly looking forward to seeing Josh tonight. He had a skateboard park in his back garden. But for now he was content watching. The world hung there in mid air in front of him, turning gently, it's billions of people going about their daily tasks like a vast army of ants. Of course, it wasn't really the world, just a map... but the biggest, most detailed and fascinating map you'd ever seen. He could lean into any bit of it and that section would grow more detailed, as if placed under a magnifying glass. In this way he could see every little person and event as it unfolded. It would have made for a cool geography lesson.

God gave the globe a little spin and reached down into the ocean just between Australia and Fiji. He reached right down to the sea bed where the time dial was. He was surprised that none of the scientists had discovered this one yet. They were a strange bunch, scientists. So engrossed in their discoveries they missed the blindingly obvious.

God carefully turned the knob backwards to 6 May 1932. He then swivelled the globe again and his eyes honed in on Denmark. He watched a particularly stunning sunset and then reached down and rested his finger on the forehead of a small boy called Samuel, laying there asleep. The boy wasn't particularly important or famous... not yet anyway... but God wanted to inject a little thought into his mind whilst he slept. A thought that maybe would grow into something else, may even one day change the world. It "may" change the world, or it "may not". That would all depend on the decisions of little Samuel over the next twenty years or so... what he did with the thousands of trillions of thoughts that would pass through his brain between now and then. Nothing was certain. Everything was possible. And so the world worked. It was so unbelievably, humongously complicated, a truly amazing creation. As if to reinforce the thought God blew a gentle breeze through the open window and caused the pages of the large book, laying here on the floor, to flip over to just the right place.

Of course it was a fine balance in such a world as this. The fine balance of letting these people think and do and choose for themselves whilst now and again injecting a thought here or a little miracle there, or sending an angel down to help him or placing a hand of protection over her. God had decided many years ago that he would only interfere with the little things. He would put the little thoughts in and concentrate on the little people, and he would let the big things take care of themselves.

But God took his time... after all he had lots of it. He could adjust the time dial back and forth and continue the slow process of moulding history. He had spent about two billion years of "heaven time" on it so far.

With that task done for Samuel, God shot a quick thought into a young woman walking down the street, two blocks away. She suddenly had a strange feeling she couldn't explain and she changed route in the dark of late evening. It saved her life as she turned away from the man lurking in the shadows.

And there was God's problem. Put plain and simple, people just weren't always very nice. They didn't "see" did they. And he couldn't just zap them and make them nice, otherwise he would have nothing more than a world of rather rubbery looking robots. Maybe he should have made their brains a bit bigger instead... no, that's no use. They only used ten percent of them anyway.

No, they had to live their own lives. And so this world he watched had life... it was beautiful and it was frightening too. It was a bit like the biggest game of chess in the universe.

The Map Room was very spacious. And were you or I to walk into it, we would be struck by how odd it all looked. God's red satin armchair sat in the middle of a beautiful green pasture. On his right was a dusty stone path and beyond that a wooden fence. On his left the green field ran down to the stream at the bottom of the valley. A huge old gnarled tree grew next to the stream. In fact it was so broad that the tree grew on both sides of the stream and its gigantic trunk arched across from one bank to the other. It was the oldest tree in the universe, and God liked to keep it in the Map Room. High above the ground where you would normally expect to see a  shining orange sun and a cloudless blue sky on such a glorious day as this, the sky was actually quite dark and the stars twinkled brightly. This was the highest point in heaven. The planet Earth, hanging in mid air, and the night sky on such a gloriously bright day, were not the only strange sights to the uninitiated. There were lots of strange objects which just sort of hung there or slowly moved around the room. Some were round, some square or all sorts of other shapes and sizes. The Map Room was only one little room up here, but after all there was no shortage of space in heaven.

A very tall man in jeans and a baggie t-shirt entered the room and marched quickly up the dusty path towards the red satin chair. He must have been ten foot tall and you wouldn't have passed him in the street without noticing both the height and the strangely long face. He definitely had a strange inhuman look to him. His eyes shifted uneasily from one side to the other and his eyebrows came together in the middle in a rather serious, strained look. God stirred from his observations and looked around, a smile breaking out on his face.

"A message from the Watchers, Chief," said the tall man. He spoke in a rather stern voice and handed over a piece of paper folded over a number of times.

"Thank you, Gabe. Everything progressing to plan?"

"Yes, Chief!"

"Would you like to sit down?" asked God. The angel frowned uncomfortably. God played with the idea of offering him an ice cream cornet, but then he thought that would be teasing him just a bit.

Angels... there was a different problem. They saw much better than humans... they were brilliant forward planners and pretty good chess players. They could plan a million moves forward in this giant chess match of the universe. They were also absolutely indispensable. He relied on them for so many things. They were totally reliable, of course, but just a tad too serious sometimes. More like a highly organised army than a friend you could have a laugh with. God sighed. All except for a few, like Rafe, who came immediately to mind. God chuckled to himself. Some, like Rafe, were a little different and he had some special tasks for them.

God placed the folded note on the arm of his chair. After all, he didn't need to read it, he knew what it said anyway.

"Thank you Gabe. Tell the Watchers that I am pleased." A hint of a smile crept onto the angel's face.

God flicked the time dial back to very near the beginning of time to give some encouragement to Noah who was feeling rather discouraged at the moment, building his ark. Noah's friends were giving him rather a lot of stick about it. Everyone seemed to have very stuffy ideas about God. It annoyed him sometimes. No-one down there seemed to think he did very much, and when they thought about God they tended to think of stuffy old churches, vicars in dog collars and very long boring church services, which wasn't what he was about at all. They seemed to forget about all the best bits he had created... coral reefs, snow crested mountain tops, a hundred thousand different varieties of sea monster, the bend in the banana, earth worms which have a brain at each end, and oh yes, skateboards! God actually worked in some very strange ways. Take Noah for instance. Who would have guessed that God would work through getting this one man to build a boat in the middle of the desert? God loved doing the unusual and the unexpected. He rubbed his hands together.

"Right Gabe!" He turned the time dial yet again and spun the globe. His fingers played with the note still sitting on the edge of his armchair, and he edged forward in his seat, a look of excitement coming onto his face. He had two gifts to give. He loved giving gifts, it was one of his favourite things... and especially if they were unusual gifts. For the first one, his eye rested on Africa. Senia was a small girl of ten sitting in a make shift class room, where they used upturned banana crates for desks and the rain splashed through the corrugated iron roof when the storms came. James Cogan was a missionary. He sat at his desk at the front of the class room. Senia was the last child in the classroom that day. The sun was blazing and the sound of exotic birds outside could be heard. God reached down and placed his finger on James Cogan. The thought drifted into his mind. What would he do with it, God wondered? Cogan had a number of items to give out, some toys, drawing kits, models... simple stuff like that. He reached into his satchel and his hand hovered amongst the presents for a moment. Which one, he wondered? Then he withdrew the writing set. It was a nice set, leather cover with a blotter to write on, a pad, writing pens and drawing felt tips. It had a black African Elephant motif on the bottom right corner. He gave the gift to Senia.

"A writing set? Why a writing set?" asked Gabe. God smiled at the angel.

"Just wait and see. It all depends what she chooses to do with it." He spun the globe again and focused in on a little island just off mainland Europe… England. He honed in on a small house. It was Christmas dinner. He reached down quickly and placed one extra gift under the Christmas tree. It was a box of chocolates.

Gabe looked sceptical but said nothing. He'd seen so many of God's strangely crafted plans.

God read his thoughts (being God, he could do things like that) and gave him an amused smile. "Don't forget our motto, Gabe. We chip away with the chisel. But sometimes when the message doesn't get through—"

"We use a mallet, Chief," Gabe interrupted. "I remember."

"Well this time it's more like a jackhammer, I think, Gabe. It takes a lot to reach some of them. Might need to get the bulldozer out next!"

God lent back in his chair. "OK Gabe. I may need a protection detail on those two. Should we awaken the sleepers, do you think?"

"Yes Chief." Gabe saluted and left.

Yes, thought God. This would be an interesting little episode in our rather big complex world. And it would be an important one. I wonder how it will play out?

As the angel left, the door behind God opened once again and a rather old looking man came in pushing a large trolley. It was Bill and the mail trolley. God smiled and zapped a rather nice reclining sofa into existence next to his armchair. Bill wore blue overalls and a cap. He pushed the trolley very slowly up the dusty path. It bumped over stones and twigs. God watched and smiled.

"Bill!" he exclaimed. "Come and sit with me for a while." The old man pushed the trolley to a halt and sat down on the sofa next to God. The two sat in silence for a while as they watched the world at work. Bill had been a postman once down on earth. When he arrived in heaven he put in a special request for the prayer trolley job. How could God refuse? Bill had a heart of gold. God loved to sit and ponder the world with him. And Bill enjoyed nothing better than to sit here with God and watch in wonder as the world turned and lived.

Bill was an interesting character. Most humans, on arriving in heaven, chose to be young again… at least at first. They wanted to have the perfect new body, young, fit, and slim. That's why most of the people you saw up here looked young. But not Bill. The day he arrived, he pondered for a moment and announced that he was quite comfortable with being old, thanks very much. He had chosen to be old, he had perfected it... to be older, wiser, slower and ponder life. Life was for pondering, after all. God glanced at the earth, all the little ant-like people, speeding around like hamsters on a wheel. Too much activity and not enough pondering. To give up "doing" in order to just "watch and understand" instead, was truly a great thing.

"So what have we got today, Bill?" Bill glanced across at the prayer trolley. In it lay thousands of letters. Some were large clean white envelopes. Others were tiny, scruffy looking scraps of paper. There was the occasional parcel and as you looked at the trolley closely you could see some glints of gold... these were the gold envelopes. Bill was one of the few humanoids who had access to the Watchers. The prayers shot up from the world, were captured by the Watchers and were collected and filed by Bill. He then wheeled them up to the Map Room. There was no particular hurry to read them. After all, God had all the time in the universe. Of course it wasn't the length of the prayer, which determined if it was a large white envelope or a scruffy scrap of paper, or indeed a gold crested letter, and it wasn't the importance of the situation which had been prayed about. Neither was it to do with the importance of the person who said the prayer. It was all to do with the heart of the person who said it. The big white envelopes were real heart felt prayers pleaded by people really in need of God's help, whilst the scruffy little notes were often rather half-hearted prayers and with little thought, time or effort spent on them. It was a sad fact that many such prayers never even made it into the prayer trolley. Why, you ask? They were so half-hearted that when they shot up to heaven they slowed down too quickly, came to a stand still and got blown away by the breeze. Prayers were amazingly crafted pieces of eternity. Each moulded by words and thoughts and heart and time, and often out of pain which people had felt and tears they had wept. Some prayers were written in an instant and shot up to heaven, whilst others were constructed over years, and were part of a rich tapestry of correspondence with God. And each one would have an effect on eternity, because God would read each and every one of them and would respond. It was one of the rules he had set himself in this colossal chess game. He would only interfere in the little things... but when people asked, he would do more.

God raised a hand and a string of golden envelopes shot out of the prayer trolley and zipped through the air into God's hand, as if yanked on elastic. The first one rose up into the air in front of God and opened itself. God scanned it and smiled. He wrote in the air with his finger and, as he did, writing appeared and the letters and words sort of hung there in mid-air. As God moved onto the next line, the first line shot off towards the large globe of the world and disappeared. The second Gold letter opened itself and God gave instructions to Bill to pass on to the Watchers. The third Gold letter put lines of worry across

God's brow. He immediately turned the globe to find the writer of this particular letter. He touched them lightly and then put that gold letter in his pocket. And so God and Bill worked through all the gold ones, God giving various instructions for Bill to take back to the Watchers. Bill sat with a notebook and ballpoint, taking notes (he still wasn't all that keen on angelmail, and preferred his trusty notepad).

Bill stared at the globe in front of him, at the spot God was watching. His eyes lit up and followed all that was happening.

"So, it's young Monty then?" His voice was slightly cracked, but his eyes and mind were razor sharp. Of course they were, he was in heaven now, all aches and pains and problems gone. "You're going to call him?"

"Yes," replied God. "I thought I would. What do you think?" Bill saw the box of chocolates, which God had placed under the Christmas tree and chuckled. He always enjoyed watching God at work, seeing people's lives being changed. He rubbed his chin and considered before he responded to God's question.

"A bit touch and go 'aint it? He's weak. He'll need 'elp."

"Yes, you're right, we'll give him help. And at the end of the day, it's his choice."

"Always 'is choice!" Bill echoed.

"Oh, and Bill." God pointed into the large globe, to the Christmas tree squashed into the small front room. "I'd like you to watch out for the prayers from Monty."

"Gotcha!" replied old Bill. "Will do!" And God knew that Bill would make a mental note and would not let him down.

Then God looked at his watch, patted Bill on the shoulder and made his way out of the Map Room. It was time to visit the building works… sector four on Realm three.

George was an investment banker from Wall Street in New York… or at least he had been in his previous life. Anyone on earth would have looked at him as a great success of course, such was the way of it. He had made a tonne of money working twenty hour days in the stock markets. But in fact George's life had been a sad one. His real ambition, his dream, had always been to do something with his hands, to build his own little cottage in the country, miles from anyone else. He had never got the chance though. Making money was just too addictive to put down. "Next year," he had always told himself, and then when he was forty five his luck had broken. In one day he had lost twenty five million dollars of his and other people's money. It was more than he could take and he shot himself at two am in the morning with a rusty old shotgun he kept for weekend rabbit hunts.

And so now, up here, he fulfilled his ambitions. His hands worked on the wooden beam frames with the precision of a master woodwork craftsman, which he was. The grey hair and wrinkling features were gone, for George was no longer the fast aging stressed forty five year old. No, here his features were more akin to someone of eighteen or nineteen years old, his blonde hair ran long, down his back, and his face sharp and young.

God stood for a few seconds and surveyed the property. He stretched out his hands extravagantly.

"George, this is magnificent! I don't know how you manage it."

George jumped down, a smile beaming from his face.

"Hey, come round here, I've got something to show you." He led God around the back of the building, where the garden was unusually large. Just as God had asked for when he'd shown the plans to George a long time ago. About thirty years back in fact, but then time was no object up here.

"George, that's marvellous."

"You said you wanted lots of tall trees."

"Yes, lots of trees." God cast his eye over the forest like garden. He had a specific purpose in mind for this place. "It's perfect!" he said.

George beamed.

George wasn't in charge of the building works of course. There were many other people there, and after George's disaster of being in charge of things down there on earth, he had chosen not to do anything here except work with his own hands. God smiled. He hoped in another few thousand years the bad memories may fade and George would be willing to be a little more adventurous again. But all in good time!

Chapter 4

The George...

Downstairs
Galaxy ref: P5763EARTH
Grid: UK742~BCz87

It was Wednesday, the first real day after Christmas when everything was open in town, and I was in the shopping arcade with Dad. We were queuing up in the bank. Dad to pay his bills and me to pay my Christmas money into the escape fund, as I affectionately called it. I had more cash stashed away now than Mum and Dad would ever have guessed. It was one of my obsessions. Well, if Dad intended to frog march me down to the army recruitment office on my sixteenth birthday, then I intended to leg it the day before, and I had it all planned... where I'd go, the money I'd need, where I'd hide out. Charlie and Hash, my best mates from school, didn't reckon I had the guts to carry it out, but this was my lifeline. It was the one thing which helped me endure my dad's ravings.

But for now there was a more pressing worry. School was getting far too close for comfort. The school holidays were coming to an end and the prospect of the long slog till Easter seemed like a prison sentence.

Ding. The counter became free, five people ahead of us, and we shuffled forward obediently in the queue. I clutched my paying in book. Dad seemed lost in dream land... laying a secret night time assault on the enemy, just outside Burma, no doubt. We stood in silence.

I needed something exciting to happen. A meteor to shoot out of space, for instance, and score a direct hit on the school. I didn't want it to do any other damage. Just enough to obliterate every offending square inch of school would be perfect.

Dad gave a sigh of satisfaction. "Burma," he mumbled.

"What?" I glanced up.

"Burma," he repeated. "Don't you think it would have been fun, Monty? Being out there like paps was. Travelling the world, sleeping under the stars, taking your life in your hands, the glory of fighting for God and country..."

Yeah, and lying on your belly in a snake infested mud patch for eight hours at a time. Sounds swell.

"When you're on your postings Monty, I want you to write every week. I wanna know where you are and what they've got you doing. You're gonna have such an adventure out there, Monty!"

Ding. Four in front. We shuffled up the queue. I clutched my Christmas money nervously, thinking I could just withdraw everything now and make a run for it. That would solve the problem of school as well. Charlie and Hash reckoned my dad wouldn't go through with it. "When it comes to it," Charlie had said, "your dad will let you do what you want." I wasn't so sure. I glanced up at Dad. He winked at me.

"Capow, capow!" He closed one eye and pretended shooting off a rifle. Good grief, he was obsessed!

Ding. Three to go. Shuffle, shuffle.

"Cash!" said the man at the counter. He was tall, duffle coat, carrier bag. Sorta scruffy with long greasy dark hair.

"Tens or twenty's, love," replied Charlene. She always served us at the bank. She was dating Charlie's older brother.

"All of it now. In the bag."

"Sorry dear?" Charlene looked confused. Oh great. It always happened didn't it? Murphy's Law... Queue for three hours and just when you get to the front someone has a huge long request which takes half an hour. Either that or you get some foreign geezer who thinks he's ordering kebabs at the chippie.

"BAG... NOW!" the duffle coat guy hissed. He seemed to pull something out from under his coat and point it at Charlene. A gun... my brain took a couple of seconds to register. A GUN!! This was a hold up; duffle coat was robbing the bank... Unbelievable! This didn't happen in real life; it was only supposed to happen in the movies. I could see that the guy in front of us had realised what was going on. His eyes had gone wide and he had gone stiff as a board. My dad was still in a world of his own, blissfully unaware and the people behind us in the queue were too far away to have noticed. They were still mumbling and moaning about how long this was taking. Charlene hadn't moved an inch. She was at a total loss. Charlie always said she was a bit short in the brain department. He's got a gun, kid! Give him the cash, I wanted to scream. On second thoughts, that's my escape fund she had up there, all the cash I'd been saving for years. Give him that, Charlene, and I'll personally string you up.

Panic hadn't yet registered. All the people standing around me still seemed calm. Then duffle coat turned around, shot a round into the ceiling and shouted for us to, "hit the deck."

That was definitely a good time to panic. Dad grabbed my shoulders, swivelled me round behind him and pushed me down hard. We both hit the floor, along with everyone else.

Duffle coat was now wearing a balaclava mask, and I now noticed another guy peering out of the window. Shotgun, balaclava and a red cap. He looked really stupid wearing a red cap over the balaclava, and it did strike me that it made an excellent target for the police.

The smell of the grimy floor hit me. A large piece of dust had settled on the end of my nose. It was itching ready to bust and I was desperate to reach up and scratch my nose but I dare not. I was concentrating hard on trying not to sneeze. I could hear various people crying or screaming. Duffle coat was still shouting at Charlene for the cash. Good on ya Charlene! She had a wide eyed frozen expression, a bit like a rabbit caught in the headlights of an oncoming car, and wasn't handing over a thing. She'd probably wet herself. These guys were hopeless! I could get cash out of Charlene quicker than that! I heard some faint sirens in the distance.

"Hurry it up!" called red cap from the window. There was a screech of car breaks outside the window. Red cap ran across and started shutting the bank's front doors.

"Hostage scenario... SAS fifty two," Dad whispered, lying next to me.

A hundred horrible thoughts ran through my mind. OK, I admit I had been praying for something interesting to happen. Now, I just wanted it to stop. My chest felt tight. For a few seconds I was finding it hard to breath. I had a sudden urge to leg it for the door before... Clunk. Too late, it was shut and bolted.

"Monty, you OK?" Dad whispered.

Oh yeah, just great, I thought. "What d' you think?!!" I hissed.

"Breath son, breath. Don't worry, I've got an idea."

Why did I not feel comforted by this? I suddenly had this ominously worrying feeling in the pit of my stomach. My nose was now screaming, "SCRATCH ME!!" I tried to blow the dust off. That just made it worse.

"SAS survival guide, page forty three, Monty." And suddenly Dad was up on his feet and on the move. Oh good grief. What was he doing? Here I was, seeing how insignificant and small I could make myself, and going about the important task of desperately trying to remove the dust from my nose, and Dad had suddenly grown red underpants and a cape and seemed to think he was superman. I lunged for him to pull him back, but I was too late. NO! I wanted to scream. They would shoot him. A million happy memories of Mum and Dad flooded my mind. It was as if I was no longer in control of what I was doing. I jumped up. Dad was running for duffle coat. Duffle coat was turning. I could see the shot gun in his hand. Everything seemed to have turned into slow motion.

"DAD... NOOOOO!" I screamed. Next thing I knew something whacked me right on the back of the neck. It was so hard I fell like a sack of potatoes and pain shot down my back and screamed in my head. Stars, bright lights and bunny rabbits seemed to be dancing in front of my eyes. I couldn't make out anything else. It was all black.

Next thing I remember, I woke up. I was in a bright white room. Heaven! I was in heaven. Someone leaned over me, beautiful face... an angel dressed in white. A wave of panic hit me. I didn't want to be in heaven yet, I'm only eleven! I turned my head all around, trying to gain some clue to what was going on. Sharp pain throbbed in my neck. More stars and bunny rabbits. One of them looked like Charlie... No, it was Charlie! He was heavily built, with a large mop of greasy blonde hair... unmistakably Charlie. He was sitting next to me. He was in heaven too! The angel leaning over me pulled back. She was a nurse. A rather pretty nurse. Hospital, not heaven. I relaxed. She smiled.

"Just lay still. Try not to move your head. You've taken a nasty knock on the back of your neck." She looked up at Charlie and Hash sitting next to the bed. "Five minutes," she said and then left. I lay and let my head spin for a moment.

"Brought you some sweets," said Charlie. He was a ball of excitement which lasted about ten seconds then exploded. "Wow, Fish! It's incredible... What you did... Hero and TV....Have you seen the papers?" He was on his feet and pacing the room. He was babbling. I didn't have a clue what he was talking about. Charlie was a strange one, a right moody git one day and drifting on cloud nine the next... emotions like an elastic band. Today was obviously a high day. Hash, on the other hand was tall, quiet, wafer thin and shifty looking, with eyes which were always darting left and right as if expecting a double decker bus to jump out and suddenly mow him down.

Charlie finally saw the confusion on my face and started again.

"We're just doing the afternoon bedside shift while your mum got a bite to eat," put in Hash. At last someone who made sense. He gained the name Hash at McDonald's where, legend had it, he regularly consumed fifteen hash browns for breakfast. Why? Who knows... there were things about Hash you didn't try to understand.

Then it all suddenly flooded back... Christmas, the bank!... Duffle coat, my dad.

"My dad! Is he dead?" I blurted.

"Dead?" Charlie looked confused. "He's a hero, Monty! So are you. You distracted the first guy and your dad took out the guy at the counter. Least, that's what the papers said."

"Papers?"

"Papers! You're front page news, Fish! You don't get it do you? You're dad's a national hero. He's not here, 'cause he's giving TV interviews!"

Hash tossed a paper on the bed in front of me and nodded at the cover. I fought through the pain and sat up. I grabbed the paper. Sure enough, front page, my dad grinned up at me. Bottom left was a smaller, grainy picture of Dad diving through the air towards duffle coat.

"They got that one from the CCTV," said Hash.

But what really caught my attention was the picture on the right. I just stared at it. I couldn't believe my eyes. It was the cross.

Charlie was hovering over me in a sort of uncomfortable half sitting position, as if ready to pounce. He was obviously desperately waiting to launch into his next speech but waiting for me to finish reading. He saw where I was looking and couldn't wait any longer.

"Yeah, isn't it amazing!" His arms went wide as if he was trying to grab hold of the whole world. "It's just awesome, Fish! They're awarding your old man the George Cross. Look, that's a picture of it there."

I couldn't take my eyes of it. I glanced at the headline below the picture. *"The highest medal awarded by the Queen for civilian bravery, is to be awarded to Ronny Pilchard, our very own Superman!"*

My mind drifted back to the box of chocolates. *"The Queen's hero,"* that's what it had been called. The chocolate had been a square, Celtic style cross. And here it was... The George Cross. This picture... this medal, was the exact image of the chocolate I had eaten. Was I going mad? Or maybe I'd been hit a bit too hard? This couldn't be a coincidence.

Charlie told me everything he had gleaned of the day's events. As chance would have it, I had stood up just as red cap was lining up a shot, which is why I had ended up with a crack on the back of the head, as red cap had thumped me with the butt of his gun. Dad had shoved Duffle Coat hard against the counter, doing enough to put him out for a minute or two, and then the police had stormed the doors. Apparently Duffle Coat and Red Cap were first timers - it showed. The papers and TV stations had all turned up and been snapping away, and I was now in my own private hospital room since my dad was now an instant celebrity. The hospital desk were having to fight to keep the reporters out of my room.

I quickly explained about the chocolates, before the nurse returned, and I dispatched Charlie and Hash with orders to retrieve them and bring them in.

Nurse Heartly was blonde, young and drop dead gorgeous. I had been looking for a plan to stay off school as long as possible and all I had to do was play up the neck pains and I could stare at her smile for weeks.

Mum came and smothered me with kisses, blabbering on about how she thought she had lost me. Mothers can just be so uncool sometimes. She apologised for Dad but he was in makeup getting ready for a TV appearance and would get along when he could.

Next visitor was Jacob, who came empty handed since Nurse Heartly had confiscated the bottles of stout. We played cards and discussed Nurse Heartly. Jacob said she reminded him of a nurse who'd looked after him in the war.

"I didn't know you'd been in the war!" I blurted.

"Oh yeah. I played cricket for the medical corp. Got knocked out stone cold by a fast bowler from Chantry. A leg bouncer it was. Real mean ball." I told him about the cross in the paper and the chocolates. He pondered this for a minute.

"Ya know, I saw som'ink like this back in forty one." More silence and pondering. So... spit it out, I wanted to say.

"Shall I let you in on a secret?" Jacob reached into his pocket and pulled out an old battered silver hip flask. "My Annie gave me this before the war." He pointed to a dent on one side. "Bullet hit it. Saved my life." He undid the lid and took a swig from it. "You know, Monty, I filled this up with brandy in 1937..." He leaned into me and glanced quickly to each side as if someone might be listening in. I leaned closer, fascinated. "I've never refilled it since, Monty." There was a long pause. "It's never run out... not in over sixty years. There's something very special about this 'ere flask." He nodded. "It was a...special...gift." He nodded in a "you know what I mean" sort of way.

"Nah!" I objected. "You're kiddin' me?"

He shook he head. "All sorts of things are possible, Monty." He prodded a finger in my chest. "Your box of chocolates, my hip flask. Yeah... Life hands out some very strange gifts, it does sometimes, Monty. Whoever's in charge up there has a strange sense of 'umour."

I stared in wonder for a few seconds... then I snapped out of it. Jacob was clearly barmy as a banana tree. No-one was in charge up there. He obviously just drank very slowly.

Next visitor was Rupert. He was even wearing his yellow check scarf. He looked really stupid. He obviously felt safer wearing it outside Sunday youth group. I looked around him hopefully but he hadn't bought me any presents. To my horror he had come armed with bible verses instead. I couldn't believe it. I didn't want bible verses, I wanted sweets! I ducked low under the covers and hoped Nurse Heartly wouldn't come in and see me with this dimwit.

Ugly and Missus Agnes brought me some fruit. Missus Agnes looked awfully tired. I asked them how my bedroom was, with as much annoyance as I could put in my voice, but they didn't get it... straight over their heads.

It got to nine and I found myself praying that Nurse Heartly would come and read me a bed time story, but apparently she had gone off duty. Very inconsiderate, I thought.

Charlie and Hash somehow managed to wangle there way back in at nine thirty, and we stared at the chocolates, all totally dumbstruck.

"That ain't no coincidence, Fish!" said Charlie. "It's spooky, that's what it is... Spooky!"

"Maybe it's supernatural," said Hash.

"Jacob called it a gift from... up there," I pointed up and immediately regretted it.

Charlie rolled his eyes at me. "Look bozzos, if God were to give you something... which he probably won't since he don't exist... it's hardly likely to be just a boxes of chocolates, Fish, is it!"

"This isn't just a box of chocolates," I replied.

"Well, only one way to see," said Charlie. "You'll have to eat another one." I stared at him in astonishment. "You know, just to prove it," he added. "Don't you see? If something else happens then we know for sure don't we?"

"Are you serious!?" I retorted loudly. "Can I remind you, I got injured and ended up in hospital! You eat one!"

"Na, wouldn't work, mate."

"Why?" I asked, feeling a stitch up coming on here.

"It's a scientific experiment we have here, Fish. It's gotta be you to keep all the elements the same in the experiment. Everyone knows that."

I twitched, annoyed at not having a good response and not wanting to look ignorant on the important subject of scientific experiments.

"And anyway," Charlie went on, "being injured doesn't seem to be doing you too much harm. Off school. Personal nurse."

I was defeated. I reached for the box of chocolates and carefully selected the long sea-like, wavy one at the top of the box. "*The Dream Warrior.*" I turned it over and, sure enough, carved into the back of it was a small inscription, which read, "*In our dreams we find out who we truly are.*"

I was never one for guessing games.

"I don't think this is a good idea," said Hash. I paused for a second, undecided, and then took the plunge, taking my first bite.

Chapter 5

The Alien, the Biops and the Trainee Angel...

Upstairs
Realm 3... Moweoran Quadrant
Main Street, Floogier House

"D us... ster?"

"That's right!" replied Creevy, taking another swig of floogier juice.

"Dus... sioter," repeated Stex, awkwardly. Then he smiled. "Na! You guys are having a laugh. I don't believe you!"

"No, it's pronounced DUSTER. And it's no joke." Creevy said, rolling all three eyes. Stex looked across to Rafe. Rafe nodded.

Stex crinkled up his nose. "What and they're bits of cloth, right. Which they use to wipe round their house?"

Creevy nodded and beamed. "Yep, that's right!"

"Why?"

"Well, to clean up the dust of course!"

"Dust?" Stex wracked his brains for a moment. "Oh yeah. That's the little bits of dirt which float around in the air, right?"

"Well, yeah, sort of," replied Creevy.

"That's disgusting! Bits of dirt just floating around. Strange place!" concluded Stex and had another gulp of his floogier juice. He flipped over the page in the Biops Orientation Training pack and stared at the next picture... Light Bulb. What was the point in that? Light just shone out of the ground.

Everyone knew that!

The trio were very unlikely friends. To anyone walking by the Floogier House, they looked a strange group to be drinking together. Rafe was an angel, mind you only a very junior angel. But still, any angel was an impressive sight on Realm three of heaven. Creevy was green, a sort of round shape, with three eyes and numerous arms and legs, for of course humanoids were not the only beings to be granted heaven rights. He was a being from the planet Svenerion Xertox, or should I say, had been, until he died and moved on. He was very young in heaven eyes. He had died on Svenerion Xertox in a freak space ship accident. One in a million. Just flying out of a red gas cloud, a few seconds of blind flying, and bam! Hit another ship. Vaporized in a millisecond. But there you go. He'd been here a few hundred years of heaven time. And then there was Stex. He was from humanoid origin, but then he was a Biops, which basically meant he knew nothing about nothing. No, that was overstating it. He knew less than that.

"And you're saying they don't even have floogier juice down there?"

"No floogier juice!" Creevy shook his head.

"OK, I got another one for you. Ready," said Stex excitedly. "A light bulb. Explain that one to me. I mean, I just don't get it?"

They were sitting on Main Street. It was a great place. It was very long. One end of the street ended in the Great Square, meeting place for many announcements and celebrations, and the other end finished at the wall. The wall which surrounded the whole of Realm three was magnificent. Made of gold, over a thousand miles high, with huge gates which opened up to deep space. Rafe loved to sit on the wall and star gaze into space.

"What do they teach you on Biops orientation? It's useless, whatever it is."

"No, I'm getting there, honest." Stex argued. "I really think I'm beginning to get the idea. Our motto, lesson fifty-seven: Pre-world teaches us the importance of... er... food. That was it... no... God. Pre-world teaches us the value of God. With no God, life breaks down, like an old rusty space ship, hey Creevy! See, I got it," Stex beamed. "Do people really have to eat and drink to live? And if they don't, they die? I thought we just ate and drank for fun?"

"Another three floogiers, please, Boris!" Creevy called over to the bar, waving five hands franticly to get attention.

"Come on," said Rafe. "Let's go down to the wall." The Floogier House was a great place to meet and relax. They sat in a small booth, drinking the cool liquid which seemed to warm the heart. Of course in heaven you didn't have to pay for anything, like food or floogier juice. There was no money up here. Everyone gave and everyone seemed to have enough. It just... worked. Stex wrinkled up his nose in concentration. He just couldn't understand why the same wasn't true on earth. Every now and then when he concentrated hard enough he thought he caught just a glimmer of understanding, but then it floated away, just out of reach. Earth, or Pre-world, as they called it, must be a very strange place, he thought.

As they walked down Main, Creevy explained the intimate purpose of a light bulb to Stex.

"Creevy, it's no use," Rafe said in frustration. "He's a Biops. He doesn't get it."

"Well, I'm trying!" pleaded Stex. They walked in silence for a few minutes.

"It seems amazing to think that I was down there once... on earth," said Stex. "If only for a few days."

"Trust me. It's no big deal kid, living in pre-world," replied Creevy.

"But you were on Svenerion, not earth!" Stex protested.

"Yeah, it's all the same though, this is pre-world stuff. You're under attack all the time. It's no fun. You have pain, cravings, temptation, problems that just come up and hit you."

"What's pain again? I can't remember. You did explain once I think."

Creevy ignored him.

"It's no good," said Rafe. "You have to see it to understand." They climbed the steps and sat on the wall and gazed out at the hundreds of millions of stars in space.

"So which one was my galaxy?" asked Stex.

"Forget it," said Rafe. "It's unhealthy to think about it all the time. This is better."

"Yeah, but it's alright for you. You're applying for the Watchers."

"He got turned down again," whispered Creevy.

"Oh... Oh, sorry," said Stex. "Wish I could be a Watcher and just, you know... watch them."

"No - Biops - in - the - Watchers!" said Creevy. "You know the rules. Not for the first billion years."

"And until they've lost their longing to go back to earth," put in Rafe, casting a doubtful eye on Stex.

"Yeah, yeah. I know. It would be fun though."

"Yeah," replied Rafe with feeling. He was dying to get into the Watchers. He had applied seventeen times. He had spoken to the Lord about it. The Lord had just smiled. "Be patient. Your time will come," he'd replied.

Rafe eyed Stex next to him. Best friends with a Biops. Who'd believe it! Angels didn't much like Biops's. Whilst angels worked hard to serve the Lord and be perfect in everything, humanoids were weaker. That's why they were given "Pre-world", an extra life before they reached eternity in heaven. The idea, as it had been explained to him, was to teach them. If you showed them pain and trouble and all the things which went wrong when God was not around, then they would learn... they would learn the value of God. Angels thought letting humans in at all was a risk. But then the Lord loved them so much he even let the Biops in too! The Biops... definition: a humanoid who dies before the age when they can recall, normally about four years old, but variable per humanoid. They were the exception to the rule... they were a risk... A HUGE risk... A risk the size of the whole of Realm Three!... but then the Lord didn't shy away from taking risks did he? What did he always say... If love requires us to take risks, then we take risks. But they knew so little, the Biops! They were hopeless, which was why of course, they had the orientation. But then, that didn't do much good; Stex was living proof of that. Without first hand experience how could they understand what it felt like to have the enemy tempting you, placing carefully crafted evil thoughts directly into your brain, manufacturing circumstances to cause you pain... basically out to kill you! And so angels tended to shy away from Biops. To the strong, tough angels, who tried so hard, the Biops was just so weak, and had been let off the toughest bit of their training on earth, just to enjoy the comfort of heaven. It was too dangerous.

"So which one was my galaxy?" repeated Stex.

Rafe smiled. Despite it all, he really liked this kid, dangerous or not. "Look," he pointed. "You see the gas cloud, left a bit."

"The bright one?"

"Nope. Next to it. Then count down five."

Stex looked left and counted down five stars... He gazed. "Earth." Wow!

"Well, technically no," said Creevy. That's just the Milky Way galaxy sun. You can't actually see earth from here. It's so tiny.

But Stex wasn't listening. He was just gazing. Amazing. He had been there once.

Something caught Rafe's attention. There was a small patch of light buzzing around, like a glow fly. As it got closer it got bigger and then stopped in front of the three of them.

"Good day, Rafe."

"Beorn! Nice to see you," Rafe replied. Beorn was a messenger angel. He glowed gold as he hovered in mid-air. Rafe himself was in between jobs. He longed to be back in action again. Beorn handed him a letter.

"From the Chief," said Beorn. Rafe looked down. It had "S.A." written on the front of the envelope. Rafe was immediately on his feet. Those letters meant one thing only.

"A Special Assignment!" There was a sudden look of excitement in his eyes. "Gotta be off guys. See you." Rafe tripped over his cloak as he turned and ran down the steps.

Beorn shook his head. "Rafe, honestly. Dignity, angel. Slow and dignified, please. Come on, fly with me."

"No thanks!" called Rafe. I'll go this way. It's quicker for the Map Room."

"I can fly you," shouted Creevy. Rafe just turned and waved. Beorn nodded politely to Creevy and Stex and then launched off again in a neat arc towards the stars.

"Good on ya, Rafe!" said Stex with a smile on his face. "I'm pleased for him. What's a Special Assignment, anyway?"

"Special Assignment from the Main Man. It means he has a special job for him. One step closer to the Watchers if you ask me." There was a pause as Stex returned to gazing at his star.

"You wanna chase some space?" asked Creevy.

"Oh yeah!" Stex enthused.

Creevy put two fingers up to his left hand mouth and let out a high pitched whistle. Around the edge of the wall to their left appeared the space ship. It was large and silver but didn't appear to be made of metal. It was more a kind of rubbery substance which bent and stretched as the ship changed directions.

"Hey, we can play chicken with the angels."

"Cool!"

Chapter 6
The Dream Warrior...

Downstairs
Galaxy ref: P5763EARTH
Grid: UK742~BCz87

I was a bit apprehensive having eaten my second chocolate, but I woke up the next morning and all my bodily parts were still in place and nothing awful seemed to have happened so I relaxed. Nurse Heartly brought me breakfast with a smile and I flicked on my own personal TV. This was the life! The TV sparked up... It was the news... boring! What was this? My dad's face smiled back as the news reader recounted the bank raid story, pretty much as the papers had it. I flicked it... Breakfast with Frost.

"And our special guest today?" announced David Frost, "Ronny Pilchard!"

Oh, good grief! I turned it off again. There was a slight annoyance in my stomach. Why hadn't Dad come to see me? After all, I'd almost been killed! He should be here, apologising for being so stupid.

Another few days passed. Mum visited every day as did Charlie and Hash. Luckily there was no sign of Rupert... but also no sign of Dad (except on the TV, in the paper and, would you believe it, on a set of special presentation stamps by the Royal Mail!) Nurse Heartly's first name I discovered was Honey... (Honey Heartly? Cool name.) She was seventeen and still in her nursing training. Why couldn't I be seventeen? I found myself trying to act older and flicked over from the cartoons whenever she entered the room. School was getting dangerously near and so I had to have a relapse and complain about my neck a bit more.

Eventually I checked out of hospital. I was desperate for Nurse Heartly's phone number but didn't have the guts to ask. As I left the hospital I couldn't believe it. There were lines of reporters and flashing cameras. I covered my eyes and ducked into the waiting car. At least at home I could stretch out the agony in my neck for a bit longer and avoid school. And I got my room back. There was no question of demoting me to the spare room whilst I was so near death's door, so Ugly and Missus Agnes had finally been booted out. Mum was so upset and astonished at all that had happened that she waited on me hand and foot and would basically get me anything I wanted. The next day Charlie visited and showed me the newspaper. I was front page news... again! There I was covering my face looking appropriately humble, ducking into the car. This was great, I was famous, and with Mum running after my every need, I was a King!

A week later Dad finally appeared.

"Monty!" he enthused, peering around the bedroom door.

"Where have you been while I've been lying here dying, you rat!" was what I wanted to ask, but I didn't.

"So how's the neck?" he asked, giving it a brief examination. "Nasty knock, that. Incredibly brave, you were!" I swelled inside and instantly forgave him. We chatted for an hour. He gave me a blow by blow account of the bank raid. He seemed on top of the world. But there was more than that. He was relaxed, and he never mentioned anything about me joining the army the whole conversation. It was as if he was no longer trying to prove himself. I couldn't remember ever enjoying being with him so much. He finally seemed like a real dad should be.

"Anyway, I've got to dash, Monty."

"What? Why?" I blurted. I was suddenly missing him already.

"Flying to the States. Giving some lectures on security techniques."

"Really?"

"Yep. It's incredible Monty. You wouldn't believe it. I've got invites all over the place."

"What about your job?"

"Oh, the double glazing company love it. They've never sold so much stuff since the bank raid. I just have to set foot in town and they instantly sell windows."

Dad jumped up from the bed and just like that he was gone again. His head popped back around the door.

"I'm glad you're OK, Monty. Love you, mate."

"Love you too, Dad." And for the first time I meant it.

That evening, remembering it would soon be Sunday, I dutifully closed my eyes and opened my bible at random. It was a story about some guy called

Balaam and a talking donkey... I mean, be serious! A talking donkey!... Come on, I'm not a total moron... God just doesn't do that sort of thing. Where did they think this stuff up from? I could hear sudden shouts from downstairs. Something was up. I shut the bible, tossed it into the corner of my cupboard, and went to investigate. I was going to have to stop reading my bible. It was a total waste of space. It would mean facing Rupert though. That would be tough.

Missus Agnes was a strange one. I had never quite worked out what was going on with her, but she never seemed to eat much, was as thin as a rake and had big bags under her eyes. She had a sort of ill look about her. She was constantly round at our place and, for some reason, unknown to me, Mum and Dad allowed her to stay over. Every now and then there would be a great kafuffle and Missus Agnes would burst in the back door in floods of tears, with Ugly in tow.

I hovered at the top of the stairs as the storm rolled in the front door yet again. Missus Agnes was hysterical and Ugly was chewing gum and looked bored. I retreated back to my room. At least I was fairly safe tonight. After all, I was seriously ill and Mum was doting on me. No way would she kick me out of my room.

I can't believe it! Life is so unfair. Here I am, squashed in the spare room under the stairs again! What do I have to do to keep my room, sick up a kidney or something?

The spare room was cramped and dark. The only window looked out onto a brick wall and the stairs running above the room meant there wasn't much headroom. If you didn't remember quickly when you woke up, then you sat up and immediately bashed your head on the sloping ceiling... not a nice wake up call, but fortunately I had done this enough for my body to know not to sit up in the morning.

It was late, the moon was shining through the little window and the house was silent. I was reading, and just getting to a good bit of my book, but I was desperately tired. It was a detective book set back in the gangster days. I'd just read a couple more...

Dreams are funny things. You know that feeling when you know you're in a dream but it still feels so real, you're terrified of the things you see, and you're convinced that were you to die here, dream or no dream, you'd be dead forever.

I'm falling through the blackness of a tunnel, walls rushing past on every side. I reach out and my fingernails scrape over a wall of bricks, but I can get no grip. I'm falling so fast, the brick swirls around me like the black clouds of a storm. Suddenly the swirling stops. I look down... solid ground. I sway uncertainly almost losing my balance, dizzy still from the fall. I'm in a hallway, stairs ahead, door on my right. It's all dark but there is shouting and a glint of light from a doorway beyond the stairs. The door is almost shut but not quite. It's a man and woman shouting at each other. My first thought is: where am I? I don't recognise the hallway. I'm frozen to the spot. What am I supposed to do now? Am I supposed to approach the door? If I do, will they know I'm there? I recognise the woman shouting. It's Missus Agnes. Her voice sounds younger and more fiery than I know it. Why's she in my dream? A hand appears around the door and it begins to swing open. Somewhere to hide, quick? Nowhere! It's the man, he's stepped through the door; he's staring at me now. This is definitely not good.

The scene grows hazy... black swirling walls again, except this time Missus Agnes is falling with me. What's going on? I don't understand it. It's as if this is her nightmare rather than mine. I don't recognise the places or understand any of the things I'm seeing. Missus Agnes gives out an almighty piercing shriek. She's pointing, eyes wide, a terrified look on her face. I follow her gaze. It's the ground! It's racing towards us. I want to scream but it's stuck in my throat. I can't breathe any more. Too late... WHACK!

I open my eyes. I'm not dead. That's cool. I'm in a field. The sun is blazing down. No, it's not a field, a plain with forest behind and what looks like a castle, as a tiny dot in the distance on the horizon.

"Right you are, squire!" comes the gruff voice from behind me. As I swing round to see what's going on, a strange sight meets my eyes.

"Right sir, first your chain mail."

This guy is dressed all old fashioned, in a leather tunic, and he's strapping chain mail to me. More worrying, there's a rather large looking horse trotting around in the background. Missus Agnes is nowhere in sight.

"Er, sorry, what?" I blurt, not quite sure how to phrase the question.

"Breath in," he orders. I do as I'm told. A rather heavy old metal breastplate is strapped on, held by fastenings at the shoulders.

"But—"

"Hold on, sir," the man interrupts and he heads off to catch my horse, which is trotting around behind us.

I'm wracking my brains. What is going on? Funnily, the head to foot armour doesn't feel too uncomfortable. It feels almost familiar. By my left foot is a large oval shield, face down. I flip it over with my foot and recognise the crest immediately. It is the long flowing water of the *"dream warrior"* chocolate from the chocolate box. OK, this is what I had been dreading. The bank raid hadn't just been a strange coincidence. I read the motto written below the crest. *"In our dreams we find out who we truly are."* The words from the back of the chocolate. Why am I not surprised? I definitely know who I truly am... a coward. I want to wake up now, please. I know what is coming is not going to be pleasant.

The leather guy is back with the horse. It's huge! What am I supposed to do with that? And it's definitely giving me a hard stare, as if daring me to try and saddle up. The leather guy is waiting expectantly. I've never even been on a seaside donkey before. I'm terrified of this thing. And the horse knows it.

"Go on, sir."

Here goes. I gingerly grab the bridle and swing myself up into the saddle. Easy. In fact, too easy. I'm handed a gleaming, golden hilted sword which I take with my right hand. The metal feels good in my hand. It is as if my body knows what it is supposed to be doing in the dream. OK, let's go with the flow. I sheath the sword. The shield is strapped to the left side of the horse and a long, but surprisingly light lance is placed in my right hand, the long handle nestling snugly under my arm, against my shoulder.

"God go with ya, sir," Leather guy hands me the heavy iron helmet which for the moment I place in front of me in the saddle. I salute him and he slaps the rear of the horse. I'm off, bent low, almost flying over the meadow, the wind buffeting against the heavy armour. My left hand holds the reigns and guides the horse expertly around the rocks, down the ravine and across the stream. It's almost as if I'm watching myself from above. My body seems to know what it is doing without me, which is some comfort since I still haven't got a clue what this is all about.

As I guide the horse up the bank on the far side of the stream and we crest the hill, the castle ahead comes again into view. It is close enough to see the narrow bridge over the moat which leads to the gates. And close enough to see and hear a hundred or more angry soldiers jeering at me. I come to a halt outside arrow range. My task seems clear. I have to take the castle. My confidence is growing, since in my dream I obviously have the skills and experience of a trained knight. But is it enough? How can one knight take a castle? My horse is chomping at the bit and stamping, yearning to get moving. I pull him back.

"It's only a dream," I repeat over and over to myself but the more I look around me the more real it seems.

I've been standing here for an age, unable to decide what to do. I look up at the soldiers in the castle and I'm scared. I haven't a clue how I would attack a castle. Let's face it, I'm a school kid! But somewhere else there is a voice urging me on.

"If you just let go and trust to the instincts and skills you have as a knight, you will succeed."

"But..." My protest fizzles out as the calm voice speaks again.

"Trust me. Have you enough courage to take just one step forward? And then another."

I look at the hundred strong angry faces on the castle. They hate me! I'm terrified. I reach down with my left hand and place the helmet over my head. How are you supposed to see anything out of this thing? OK, one step forward. But what's my plan? Don't worry about it... One step forward. I loosen my hold on the reigns and tighten my grip on the lance.

My steed trots forward. I let him continue. Suddenly he's galloping. I lean forward, low in the saddle. There is a shrill whiz, whiz as arrows fly past me. I can feel some of them ricochet off my helmet and armour.

I'm being shot at!! No time to panic. I look up and automatically pull right to aim for the gate. Tighten the lance into my arm and lean into it. The arrows are raining down like a flood now. I pray none of them find their mark.

Twenty feet... ten... I'm clattering across the slim wooden bridge. "AAAGGGHHHH!!!"

CRACK... The tip of my lance slams into the wooden gates. The lance almost rips my shoulder off. I've never felt such pain in my entire life. I hold onto the lance and the reigns of the horse with all my might. I realise I'm not even going to make it through the gate. This is a disaster.

But no, the lance has pierced the gate. It is buckling. My horse rears and its front legs slam through the gates. I'm in. The lance, what's left of it, clatters to the ground. The pain in my shoulder is killing me. I can't even feel my right arm.

I'm in a courtyard. Ahead I can see the inner wall. Walls seem to be towering above me on all sides. I suddenly feel cold, sweaty and scared, like a fox in a trap. There are various steps leading up the outside of the inner wall, and high above me are overhead walkways between the walls. No time to think. Soldiers are streaming into the courtyard. I kick my heals and head straight ahead for the iron portcullis. My left arm expertly swoops up the shield and, despite the pain, my right hand draws the sword from the sheath with a ching.

Here in my dream I am the skilled knight. My instincts have taken over. I'm like a spectator watching on from the passenger seat. My horse is picking up speed. I'm not even holding the reigns. Soldiers, twelve o'clock, dead ahead. I flinch. My horse carries me straight through the first wave of soldiers. I swerve left... why? The steps. We gallop up the narrow staircase of the inner wall, scattering angry enemy soldiers. I'm now flying along the top of the wall. It's hundreds of feet up in the air, breathtaking. I'm scared out of my wits! This wall is so narrow!

Then I see it. Tower, dead ahead. I have to rescue someone. Maybe it's Nurse Heartly. I wouldn't mind rescuing her. The door of the tower is flung open and... It's Missus Agnes? I'm so disappointed. I swoop her up expertly as I gallop past.

Then it happens. I feel the sharp point in my neck, like someone's hit me with a brick. The arrow's crept in just below the helmet and above the breastplate. I drop the sword and shield and lunge for the reigns... anything to cling onto to stop me falling. I can feel myself slipping. My hands reach out but only slide over the flanks of the horse. I hit the stone with a thud, fall back and I'm toppling again. I've landed on the edge of the castle well. I cannot gain a grip and I'm falling... bricks on all sides. I can feel nothing, see nothing but darkness.

"Aaahhhhggggg!!"

WHACK! Ouch. It was Agnes. She had just slapped me!

"Hey!"

"You OK? You were screaming." She had a very concerned look on her face. I'd never seen her look like that before.

"Nightmare," I replied, trying to wipe the memory of it out of my eyes.

"Horrid!" she replied. "My mum gets those. She never sleeps well. What have you done to your shoulder?"

I looked down and to my amazement the whole of my right shoulder was black and blue. Then the pain hit me. My right arm ached like anything. "Oh, it was the lance," I replied.

Chapter 7
Night Owls...

Downstairs
Galaxy ref: P5763EARTH
Grid: UK742~BCz87

The next morning I found Missus Agnes down stairs, sitting in the kitchen, in her dressing gown. She was in deep thought, eyes glazed over, sipping on a cup of coffee. Everyone normally ignored Missus Agnes in the mornings, when she was round at our house, because she was always in such a foul mood. I was just reaching up to the cereal cupboard when she spoke to me.

"I dreamt about you last night, Monty."

I froze. Surely that was impossible. You couldn't share dreams with people, could you? That would be even better than on-line Internet gaming!

"You were a knight in shining armour..." I had heard enough. I had been desperately clinging onto the idea that this was a very odd set of coincidences. But it was obvious there was something more sinister here.

"You see, I've always had this nightmare where I was falling down a hole," she went on, eyes still glazed. Why was she telling me this? Was I her therapist or something? "But last night you saved me. Thanks."

"It was just a dream," I lied.

I needed to talk to someone about it. But who? I wasn't sure about Charlie and Hash. They would just persuade me to eat more chocolates. Jacob perhaps? The answer came a week later and from the person I least expected.

As the next week passed I was getting more and more worried. My excuses had exhausted themselves and I had been packed off back to school. No-one there was going to let me live down all the articles in the papers. After the bank raid and with my nickname of Fish, they had now christened me the "Cod father" after the gangster movie. I entered the classroom on Tuesday and there was the most terrible smell. I opened my desk to find a dead tuna fish there.

"Well, we couldn't find a cod," one of the other boys explained.

Nice, I thought.

But I couldn't concentrate on school. Strange things were happening to me. I was still getting twinges in my neck, which worried me. And when they got really bad I had to lie down on the floor.

As one kid kindly pointed out, "What you doin' Fish? Hey look, he's doin' a cod impression!"

My right shoulder was still badly bruised and to my horror, Mum decided it must be due to school bullying and marched into school to complain. I tried to tell her it wasn't, but she just said that me covering it up just proved she was right. Adult logic??

But most worrying of all, Friday came around and I hadn't slept a wink all week. I tried Monday and Tuesday but every time I fell asleep I could see myself falling down the well, bricks on all sides, darkness below me and my finger nails clinging for the walls but never able to find a grip. Then I would wake up in a cold sweat.

After Tuesday I didn't try to sleep. I read, got bored and gazed out of the window, wishing I could be out there and not cramped into the spare room. Strangely, I didn't feel tired. But I was really worried. What was happening to me?

It was Friday night when I decided to creep down stairs and raid the ice cream, and I met Ugly on the stairs.

"What you doing up?" I asked in surprise.

"Nicking ice cream," she replied. "You?"

"That's my ice cream!" I hissed. She ignored the comment. She looked at me as if undecided about something and then said, "Follow me. I got something to show you. You'd better get dressed first."

What was going on? I got dressed quick and then hovered outside Missus Agnes and Ugly's room. What was I thinking... MY ROOM, which they had viciously stolen!!

"Come on!" hissed Agnes and an arm came out and dragged me inside.

"Look," Agnes pointed to her mum asleep on the bed. "Slept like a baby all week. She's never done that before, for as long as I can remember." Then suddenly she started moving with a purpose. She wrapped a scarf around her neck, picked up her torch and pulled open the window.

"Where 'we going?"

"Come on," she hissed. "Just follow me, and stop asking stupid questions."

The night was cool but pleasant, the moon bright and the streets deserted. I didn't have a clue what time it was, I'd left my watch behind. Agnes led me to the end of our street, and down the next, in silence. There we were, at the edge of Vitenbury forest. It was a large forest reserve, rambling and deserted most of the time. Once in the forest, Agnes broke the silence and started talking.

"Thanks," she said.

"Thanks? For what?"

"You know."

I didn't have a clue what she was talking about. I stared at her blankly.

Ugly rolled her eyes as if I was stupid and continued into the forest.

"What are we doing here?" I shouted as I ran to catch her up. We were now deep in the forest. The trees were close in on both sides and their branches formed a canopy a hundred feet above us so the night sky was blocked out. Agnes withdrew a torch from her pocket and flicked it on. I heard the howl of some night animal in the distance. The only other sound was that of our shoes scuffing along the uneven path. My foot caught on a branch as I was running and I went sprawling on the mossy floor. Ouch.

"Ugly! Come back here and tell me what's going on." Whack. Something bounced off my head. It was a pinecone.

"Don't call me Ugly! I don't like it!" Agnes marched back and stood defiantly, hands on hips, looking down at me whilst I crawled back up and dusted myself down. "It's not very nice, is it? You wouldn't like it if you were called Ugly, would you?!"

"OK," I grunted under my breath, not wanting to give ground.

"OK What?" she demanded.

I'd lost the plot on this one. What was I supposed to say now? They ought to issue scripts for having conversations with girls. I could never work out what I was supposed to say. Girls were so illogical.

"SORRY!" she shouted. "You're supposed to say sorry!" Next thing I knew she had booted me in the leg and I was down on the floor again in agony, whilst she stormed off. But I wasn't stupid. Without a torch I was dead meat here.

"Agnes… Hang on!" I hopped after her clutching my leg.

"Now, follow me carefully. And don't lose your balance. It's tricky." Agnes led on. I was intrigued. She stood close to a long rock wall where the ground level changed. The wall was covered in moss and vines and branches from trees. She walked as far along the wall as she could before the trees clumped too tightly into the rock. Then she turned and winked at me. Then she disappeared. She slid in behind the vines. I followed. Yuck! I could feel and smell the moss on my back. The vines scraped over my face. Then my shoe kicked something and I almost tripped. It was a root of tree. I stepped up onto it. There was another. These were steps I realised. I couldn't see Agnes now. I frowned and started moving a bit quicker to catch her up. About ten steps up I was no longer standing on roots but on wooden log steps. I could see the ropes holding them in place. Up and up I went. It seemed to go on forever. I eventually emerged onto a wooden rope bridge. The bridge led further up and as I emerged onto a wooden log platform, I was totally gob smacked. Agnes was grinning like a Cheshire cat.

"Worth coming to see?"

"You're kiddin'! This is incredible!" And it was. I was standing on top of the canopy of trees. I must have been hundreds of feet up in the air. I could see a maze of rope and log bridges which connected wooden platforms and at various points there were huts built in the branches of the trees. They were tree houses. Everything was tied onto the top of the tree trunks which emerged from the undergrowth below me, or to the uppermost branches of the trees. I stood still to admire the sight. The world was silent. Above me I had a totally clear view of the night sky, the stars and moon. Ahead I could see the treetops running out from beneath me, as they disappeared into the darkness in the distance.

"Come on," called Agnes. She raced off. I followed her carefully. I certainly didn't want to lose my footing. She ran nimbly along a thick log resting between two platforms, her arms outstretched to balance her. I paused, wondering what would catch me if I fell off. Would the branches break my fall?"

"Come on Monty. Don't be a wuss!" called Agnes.

"Fish! You can call me Fish!" I gulped and ran speedily across the log. It was easier than it looked.

I finally found Agnes in a shed size tree house with a semi-open roof. She was lighting a fire in a metal grate in the middle of the hut. The warmth felt good. The smoke circled up and through the open roof. The fire gave out enough light to see Agnes sitting the other side.

"She never sleeps. Ever since Ronnie died." I had so many questions, but Agnes seemed to have got in first.

"Who doesn't?" I asked. Do you ever get that distinct feeling like you missed something important in the conversation?

"My mum, stupid!" she snapped back at me. Then she calmed down again and continued. "But this week she has slept soundly each night." Her eyes narrowed and she looked at me suspiciously. "It was something to do with you, wasn't it? Something to do with the chocolates?" Ugly was the last person in the world I wanted to talk to about the dream.

"Ronnie? Who's Ronnie?" I asked, changing the subject.

"I had a brother once. He died. Fell down a well when we were visiting a castle ruins in Nottingham. Mum's been falling down wells in her dreams ever since."

Unbelievable! I felt like a brick had just hit me. It was like another bit of the jigsaw had just fallen into place. So I sighed and told Agnes the story so far. She stayed quiet and pondered.

"So you're saying you shared a dream with my mum," Agnes played it back, "Let me get this right... you rescued her, and now you're having the dreams instead of her?"

"All after I had eaten another chocolate." I told her about the George Cross.

"That's spooky. It can't be true?"

"You don't believe me?" I asked. Agnes looked sceptical.

"It sounds so farfetched."

"Yeah well, I've got the bad neck and shoulder to prove it," I mumbled back angrily. "And I'm getting worried about my nights. I need the sleep!... I never sleep!"

"Well!" Agnes said, suddenly enthusiastic. "Neither do I! Never have slept much whilst my mum has been tossing and turning and waking up. So this is a good idea. We could start a club or a gang. Meet up here at night, to pass the time for you." Agnes looked like she was on a roll. I liked the idea. This was a very cool place. "Who will we invite?" she continued. "You'll have to bring the chocs down here. I want to examine them."

"Now my turn," I said. "How...?" I opened my arms to indicate the tree house and everything around.

"This? How did we make it, you mean?"

"You made this?" I blurted in astonishment.

"Don't look so surprised!" she hissed back. "I'm not as useless as you! I want to be an architect when I grow up, you know. A designer. To design really big, complicated things... like this! It's a good start isn't it?"

"But... but, you couldn't do all this on your own!"

"I did it with Ronnie, and then when he died I sort of carried it on. It's not finished yet. I'm still working on it." There was a moment's silence. "Ronnie still helps."

"What?"

"Don't look at me like that!" she shot back with a menacing look on her face. She looked down at her feet as if suddenly embarrassed. "He writes to me. Tells me what to build."

"But, he's dead!" I realised just after the words were out that perhaps I could have said something a bit more helpful.

"He - still - writes - to - me !!!" she replied very slowly through gritted teeth whilst staring daggers at me. For the first time I wondered if I was safe up here with this obviously loony girl.

She stood up and stared out of the open roof. "I love it up here. It's like being at the highest point in the world, as near to heaven as you can get. I feel closest to Ronnie when I'm here."

I was about to launch into my explanation of how I knew positively that there was no such thing as heaven, but I thought better of it. I guess Agnes wasn't so bad, after all. The ginger curly hair could be forgiven. The teeth were a problem though... as was the temper. I'd never really bothered to find out anything much about her before. I'd never even known she had had a brother. I wish I had had a brother.

"I could help you building the rest of your tree houses if you wanted." Why had I said that? I had absolutely no intention of carrying tree trunks up here. It was madness. It's just one of those funny things when you've said something wrong you sort of have this inbuilt need to say something nice to put it right.

Agnes's eyes lit up. "Really? That would be so good!"

Oh no, what had I let myself in for!

It took me a couple of days to work out who should be initiated into our new club, as Agnes called it. It had been Wednesday before I could let everyone know. Thursday night we had our first meeting.

"What on earth are we doing here?" asked Charlie, as he sat down uncomfortably in front of the fire in what Agnes called the Gathering Hut. "Look Bozzos, I'm freezing cold! I should be asleep! But you've got me in this pest infected hole of a place." It was one o'clock in the morning. He swatted a bug, which was buzzing, around his head.

"Wash your hair, Charlie," I said sarcastically. "That'll keep the bugs off."

I was excited. This was something new. Not even Charlie in, I judged, one of his bad moods, could dampen my spirits. Hash sat quietly across from Charlie. The night was cool but not unpleasant. The forest had an eerie, menacing sort of feel to it, especially in the silence of the night. The fire hissed and the smoke rose through the circular hole in the ceiling. It was actually a brilliantly designed room. The log walls of the tree house kept the breeze off us but the open roof allowed us to star gaze and take in the glory of the surroundings. I rose from my place and wandered just outside the door of the Gathering Hut, onto the rope bridge. I was growing to love this place. It was, as Agnes had said, like standing on top of the world, and I guess we were, hundreds of feet up on top of the forest. It was going to be so cool meeting up here. I had my plan. I could hear the oooh's and aaaah's of Donny as Agnes guided him up the steps. Everyone had been similarly stunned and enchanted as I had… everyone except Charlie that was, who was mister grumpy git today. "Agghh, there'll be beetles and spiders and stuff," I could hear Donny mopping. He wouldn't get much sympathy out of Agnes, I smiled to myself. Agnes and Donny appeared over the entrance bridge and so we all settled in the Gathering Hut.

"Right, let's get started," I announced. "I want to start by welcoming you to the…" I paused for effect… "The Night Owls. This is our first meeting. Agnes is going to start with her forest story. Then I'm going to tell you the rules. Then you'll understand." As expected, a mixture of blank faces and total confusion. Donny raised his hand as if he was in class at school.

"Can I ask a question?"

"Er, no," I replied. "All will become clear. Agnes?"

Agnes took them through the same spooky story she had told me. It was even more frightening by the firelight. There was a look of wonder in everyone's eyes by the time she had finished. I noticed that she had left out the Ronnie writing her letters bit. Hash wondered in his low suspicious sounding voice, whether Ronnie's ghost might still be haunting the trees. Everyone looked around the hut wondering if a semi-transparent Ronnie might just jump out of the walls and say "boo".

"Don't be stupid," said Donny with his best religious mode switched on, "ghosts don't really exist."

"Rules!" I announced. At that moment there was a noise from far below us. A thump and an "ouch". Someone was moving around. Agnes moved quickly out of the hut to the spy deck, ten feet down dropping just below the tree tops. From there she could see everything going on below. "It's some old geezer," she whispered across to me.

"It's Jacob!" I announced and rushed off to get him.

Jacob was not young anymore and I could see the aches and pains in the look on his face as he struggled to make the climb.

Jacob rolled uneasily into the Gathering Hut.

"Monty. What on earth's goin' on 'ere?" I sat him down. Charlie and the others also looked uneasy. Jacob wasn't a kid like the rest of us. I had umm'ed and arr'ed about Jacob but at the end of the day he was like the older brother I had never had and I wanted him in.

"Right!" I repeated. "Rules! We are the Night Owls—"

"So what is that?" said Donny, confusion evident. "Is it some sort of gang? I don't want to get involved with anything dangerous or illegal."

I could see Charlie rolling his eyes.

"Don't worry Donny. You'll enjoy it. Rule number one," I continued. "You're not allowed to tell anyone about this or bring anyone here, unless the rest of us agree. Two, we all make an effort to come here as many nights as we are able. Three, we bring food."

"Beer!" announced Jacob. "I can bring beer?" I nodded encouragingly. I looked around the wooden log hut. Jacob was already going up in everyone's estimation (unlike Donny).

"Four, each night we will have a subject for debate or something we do, and whoever gets here first gets to choose it. Five, and this is the risky one, we always tell the truth here. Whatever we think about the subject under discussion, we say it, however hard it is." Silence. Was that good? "That's it."

"We could call it the Pact," announced Charlie, who had suddenly swapped over from grouchy to mad eyed enthusiasm, as if with the flick of a switch. "And anyone who breaks the Pact could have a punishment!" He leered at everyone around the hut, as if tempting anyone to ask what the punishment would be. Donny looked positively petrified.

"We need a secret handshake or something," put in Hash.

"We could all cut our palms open and rub our blood together as a sign of the Pact!" Charlie announced.

"Err, I don't think we need to go quite that far," I said. In the end we agreed on everyone having a dead arm punch as a sign of joining the Pact, and a good duffing up if they told anyone else. Charlie administered the dead arms, and Agnes volunteered to give him one, which I must say she administered with some vengeance. We nicknamed her, Buffy, the vampire slayer after that. She had a vicious streak, and no-one liked to cross her, especially up here in her domain of the tree houses. Charlie continued to call her Ugly, until two weeks later when she crept silently up behind him and knocked him out of the trees. He was only saved by the spy deck. It took him a week to recover from the shock, and he was positively scared of Buffy after that.

Anyway, for now we settled down for our first evening and I gave the floor to Agnes (or should I say, Buffy) to talk more about the Tree Houses and how she had built them. The fire sparked and fizzled, casting a dim glow which just about lit up everybody's face. There was no doubt that everyone was a little frightened. Buffy definitely knew how to tell 'em and every now and then the fire would give off a loud pop as it burnt up a damp log, and everyone would jump. Jacob and Hash then continued the night with spooky ghost stories, and Donny almost flipped out when Charlie crept up behind him, hissed and placed a long rubber snake on his shoulder. (Where did he get that from in the middle of a forest?) All in all it was a good start to the Night Owls, I judged.

Over the next week, the Night Owls met every night. Buffy and me, we hadn't planned things very well. I guess we should have anticipated some of the problems, but we just hadn't thought that far ahead.

I was always there, since I never slept. One of the huts was set aside for the food and beer, which Jacob, true to his promise, provided. Agnes came three nights in that first week, as did Charlie. Jacob and Hash came twice and Donny turned up just the once. Our debates varied considerably. We discussed girls the second night, since Agnes wasn't there, and Charlie was squirming in his seat before confessing that he fancied one of the teachers at school. Mind you, I wasn't much better, what with Nurse Heartly.

We considered strategies for me to get hold of her phone number.

"Just walk back into the hospital and ask her," said Hash over the firelight whilst sipping on his bottle of stout. We all stared at him as if he was stupid. How could he make it sound so simple?

"No! You gotta really impress 'er, Fish." It was Charlie in one of his enthusiastic moods. I had to be careful or he'd have me putting up "I love you" posters on the advertising hoardings opposite the hospital. I'd lost count of the number of times he'd talked me into doing really stupid things.

"It's very tough, young Monty. Love is not an easy thing to start." It was Jacob talking this time. "It takes courage to ask, and even more courage to stick with it when it gets tough." I didn't understand what he meant about sticking with it. Give me Nurse Heartly and I'd be besotted for life!

"You married, Jacob?" asked Hash. I looked across. I could see Jacob through the firelight. He glanced down, a mixture of happy memories and pain on his wrinkled face. It was a face which had seen a lot of life.

"Was once," Jacob replied. "A long time back. She died." There was an awkward silence. I guess our little gang wasn't ready for stuff that personal yet. No-one knew the rules for these sorts of discussions. "She was very beautiful, my Annie. Had a sor' of sparkle in 'er eye, she did."

"So, have you got kids?" asked Hash.

"Nah, just never got round to it and then, well... it all happened, di'n' it and the chance was gone." Awkward silence again. Everyone wanted to ask how she had died, but no-one had the guts... me included.

"So, Monty," Jacob continued, suddenly more upbeat. "The moral of the story is... Don' wait. Say it now, mate, whate'r 'tis ya gotta say. May ne'er get 'nother chance."

Third night, Jacob brought his pack of cards and insisted on teaching us how to play poker, and Donny wanted to discuss religion. (Boring - I was beginning to think including Donny had been a bad idea). They also bullied me into agreeing to bring the box of chocolates in the following night.

And so, on the forth night we debated the mysterious box of chocolates, which I reluctantly brought along and it took up residence in its very own "Mysterious Hut" as we called it. We had our most fierce debate, on the subject of whether it would be safe for me to eat another one. Everyone seemed to ignore me when I said, it didn't really matter since I definitely wasn't eating any more, anyway. Jacob drank too much stout, sang much too loudly and fell out of the tree. We had another argument with Buffy since she insisted we should take him to hospital. In the end Charlie pinned her down and I half carried Jacob back, abandoned him on his hallway floor and raced back home far too late, almost getting caught absent from bed by Mum's early morning trip to the toilet. The next day I checked on Jacob, who was fine.

On the fifth night Hash wanted to discuss angels for some reason. Boring! Jacob insisted that he had been rescued by one during the war. He sat under the moonlight and unfolded his story. He had been too slow out of the trenches when they had retreated, and he had been left behind, lost within the ranks of the advancing enemy. One other soldier had come to his rescue. The strange thing was that when the soldier had finally carried him back into camp, the other soldiers swore blind that they had seen Jacob stagger in alone, not with anyone else. Jacob had searched for the mysterious soldier but he had vanished. Hash was intrigued and got Jacob to describe the whole incident in rather monotonous detail.

And so the Night Owls continued. Each night was better than the one before. This was a perfect time. We became a close nit little group.

Friendships deepened, mammoth amounts of food were consumed and we worked through some difficult subjects, all because of the Pact. We also developed a brilliant game of Tree Tag. It was quite spooky, sprinting across the narrow walkways, hundreds of feet up, with nothing but moonlight to guide us. Buffy was bril at it but it took the rest of us a while to get used to taking our life in our hands, across the rope bridges and climbing vines. We usually did this when Jacob wasn't there, since he wasn't up to it. All in all, I even became quite pleased that I never slept. Sleeping was for wimps!!

Within a couple of weeks a sort of competition had erupted. Hash had said he wanted to talk about death and so everyone was trying to ensure they got to the Gathering Hut before him so he couldn't chose the subject. When Hash finally arrived first, one evening a week later, and announced the subject of "death" we all gulped, Agnes went quiet, and Charlie looked as if he was suddenly very uncomfortable. It was a Monday night. We had no Donny tonight but everyone else was there. It was surprising since it was peeing down with rain. We had abandoned the Gathering Hut and were locked in the Food Hut, door shut against the howl of the wind and rain. Hash gazed across at Charlie, his eyes unflinching. What was he up to, I wondered? Hash, Charlie and I were best mates. But here, now Hash seemed to be picking on him. Maybe he thought it was about time he talked about his dad.

Charlie's dad had died two years before in a boating accident. Charlie had never been the same since. That's why he had high days, when he was determined not to let it get to him, and low days, when he couldn't put it out of his mind. We all accepted Charlie whatever his mood. We knew it was tough for him.

Looking around the Food Hut, most of them had had someone close to them who had died... Buffy, Charlie, Jacob. I didn't know about Hash.

Charlie sucked in breath through his teeth, very tense. "The real killer is, they never found his body," said Charlie. He seemed to relax, having said the thing which was weighing on his mind. All the slatted shutters were shut tight to the storm. The light came from four candle lamps, swinging gently as they hung from the roof.

"It's like..." Charlie paused, crinkled up his face and closed his eyes. He looked like he was desperately trying to grab a stray and elusive thought before it fluttered out of the hut and disappeared forever. "...Some days I wake up and I just wonder if maybe he'll turn up at the door, alive and well. And we'll all be back together again."

We all stared at him. What could you say? A blast of wind, from the storm raging outside, rattled the shutters. The little hut shook, and two of the candles flickered out, as if a ghost had swept through the room, listening to our debate. Charlie didn't seem to notice.

"I know it'll never happen. If he was still alive he would have come back by now. I just can't stop the thought. And then, it's like it all comes back again... all the hopes, all the possibilities, all the memories... and I'm back to square one and I can't get over it."

I'd never heard all this before. Well, it wasn't your normal sort of playground chatter at school, was it?

There was a moment's silence.

"I lost my Annie to cancer," Jacob said suddenly. I was beginning to feel a bit of an under performer, never having had any deaths.

"You're never ready for it," said Jacob. "It was all too soon. We had our ideas and plans, a life all laid out before us, but then it's the doctors one day, then the hospital and before you can take it in, you're standing by a grave stone, in a daze, wondering what just happened."

I had to admit, it was a raw deal.

"Life... Life's what happens to you when you least expect it." It was one of Jacob's sayings. I had heard him say it before.

"I'll see her again one day," Jacob went on, a dreamy, heaven gazing look in his eyes. "We'll talk things over, reminisce, finish all those plans and discussions which were cut short."

"Ronnie still writes to me," Agnes suddenly announced. Everyone stared at her.

"What?" said Charlie.

"He does!" Agnes insisted defensively. "He sends me letters." We were all a bit scared of Buffy, ever since she had pushed Charlie off the log bridge. So no-one was going to argue with her now.

We all went away from that night feeling rather uneasy. It had been strangely warming, I thought as I lay awake in bed. I had seen their pain and hurts. That was something people didn't often let you see. It was like we were an even closer group now... sort of like a family.

I was still worried about all the stuff with the chocolates and not being able to sleep... but for once I realised I was pretty lucky. Some of the other guys had a really raw deal. I couldn't feel sorry for myself tonight.

Chapter 8

Gone Fishing...

Upstairs
Realm 3... The Wall, Dock 7

H ey Stex! What's cookin'?" said Creevy as he stacked crates in his
ship. The spacecraft hovered at the end of the docking ramp, which
was near the top of the golden outer area of The Wall. It was
powered up and it sort of wobbled, stretching and contracting as if made of
rubber or as if it was breathing.

Stex had a bored expression on his face and, as usual, his orientation
training manual under his arm.

"Where you going, Creevy?" He watched as Creevy's arms, loads of them,
all seemed to move independently doing different tasks, some stacking, others
adjusting knobs and dials in the maintenance panel. They seemed to stretch
longer and shorter as well. "How do you do all that with your hands, Creevy?"

"All what?" Creevy looked up. It was second nature to him. "Rafe's off
on S.A. Thought I'd do a little fishing."

"Fishing?" asked Stex.

"Yeah, you know. Skate with the stars, chase some space. Just... sort
of... get out there." Creevy looked longingly out into space. It was calling him.

"You miss it don't you, Creevy?"

"Not miss it, no," the alien replied. His many arms paused for a moment.
"The Main Man said I can go out there any time I like. It's what I do, you
know. I feel... alive out there."

"More alive than in here?" Stex asked.

Creevy made a throw away gesture with three of his hands. "You wouldn't understand. This is what I did, where I lived."

"No, I do understand! Really!" Stex replied eagerly. He pointed to the thick manual under his arm. "It's in there... in the orientation manual. There's always an adjustment period from Pre-world."

"Yeah, yeah! OK." Creevy dismissed the subject.

"So what do you fish for?"

"Chase some angels, pick up some space debris, that sort'a thing. The Main Man's good about it. As long as I steer clear of the war zones and the inhabited planets, he's cool with it all."

"Can I come with you?" Stex asked excitedly.

Creevy scratched his head with one hand as the others did the standard checks around the space ship exterior. "Well... I guess so, but can you hack it, Stex? I mean, we'll be out for a time. Some guys get a bit claustrophobic out there, you know."

"Oh yeah. No problem." Stex hopped onto the left wing and up to the entrance arch.

The sides of dock seven zipped past on both sides and then they were out. Stex stared out in wonder. It wasn't his first time in Creevy's ship. He had been in it many times before, but it always gave him the same feeling of exhilaration.

"Wow! Can we spin it?... Please, pleeeease!"

"Ohh, Stex, no, that's kid's stuff!"

"Go on, please... Pretty please."

"Ohhh... OK, OK. Just stop doing that grovelling thing!" Creevy agreed reluctantly. He yanked the stick left and down, pulled right underneath the canopy of Realm Three, spun the ship three sixty, notched up the speed. As the ship sped up, the rubber-like exterior stretched longer and thinner and spun at precisely the right angle to zip through the golden Wall arch, just inches to spare on each wing. They shot over Main Street and then banked out, back into space. Creevy felt the feeling again... he wasn't a green alien, he was part of the space ship, he lived it... breathed it... he could guide it precisely within a millionth of an inch.

"WOW! So cool!" said Stex, positively jumping with excitement.

"Yeah, yeah. Come on. Enough tricks. Let's do some real fishing." They sped off into space.

Coloured lights, dials and switches, stared at them from the dash. Creevy's hands moved swiftly over the panel expertly. Stex stared out of the front screen which showed a hundred million stars against the black night backdrop. It was magnificent.

"I got an idea, Creevy."

"Oh, here we go! I knew this was a bad idea."

"It's just a little idea," Stex went on. "Just a tiny, weenie, really small, sort of... detour."

Creevy weaved in and out of some gas clouds just for fun. "Detour? What, what? I gotta hear this?"

"Well, you see that galaxy there... five down." Stex pointed out the front screen.

Creevy laughed (with both mouths).

"Absolutely no way, Stex. It's just not allowed. It breaks all the rules!"

"But... It was my home! I never got to see it—"

"NO BUTS! I'd never get through anyway. It's a waste of time."

"You can fly through anything. You're brilliant, Creevy! I've seen you flying... like when you spin it through the arch." Stex pleaded.

"This is a space ship. You're talking about breaking through the angel zone. It's IMPOSSIBLE!"

"But it's EARTH... my world! I don't remember it, Creevy. You don't understand what it's like! If I could just see it... smell it... Just once!!"

"NO!"

Chapter 9

The First Letter...

Downstairs
Galaxy ref: P5763EARTH
Grid: UK742~BCz87

D ad arrived back on a Wednesday, laden with presents from America. It was cool to see him. I stood there in my Stetson and cowboy boots and realised I'd missed him loads.

"How's the neck, Kiddo?" he asked.

I said it was OK. Actually it still throbbed sometimes and my shoulder still gave me jip from the lance as well. But my dad was a battle hardened war hero now, so I didn't want to sound like a "wuss", as Buffy would put it.

I'd given up watching TV, for two reasons. Firstly because, inevitably, I saw a glimpse of my celebrity dad on there, either in an interview or on the news or even advertising washing powder. And I didn't want to see him on TV, I wanted him here. And secondly, you watch TV to see adventures, strange and exciting things happening to people, I guess because your own life is too boring. But my life was already full of enough strange and exciting things that I couldn't explain, I figured I didn't need TV.

"Can Monty stay off school today, love?"

"No Ronald!" Mum replied testily. "He can't."

"How long you here for, Dad?" I asked.

"No more filming for a whole week or so! You wanna do something at the weekend, Monty?"

I was pleased as punch as I put my football cards in my pocket and walked to school. And still no talk of packing me off to the army. I was even beginning to think about what I could spend the escape fund on. I may not need it anymore.

I picked up a letter addressed to me from the front door mat as I hopped happily out of the house. I had a full half mile to walk before Hash would be waiting for me at the post box, so I dawdled along and ripped open the letter.

A lot of strange things had been happening to me lately, and generally I was pleased when I had "normal" days. The Night Owls I counted as normal these days as it had become part of my every day routine. But I hadn't eaten anymore chocolates so I figured I was safe. But today was to be anything but normal.

I hadn't noticed the post mark on the letter until after I'd read it. It had come from Africa! I didn't know anyone in Africa, except Uncle Frank, and he didn't count as he was a moron.

I ripped open the envelope and unfolded the single piece of smart writing paper. My immediate thought was that it had to come from a woman. Women always used posh writing paper for letters, men always made do with scrappy bits of paper. It was just one of those unexplained facts in the universe which sat alongside black holes, life after death and why the egg never popped up from the toaster when you did egg on toast.

I had a sudden thought. Maybe it was from Nurse Heartly to say she missed me terribly and couldn't live without me. I scanned it quickly. It wasn't. It was, without doubt, the strangest letter I had ever received. It read:

"Monsieur Monty,

My name is Senia. I am ten. I live in the village of Bombering in the tribe of Villtourage in Botswana. My English French not good. Please excuse. Monsieur Cogan taught me to write. I am pleased to be able to write to people all over the world. I write when the sun is up and when I am given words. I love animals and I have a pet Lima. The tribe want to eat him but I won't let them.

The God who created the same sun which shines over you and me, gave me words for you. I do not understand them, but Monsieur Cogan said I should write them anyway as they will be important to you.

The message is, to keep using the gift given to you and not to be afraid.

The floods are coming here and we will need to move to the higher land when the mountain season closes. We know the floods come as the shadow moves over the plain.

From Senia."

What did that mean? What gift? Who'd given me a gift? And how did a ten year old in Africa get my address? My immediate thought went to the box of chocolates. It was the only strange gift I had received. "Keep using the gift" the letter had said. I had a horrible thought that this snotty little kid in Africa wanted me to eat another chocolate. No way, hosay! Was this Charlie having a laugh again?... Charlie trying to persuade him to eat another of his deadly chocolates. I was definitely suspicious. I decided not to tell anyone about the letter and I'd see if Charlie hinted at anything. One thing I knew for definite. I had not eaten any more chocolates and so I was safe. Nothing else weird could happen to me. With that happy thought and the knowledge that Dad was home, I went to school.

That evening Dad treated us to a take away from the local Chinese. Buffy and Missus Agnes had gone back next door now that Missus Agnes was sleeping better and I had to admit, though I liked Buffy a lot, it was a great evening, just the three of us. Dad showed us his slides from America and Mum and Dad let me teach them how to play Rummy. We sat round the dinning table playing and just enjoying having Dad home. I cleaned them out at Rummy of course, but I didn't tell them how I'd got so good at it.

At five to midnight I lay in bed smiling to myself. As the clock struck midnight I rolled off my bed and landed silently on the carpet, ready to grab my torch, which was always placed under the bed resting against the skirting board. I noticed a slight gleam of reflected light which glinted off something metal under the bed. I was intrigued. I reached under and pulled out a metal box. It was a slightly rusty, slightly battered old tin box, whose original use had been to hold soap powder. I pulled it open. Inside I could see various trinkets... an autograph book, a necklace, one of those velvet covered ring boxes and various makeup bottles. I immediately realised it must be Buffy's, left over from the many nights when I had been kicked out of my room. I would return it to her in the morning. I was about to close it when I noticed the envelopes. I hesitated since this was her personal stuff. Then my curiosity got the better of me. There was a pile of them, tied with a neat pink ribbon. I took out the pile and then pulled the top envelope out from within the ribbon. It was addressed to Buffy, the top of the envelope already ripped open. I extracted the letter from within. I was feeling quite uneasy... even guilty about this. Buffy would rip my head off if she knew I was reading her mail. It wasn't the right thing to be doing. Oh well, as gramps always used to say, "in for a penny, in for a pound." There was no point in getting all queasy about it now, was there?

I unfolded the two sheets of letter writing paper and glanced immediately down to the sign off at the bottom of the second page. It was from Ronnie, Buffy's brother, obviously written before he had died. It must be one of the things she kept to remind her of him. The date on the first page read... hang on... Last year?! That made no sense... He was dead...

"Blooming heck!" I blurted. I hadn't really taken Buffy seriously when she had said her dead brother had written her. I counted the letters... sixteen. This wasn't possible, was it? I didn't believe in afterlife. It was all mumbo-jumbo. Death was sad and all that, but dead meant dead and anything else people said, even all that stuff the other night, was just 'cause they couldn't cope with it. But if Buffy had people writing to her from beyond the grave... well, that changed things a bit. And that made me uncomfortable. I wasn't ready for my beliefs to be rocked like that.

I scanned the first letter. I was stunned. Ronnie talked about dying, heaven, and then he went into detailed instructions about how to complete the tree houses. I pulled out more letters, read them, carefully analysed the postmarks, but none were clear enough to see where they were sent from. The heaven descriptions built up through the letters. He painted a picture of a sort of, hazy spiritual experience floating round with the clouds. I wasn't convinced. It didn't sound authentic. And if he was in heaven why would he care about finishing off the tree houses? I shook my head. It just didn't hang together. Yet, who would have written sixteen detailed letters to Buffy, pretending to be Ronnie? It made no sense. Then I suddenly had a brainwave. I ran over to my chest of drawers and rummaged through until I emerged with what I was looking for. It was the list of Night Owl rules, which Buffy had written out neatly. I laid it next to the first Ronnie letter and stared at them both, lying on the top of my bed spread, the torch as close as I could get it. My suspicion was confirmed. The writing was Buffy's. It suddenly made me feel queasy to think about it. She had written sixteen letters to herself. Why? Not because she was mad or stupid. But because she hurt. I stared again at the writing. It was definitely hers. The letters all sloped the same way and when she crossed the t's she flicked it up at the end. The neatness and the smart paper told me it was a female writer as well.

For just a moment I lay still on my back and tried to imagine what Buffy had gone through. She had hurt so much, that she wrote secret letters to herself... and she had never talked about it with anyone, not even the Night Owls. It wasn't the way life should be.

I shook my head, glanced at my watch (half past twelve) and after carefully replacing everything in the tin box, slipped on my jeans, t-shirt and shoes and headed for the window. I was still thinking about Buffy as I climbed out of the window. That's probably why I wasn't concentrating particularly hard on what I was doing. The inside leg of my jeans caught on the window latch as I climbed out. I looked down to see what was caught, my foot slipped and before I could do anything about it, there was a loud ripping sound, a searing pain in my left thigh, as if someone had just punctured it with a screwdriver, and more worryingly I was falling. Moments like this only last a second or two but it's amazing how many thoughts go through your head in that time... why did I let my foot slip?... how far is it to the ground?... why couldn't I have pasta for tea?...

I hope I don't get blood on my jeans... would my foot still have slipped if Mum had given me pasta for tea?... I wonder how much this is going to hurt... I don't want to be late for the Night Ow—

THUD!

"OH XXXXXX!!" (X= unprintable word).

I landed in the holly bush. I wasn't sure whether to be pleased there was a bush there to break my fall or annoyed it had to be the holly bush. My back ached as if someone had stapled it to the ground. I rolled out of the holly bush. My t-shirt got, sort of, caught on the sharp leaves and tore as I pulled it free. I sat on the front lawn and glanced down at my jeans. There was blood oozing from the top of my left leg and a huge rip in my jeans, crotch to knee. Oh great!! If I ran into anyone they'd think I was a streaker who'd got mugged!

I was in two minds as to whether to go to the tree houses or back in the house. But I'd only be lying awake in the house, and I thought my leg might hurt too much to climb the drainpipe. So I headed for the forest.

I arrived at the gathering hut to find the whole place deserted. I was slightly irritated, after all the agro it had caused me trying to get there, that no-one else had made the effort. I sat down, dabbing my leg with my handkerchief, and decided to use this night as thinking time, to try to solve the growing number of strange mysteries, which were now piling up. First I got a cold pizza and two bottles of stout from the food hut. I popped the lid on the first bottle, stared up at the stars through the open roof and started to think. This was definitely a calm place, a place for solving mysteries. We had discussed many things in this very room. The place had a particular feel and aura to it, as if Charlie, Hash and Buffy were now engrained in the walls, ready to help me with my thinking. It was as if I had my very own murder mystery to solve (except there had been no murder, of course.)

So, of course, mystery number one was the box of chocolates. I had already dismissed my original theory that this was a coincidence. The strangeness of the chocolates themselves, the bank raid incident and medal after eating the cross shaped chocolate, and the Missus Agnes dream which shifted her sleepless nights to me... no way could that all be coincidental. And, very worryingly, with each thing that happened, I seemed to come out of it worse off. I had considered that this might be some trick of Charlie's, but it was too elaborate and I just couldn't see how anyone could arrange a bank raid and a dream as part of a scam. No, it wasn't Charlie. Which left the final option, which I had been putting out of my mind. It could be supernatural. Either someone sticking a voodoo doll of me with pins, which was a worrying thought, or something to do with God. I put the chocolates on hold for a minute. My brain couldn't take that any further.

Mystery number two, a shared dream with Missus Agnes. Were shared dreams possible? I made a mental note to visit the library and look it up. My mind was a blank. There seemed no logic in it at all. Move on.

Mystery number three. A letter from a girl I've never heard of in Africa. Which was probably... but not for definite... alluding to the box of chocolates, telling me to carry on eating them. Again, I had thought it was a hoax but Charlie had said nothing about it at school, no unusual behaviour at all. So it looked as if it might possibly be genuine.

What was the link? The letter had mentioned God. The gift tag on the chocolates had said it was from the man upstairs. Was this also God? Donny reckoned it was, but then he was a nutter. Jacob also seemed to have some sort of belief in God, and I'd trust him in anything. No, I shook my head, I didn't believe in God; had to be another explanation. And anyway, more worryingly than who was behind this, I hadn't worked out the reason why yet? Bank raids, shared dreams, strange letters. What was the point?

I was no further on. There were two good outcomes, though. We now had the Night Owls, although I wondered where that was going. And of course, I had my freedom. My life, which a few months back, had been planned out by my dad with breathtaking finality, now appeared to be wide open before me.

The final mystery was Buffy's brother talking from the grave, but I had already solved th—

There was a flash of light from the open roof. I looked out but it was gone. I hobbled to my feet, clutched my leg and headed for the door to see what was going on.

Chapter 10
Playing Chicken...

Upstairs
Realm 2... The Watchers Restricted Section,
Perimeter Monitoring room 151

W e've got a runaway, Sir!"

"Quadrant?"

"Eight niner seven alpha."

"Identify?"

"Creevy."

The angel on watch relaxed. "He's friends with the Biops. This is a Biops screamer. It's OK."

"Sir?"

"Biops screamer. It happens to all of them. They have no Pre-world, so they tend to stress out, go a bit barmy. A high number of them actually try to return to earth."

"Return, Sir? Why? Why would they want to go back?"

"That's the point. It's not back for them. They don't remember. This is all part of their learning. They have to go through it. The Chief says it's how they will start to understand."

"What do you want me to do, Sir?"

"Nothing. Just leave them. They'll never get through the boundary, the angel zone. Just monitor them till they're brought in."

"Er... But Sir..." The angel sat looking at the monitor in front of him as the little space craft zigzagged through the outer defences. "... He's through the angel zone, Sir."

"What?! That's not possible."

"He's flying like the clappers, Sir. I've never seen anything like it. He's playing chicken with the angel guard, Sir."

Chapter 11
The Sighting...

Downstairs
Galaxy ref: P5763EARTH
Grid: UK739~DXy94

I limped as far as I could across the tree-top rope bridges. Then I had to climb down to the forest floor again. My leg was killing, but I was following a very distinct light, which was flashing intermittently ahead, and a strange sound which seemed to be a combination of a splintering, crushing sound and a mechanical whirring.

I flicked on my torch and shined the thin beam of light ahead. I didn't feel totally comfortable. I knew my way around the tree tops but I didn't know this bit of the forest. I didn't want to get lost. Also, I wasn't sure what other animals lived here at night time. But, then again, I was being stupid. This was a small isolated wood near a town. They wouldn't let anything deadly live in here. My trainers crunched on the dried leaves and twigs. I wasn't cold since I had my thick fleece on, but I could feel the cold down my leg, where the rip in my jeans was. Also, I felt damp from all the wet branches and leaves which kept flicking back into my face as I walked quickly through the thickening undergrowth. There was no doubt, the trees were getting closer together and harder to fight my way through. I shined my torch down onto my watch. Three am. It was the early morning dew making everything wet.

The light ahead was giving a bright flash about once every thirty seconds. It lit up a wide arc across the forest, so I could see much more than from the thin beam of my torch. It flashed again. I could see an opening just in front of me where all the trees seemed to have been snapped in half about a meter up. This whole patch must have been over ten meters wide. I crouched down and waited for the next flash of light. It came and I caught another glimpse of the strange patch of broken trees. It was as if something huge, like a low flying aeroplane, had swooped down and chopped them off.

The next flash came and I could see that further into the patch of trees they got shorter and shorter and then there was a deep furrow in the ground and the trees seem to have been ripped out at the roots. Whatever was up ahead had crash landed, ploughing straight through the trees. Maybe it was an army jet. There was an air base outside town.

I ran as fast as I could down the edge of the clearing, making sure I kept hidden in the trees, until I found myself running into a large shadow. Whatever it was, it was right here in front of me.

I crouched down right at the edge, by the last row of trees. There was little moon tonight, hidden by clouds, so I couldn't make much out. There was just a dark outline. But it looked big... huge... and it didn't look jet fighter shaped. I waited for the next flash of light. It seemed to take an eternity to come. When it came, I could make out a huge circular object like a large disc, about ten meters in diameter. It was lying crooked, a large mound of earth propping up its left side as if it had slid along the forest floor, digging and collecting all the earth as it went. Then the light went out again.

I blinked. My first thought was a UFO. I had lots of discussions with Donny about UFO's. Donny swore blind that they existed. Said that logically, why should we assume we are the only living beings in the universe. Said he had a second cousin in Wales who'd seen a little green man once. It was just further proof to me that Donny was a nutter! I'd read a book about crop circles once. It said they had proved it was all an elaborate hoax. When I told Donny this, he just said it was a cover up by the US military which proved beyond doubt that they had really been made by UFO's. You just can't reason with people like that.

The next flash came. I was so lost in my thoughts that I missed it. I was annoyed with myself.

Then, all of a sudden, lights lit up the forest. I suddenly realised how exposed I was here. I was much too close and in easy view of the thing in front of me.

My first thought was: has it seen me? Is that why the lights came on? But I couldn't move. I couldn't do anything. I was transfixed. The huge metal disk... plate thing, in front of me was lit up like a birthday cake, by lights coming from the very edge of the disk, placed about a meter apart. They looked as bright as flood lights on a football pitch. Now I could see it better, I could see strange markings around the upper edge, but apart from this, there were no other bits sticking out or anything which might indicate what it was. But there was something else strange. Although it looked like slightly dulled metal, it was moving... shaking gently... almost as if it was breathing. With each breath came the whirring sound. It must be made of something flexible, rubbery.

My mind was reeling. All my thoughts seemed jumbled up. I didn't believe in UFO's! There had to be another explanation. It must be some secret military project, a prototype jet, or something. I wish I'd had pasta for dinner. I really wanted to rewind my life to before Christmas. I wanted to be back in the spare room, have Agnes and Missus Agnes acting weird again, and go back to when Dad talked about the army all the time. I could understand everything back then. It was all normal life. Just now it all seemed too complicated. It was all getting out of hand. I reassured myself that nothing outrageous could happen since I hadn't eaten any more of the chocolates.

There was a loud hiss and a black outline appeared at the front of the disc.

Oh drat! I was really in trouble. A door began to open a few meters in front of me. It unfolded downwards and came to rest on the crushed tree remains. Something was moving inside. I couldn't see what it was as the inside of the... thing... was in shadow, set back from the exterior lights. Whatever it was, it was coming this way. I wanted to run, but I was rooted to the spot. I hadn't moved a muscle since the lights all came on. What would happen if I'd seen an ultra-secret military thing? In all the films on TV, when this sort of thing happened, they hunted you down and tried to knock you off.

A single green thing walked down the steps. It was as wide as it was tall, with a huge number of arms, and a hideous head, which had two mouths.

My jaw dropped. "Oh pig snot!" That was totally impossible. All possible explanations and theories vanished. In that one instant it all went out the window. My life changed suddenly, in the space of half a second. All the things I had believed had been changed, all the boundaries I'd worked out for what was true and what was fairy tales had been trampled into the mud. I'd always been so sure! Now it was a brand new day... a new ball game altogether. In fact, now anything was possible. Maybe Donny was right, maybe the tooth fairy did exist after all.

But just now I had a bigger problem. Its eyes locked in on me. I'm dead meat! Five or six of its arms pointed at me and it started making a strange noise, a sort of spluttering. Maybe it was trying to talk to me? Maybe it was about to zap me, vaporising me in a millisecond! No, on second thoughts, it was looking over its shoulder and talking to something back in the spacecraft.

Then I heard something very strange from inside the spacecraft. It sounded like someone saying: "Yes... Yes... Creepy... It's one of them." It was definitely speaking English. What was going on? Was it going to kidnap me? Should I run?

Then the little green man ran back into the spacecraft, the door shut and the lights vanished. I was plunged into darkness. I could only see blotches of light which I knew was just my eyes playing tricks. I began to hear a light buzzing sound. Then a further crunching. I rubbed my eyes and then scrambled around the ground for my torch, which I'd obviously dropped. I found it and flicked it on. The clearing in front of me was empty. I glanced up, but I could see nothing in the dark night sky. I could just hear the buzzing growing fainter. It was the only thing which reassured me that I had actually seen something and wasn't totally loopy.

My legs began to wobble under me and I let myself collapse to the ground. My breathing was suddenly laboured and I lay there for what seemed like an eternity, my mind totally blank.

Eventually I decided I had to get up.

I looked up, after what I gloomily concluded (against my better judgment) must be a spacecraft.

I decided to add another possibility to my mystery detective work. I was seriously concerned that I was going stark raving mad... away with the fairies... gaga land. I decided I wouldn't tell the others about any of this. How could I possibly explain to them that I was seeing little green men?

Chapter 12
The African Elephant…

Downstairs
Galaxy ref: P5763EARTH
Grid: UK739~DXy94

All in all, yesterday had not been a good day. I had woken up the next morning to find Dad gone again.

"He got an important call. Had to fly, I guess," shrugged Mum. Then she asked me why there was blood all over the window frame in my room. I said I had to get to school early. It was a lie, but then I had to get out of the house. I didn't think Mum would understand if I explained that my life was falling apart. I had also made the mistake, at school, of telling Charlie and Hash about Buffy's letters to herself. I regretted it the moment the words left my lips. Charlie laughed like a drain and said she was obviously out there with the fairies. Glad I didn't tell him the little green man story. I was still getting panicky and short of breath every time I thought about it. Not sure I'd ever been quite so frightened. It was a different sort of frightened to the bank raid.

I had survived school today, though. That was a good sign. I was taking life a minute at a time, just waiting to see what it'd throw at me next. I had this sort of sinking feeling that life was getting out of control and starting to crumble. I was desperately trying to hold it together. I sat in the tree house, that evening, feeling glum. Everyone was here tonight, but I was feeling further away from them, not part of the group.

"Right," said Hash. He had arrived first tonight. We all waited to hear the topic for tonight.

"Who is the greatest person who ever lived?"

Not bad, I thought. This could be interesting. It was a clear night, tonight. The stars were bright, and empty sweet wrappers littered the Gathering Hut.

"That's easy," said Donny. "It has to be Jesus Christ." That was predictable, I thought. "He is the only person who ever—"

"Yeah, we get the idea," Charlie cut him off in mid flow. "I think it's Stephen Hawkins."

"Who's he?" blurted Donny.

"Don't be a burke, Donny. The greatest cosmologist ever."

"Isn't 'e the geezer who studied black 'oles?" said Jacob, sipping his stout.

"More than black holes," Charlie went on excitedly. "He has studied and discovered the very beginning of the whole universe."

I sighed. This was one of Charlie's fetishes. He had his own telescope and he liked studying star charts and stuff like that. Well, they were pretty and all that, but that's where my interest ended.

Charlie was on his feet now, full of enthusiasm. His large build filled the skyline as I looked up.

"Look, bozzos" he pointed. "There's a hundred million stars out there. Each a galaxy like our own. It's just..." He put his hands up to the sides of his head as if trying to pluck an appropriately big word from his brain. "...No Way... It's mind blowing to think about it."

Yes, it was. We agree. I concede the point. You don't have to convince me. Now move on, Charlie, I thought. This was getting tedious.

"I mean, just imagine being able to visit all those places." He gazed longingly out.

"So, do they all have a name?" asked Buffy.

"Yep," Charlie replied. "Every star is charted. Some of the most powerful telescopes in the world pick up new ones now and again. If you discover a new star then you get to name it. I keep looking. I'd love to have my own star to name."

We all gazed up at the small specks of white, which littered the sky. Personally, I just didn't get it. Naming a star? I mean, it was like two fleas arguing over which of them owned the dog they lived on. Futile! Whether you discovered it or not didn't change the fact that it was there. Science: spending a life time trying to explain things which worked quite well, thank you very much, regardless of whether you could explain them or not.

"Well, I think the greatest person is Sir Christopher Wren," announced Agnes.

Good on ya Buffy(!) I thought. That put a swift stop to old Charlie. I knew that Buffy wanted to be an architect one day, so it was no real surprise who she had chosen.

"Did you know," she went on, "that when Sir Christopher Wren built St Paul's Cathedral, he designed the main dome with no supporting pillars in the centre. The whole thing would be held together by the angles and precise design of the arc of the dome, resting only on the outer walls. It was not only magnificent but an amazing piece of precision engineering. He was following a design he believed had been given to him by God in a vision," she nodded to Donny. "But the overseers of the project didn't think it was safe so they ordered him to build six supporting pillars. Now Wren had a problem. He had a design given him by God and he had orders from those organising the building which he didn't feel he could disobey. What should he do?" Buffy looked around at us. We were all sitting in rapt attention. She continued. "In the end he built the supporting pillars. But it was not till a hundred years later when someone was doing routine maintenance work on the dome that they realised that all six pillars had been built six inches too short, so they weren't touching the dome. The dome had been held up for the hundred years as intended in the original design, which Wren had received in his vision."

Buffy concluded her story and we all nodded solemnly.

"Pretty impressive to have such a strong vision of what you're gonna do with your life," I said. And I meant it. I didn't have a clue where mine was going just at the moment. Then Jacob spoke up.

"I'll tell ya 'bout someone 'o 'ad a strong vision of life. Winston Churchill, that's who! 'e saved this country from the crouts, even when no-one ever believed him. For years he said old Hitler was a threat, and they didn't believe 'im. Then when the war started... I was jus' a lad then... he was the one who believed we could win it. Ya know, if ya 'ave one person who really believes, ya can achieve anything."

We went silent again as we scrambled for the last of the sweets and the final slice of pizza.

"What about you, Fish?" said Hash. "Who's your greatest?" I pondered for a minute.

"Probably thinks it's himself," Charlie teased. "Our own resident superstar! The Cod Father!!" he announced dramatically. We all laughed. I didn't mind Charlie taking the mick. He did it equally to everyone. You began to feel picked on if he left you out!

I didn't really have a favourite person I admired. I shook my head.

"Dunno really."

"Tell you what," said Hash. "You be the judge. Who is the greatest out of all you've heard? Jesus Christ, Stephen Hawkins, Sir Christopher Wren, or Winston Churchill?"

They all looked at me expectantly and I felt uncomfortable. I didn't have any strong feelings about it. Well, no way was I gonna go with Donny. And I didn't want Charlie blabbering on about deep space and black holes any more, so that left Buffy of Jacob. I decided to side with old Buf as I still felt sorry for her, what with the Ronnie letters and all. I announced my decision.

"HA!" stormed Charlie sulkily. "Siding with old fairy girl." He made flapping wing expressions with his arms and whistled. I shot him a warning glance and he said no more. Buffy and Charlie stared at each other and I knew the competition was on.

"Right!" said Buffy, in her dangerous voice. "I'm gonna get here first tomorrow and we're—"

"Over my dead body!" Charlie shouted.

"It can be arranged," Buffy replied very quietly, an iciness in her voice that stopped Charlie in mid-flow and made me shiver.

"I've got something to show you," I announced, changing the subject and fumbling around in my rucksack. I had to show them the Senia letter. I passed it around. They all read it with the same unbelieving eyes, I had. I particularly watched for Charlie's reaction.

"No way!" he blustered. "You're makin' this up, right?" OK, so I was wrong. The letter wasn't one of Charlie's jokes.

"Let me see," said Buffy, snatching the letter from his fingers. Donny and Hash gathered round to read it over her shoulder.

"What does she mean, gift?" asked Donny.

"How did she get your address?" asked Buffy.

"Did she use your post code?" said Hash.

"What?" we all stared at Hash.

"Who cares!" said Charlie.

Why post code, I wondered?

The strangest things seemed to go on in Hash's head. I didn't pretend to understand him. His eyes were narrowed, suspicious looking as he stared at the letter. Then he took it and held it up towards the moon. "Looking for the water mark," he said when we questioned him.

"Hash, stop being a turkey!" said Charlie and grabbed the letter back. I continued staring at Hash. His eyes had bags under them and he looked very tired. Only then did it strike me that Hash was the only one of us that had not said who the greatest person was. In many ways Hash didn't play by the rules here. We were always supposed to be honest, but I sometimes had the feeling that none of us really knew Hash at all. He didn't let anyone in. Why?

Just then Jacob appeared back at the doorway of the Gathering Hut. I hadn't even registered that he had gone. He was holding the box of chocolates.

"Well, I think that there letter's talkin' 'bout the chocolates. And if ya ask me, there mus' be a reason behind it. Ya can't just ignore it."

I thought 'ignoring it' was actually a very good idea. Jacob placed the box on the wooden log floor.

"I'm not eating another one," I blurted.

"But you have to," said Hash.

"Go on," said Charlie.

"No!" I replied firmly. After the day I'd had yesterday the only thing keeping me sane was the fact that I'd not eaten anymore chocolates. I was clinging desperately to the fact that if I ate no more of the stupid things, my life would eventually return to normal. "Look, it ain't you guys who got shot at, ended up in hospital, had strange dreams, can't sleep at night. I can't keep doing this."

We all stared at the box in silence.

"They didn't actually shoot at you, Fish," said Charlie, hopefully. I didn't reply.

Then Jacob announced, "Ya quite right young Monty! It ain't fair making you take all the risks. We should all take a bite of it."

Charlie gulped, Donny looked positively horrified. I nodded.

"OK," I said. I reached forward and picked up the box, removing the lid. There were only three chocolates left. My eyes fell straight on the dark, almost black, elephant in the bottom left quarter. It was called the "*African Elephant*" I knew, since I had read the golden insert before. I picked it up.

"This one?" I asked. They nodded.

"Ought to," said Jacob. "Your strange letter came from Africa, after all." He was right. This was the right choice.

"Are we all in?" I asked, staring round almost daring anyone to refuse. Everyone nodded silently; everyone except Donny.

"I dunno, Fish." He fidgeted in his place and shook his head.

"Donny, you wimp," said Charlie.

"He'll eat it," said Buffy. "I'll stuff it down his throat if I have to."

I nodded. "Thanks Buf."

I stared down at the African Elephant in the palm of my hand. There wasn't a sound coming from outside. The night was totally still, as if it was watching and waiting to see what would happen next. I guess we were all feeling the same queasy feeling. These chocolates were not normal. Things happened which you couldn't control or explain.

I turned the chocolate over and read the inscription on the back. *"There is another place where you face your ghosts and dreams."*

I wasn't sure about this, but although I was scared, a little voice said, "it's OK… remember the dream." That's right, the dream I'd had. As a warrior I hadn't known what to do but still I had ridden into the castle and, somewhere inside me, something in my head had known what to do.

I took the first bite. It tasted of dark, bitter chocolate. I winced and handed it to Jacob. He didn't flinch. Donny nibbled it very slightly. Had he really taken a bite? Hash, Charlie and Buffy all took a bite. We sat in silence, waiting.

We were stupid to think something might happen straight away. Nothing happened that night and we departed.

The next evening, just as expected, Charlie and Buffy were at each other's throats. When I climbed onto the tree top platform and ran across the log bridge, I could see that Charlie had his telescope set up and Buffy seemed in a huff, so Charlie must have got their first. I groaned inwardly. We were in for an astronomy lesson tonight. Great, I don't think!

Today was the fifteenth of May. It was a date which was to be etched in my memory forever. It was to be no normal evening.

For whatever reason, there was no Donny or Jacob tonight. Jacob was tired, I guessed, and I had my suspicion that perhaps we had spooked Donny a bit with the chocolates.

As it turned out it was a great night for star gazing. The sky was clear, there was only a slight breeze and it was very pleasant out on the canopy. This was the highest platform in Buffy's tree top paradise. From here you had a view of all the huts and, on a clear night such as this, you could see right across the top of the forest foliage. It looked like a rumpled blanket. The quarter moon glinted off some of the tree tops. There were a couple of stationery clouds, back lit by the moon. Buffy had her eye to the telescope, Charlie showing her the arrangement of the constellation of Orion. Hash was lying on his back, just staring at the stars. He looked as if he was daydreaming.

"What you looking at, Hash?" I asked.

The long, thin face looked at me. "Just trying to imagine how big it is, Fish."

"It's big," said Charlie. "Billions of light-years across the universe."

"So can I see any black holes through this thing then?" asked Buffy from the telescope.

"No," said Charlie. "You can't see black holes. They don't generate any light or particles. They are incredibly strong magnetic fields. Since nothing comes out of them, not even light, you can never detect where they are."

Buffy's head popped up from behind the telescope. "But that's stupid," she said. "How do you know it exists? Someone must have seen one."

"Er no," replied Charlie. "It's all proved by theory. No-one's ever actually found one."

"It's not really true then?" said Buffy. "I mean, if you can't prove it, it's not true is it?"

I was watching the exchange with interest. Buffy and Charlie were an explosive combination. Buffy always won arguments, and Charlie always got annoyed about it.

"Course you can prove things without seeing them," laughed Charlie. "You see their effects. Electricity, wind, radio waves. There's loads of examples."

"Oh yeah," Buffy scoffed, hands on hips in her standard Lara Croft combat mode, as if she was about to draw the guns and splatter Charlie all over the trees, which probably wasn't too far from the truth. (Lara Croft was a lot better looking though). "It's a bit of a leap of the imagination though. Electricity to black holes."

"It's all part of the theory of origins of universes. Black holes are the death of a star. What happens is—"

"All sounds like a bunch of codswallop to me! Your scientist mates are all a bit loony if you ask me," Buffy interrupted dismissively.

"Well at least I don't write letters to myself from my dead brother."

I gulped. You could have cut the silence with a knife.

"Yeah. Fish told us," Charlie snarled, unwilling to back off. "We all had a good laugh. Who's a bit loony now, 'ey?"

Oh no. I shut my eyes. This wasn't going to be pretty. Agnes had gone a deep crimson red. In fact, her face almost looked purple. It wasn't embarrassment, it was rage. Charlie stood his ground, a bit like a rabbit in the headlights of an oncoming artic. Buffy was staring at him. She was about to explode. Then there was a loud clanking of metal and I saw her foot as it kicked out at the telescope. Charlie's pride and joy toppled left and before anyone could grab it, it had plunged over the edge of the canopy. We all scrambled to the edge and watched as it disappeared, with battering, crunching sounds as it bounced of tree trunks and we saw little bits of flying metal zipping off in all directions. I glanced at Charlie. He was ashen faced. I knew he had saved up for over six months to buy it. I glanced at Buffy. She had bolted. I just saw as she disappeared into the trees. I scrambled to my feet and ran after her. I needed to explain. I shouldn't have bothered. I should have realised this was beyond repair. I reached the spy deck.

"Agnes," I called quietly. She was nowhere to be seen, but I knew she wouldn't be too far away.

WHACK!

The side of my face felt like it'd been run over by a lorry. I could see little stars dancing around the tops of the trees.

"How could you?!!" she screamed. I didn't feel too safe. She had a very wild, out of control look in her eyes, almost daring me to try to explain.

"But Agnes," I said quietly, taking a deep breath before taking the plunge. "Ronnie didn't write them." There was a long pause. What was going on inside her head? "It's OK," I continued suicidally. "I understand. You wanted him back. It's the only way you could be close to him. It makes sense. You pretend. It's not a stupid thing to do." I had it sussed now, I thought.

"YOU DON'T UNDERSTAND AT ALL!! He left... No goodbye... He never finished this!" She bellowed, pointing around at the tree houses. "This was ours, but he left it. He left me. That was so unfair, so mean." Another pause. "So he writes. He does write. He has to."

I didn't know what to say. She sounded totally lost. The anger had evaporated. My left cheek still throbbed like it'd been decked by Mike Tyson. She collapsed into a heap on the log platform. What now? I'd totally lost the plot. She was as weird as her mum. I didn't understand.

Ten minutes later we were all sitting silently round a crackling fire. No-one spoke. We all felt a bit numb. Charlie looked totally miserable, Agnes had been crying. Funnily enough, Hash didn't look phased in the slightest. In fact, I would swear he was trying to keep a smile from his face. Was he just so thick skinned he didn't get it, or was there something else I was missing? Where had it all gone wrong tonight? Was this to do with the chocolate we had eaten?

There was a spit over the fire with a mixture of marshmallows and bread toasting on it. Hash leaned in to adjust the spit. There was a sudden blinding flash of white light. My eyes were blinded by it. I heard someone scream to my left. I leaned back... an automatic reaction, and suddenly I was falling. I could see nothing, feel nothing. I was just falling.

Chapter 13
Charlie's Vision...

Upstairs
Deep Space

W hen the white light faded from Charlie's vision, the first thing he noticed was that he couldn't feel his feet, which seemed strange. The second thing he noticed was that he kept trying to open his eyes, but everything was still totally black. He thought he could feel his eyelids flitting back and forth but no change in the blackness. He tried to jump. What a strange feeling... his legs were moving but he was just floating. It was like his limbs and muscles were not responding when his brain told them to move. It was like swimming in jelly... he couldn't get anywhere.

"Not jelly," said a voice next to him, "space."

Space? Come to think of it, he could see small white blotches... he had thought these were just his mind struggling with the blackness after the flash of light from the fire. A bit like when you stare at a light bulb too long and then close your eyes, you can still see blotches of light. Were those stars? Things were coming into focus. They didn't look like he had imagined stars. Tiny white specs were moving around. Some moved very slowly, almost indiscernibly, others seemed to zip around. Stars didn't move that fast, did they? What was he doing in space, anyway? And who was this guy talking to him? And was he dead or what?

"Just relax. I wanted to show you something. Stop struggling. Being up here is a bit like swimming. You have to relax and just sort of float around."

Charlie looked around. Standing, or floating, next to him was a tall man, short haircut, jeans and t-shirt. He smiled at Charlie and demonstrated a neat somersault. Who was this bozzo? Charlie looked around him. All he could see in all directions was blackness and spread over the blackness a scattering of white dots, as if a farmer had scattered the feed randomly in a chicken yard. His eyes were struggling to get the perspective. Were they white dots painted on a backdrop or objects that were far away? There were clusters and to his right he could see a light area of grey bubbly… almost liquid or cloud.

"It'll take your eyes a few minutes to adjust. They're not used to seeing things quite this fast."

"Quite so fast?…" What an odd thing to say. "What do you mean, fast?"

The man took him by the arm and floated him around in a circle so he was facing the other way.

"I want to show you something. Look. Do you see those two stars? The bright one and the slightly dimmer one."

Charlie stared. The two stars were beautifully bright and a silvery orange glow. One was distinctly brighter that the other.

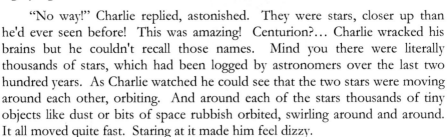

"These are what in your world are logged as stars Centurion eighty seven and Centurion eighty eight."

"No way!" Charlie replied, astonished. They were stars, closer up than he'd ever seen before! This was amazing! Centurion?… Charlie wracked his brains but he couldn't recall those names. Mind you there were literally thousands of stars, which had been logged by astronomers over the last two hundred years. As Charlie watched he could see that the two stars were moving around each other, orbiting. And around each of the stars thousands of tiny objects like dust or bits of space rubbish orbited, swirling around and around. It all moved quite fast. Staring at it made him feel dizzy.

"That stuff orbiting the stars is not rubbish, they're planets."

"Of course!" Charlie murmured. Charlie knew that… he just wasn't used to seeing it all quite so close up. Charlie's forehead crinkled up into a frown. There was something even stranger here, than floating around in space. This guy next to him kept answering all the questions Charlie was thinking. Charlie hadn't actually asked any of them out loud. It was very unnerving. How did he do that?

"Watch the brightest star," the man pointed. "You are about to see it die."

"Die? But that takes millions of years to happen," Charlie blurted. He knew his basic astronomy. Every star that you could see in the sky at night was in fact a sun, like our sun, with planets circling, or orbiting, it. The theory was, that when a star died, all the orbiting objects and planets were sucked in by the huge gravitational pull of the star and it all contracted into one small lump the size of a small planet, which scientists called a White Dwarf. But all of this was theory, wasn't it, thought up by scientists and boffins, for the simple reason that no-one had ever seen it happen, just as Agnes had said. And how could they? It took millions of years for a star to die!

"It takes billions of years, actually. I told you we were moving fast," replied the man, breaking Charlie's thoughts again.

"How fast, exactly?" Charlie frowned.

"We're in a fast time stream here. Time's shifting at around a billion years per second at the moment. That's why some of the planets look as if they're zipping around a bit too fast."

Charlie blinked. "A billion... years... per... second??!! No way! You're kiddin' right?"

The man just grinned.

"But..."

"That's right," the man interrupted again. "Your life, all your thoughts, ideas, your ambitions, mistakes and successes all last about... ohh..." the man glanced down at a rather fancy looking watch on his left wrist, "a hundred thousandth of a second. There you go... ZAP!... You're gone, bye bye, dead... forgotten... history." He smiled.

Charlie's mouth dropped open. "But that makes me feel so..." He was struggling for the word. "Small." Floating there in space, Charlie had never felt quite so insignificant in his life.

"Well... you are small," replied the man. "No getting round it."

"This is a dream, right?" asked Charlie, gaining new confidence. "It has to be, right? I mean, time can't move that quick."

"Actually time is quite rubbery really. It stretches and shifts much more than you would realise. Just think, Charlie, every time you stand at your telescope in the evening and look at the sky, the light from the sun takes eight and a half minutes to get from there to you. The light from the furthest star you can see from your back garden takes ten billion years to reach you. That means that when you look at it you are not seeing what is happening now, but what happened ten billion years ago. There you go Charlie, time travel in your own back garden."

"But..." Charlie's mind was desperately struggling to put the pieces of the jigsaw together.

"This is no dream, Charlie. Everything you see is really happening as we watch."

"Is there life on any of those planets?" asked Charlie, changing the subject.

"Not anymore. There was life on three of the planets, for a while... about a second or so, but it's finished now."

"What, dead?" Charlie replied.

"Yep. Got a bit too hot for them as the temperature rose."

"Oh." It all sounded a bit clinical. That was it then. A whole massive planet, alive for a second or so in the cosmic scheme of things and then zap, gone. Charlie was finding it all a bit depressing. Is that all life added up to?

The man pointed. "That star is just a ball of gas, Charlie." Charlie put all his questions on hold for a moment and stared at the brighter of the two stars. Something was happening. It was beginning to dim a little. It did actually look as if it was getting old. "It's already run out of hydrogen gas a while back, and it needs that to survive," continued the man, giving his running commentary as events unfolded before them. "And so then it rises to about a hundred million degrees heat, swells up, then sheds its outer skin. That's all the rubbish that orbits it... which eventually become the planets." The man put his hand to his chin and paused, as if stopping the running commentary suddenly to ponder something. "Isn't it interesting? The planets are only born because the star is now dying... life out of death. Remember that, Charlie. It's important. Anyway, that's where the life grows for a little while, on the debris, the planets circling the star. Then the star carries on struggling till it can go on no longer. That's where it's at right now."

There was a sudden flash of light so bright it seemed to shoot out across the universe. Charlie recoiled in fright and pain as the white light shot briefly through his head. All the planets floating around the bright star started to swirl very quickly, and then seemed to get sucked into the star. They almost seemed to be struggling against the pull of the star. Then the star suddenly seemed to burn out and vanish. All that was left was a patch of space where the dead star had once been, which seemed even darker than the rest of the blackness around it. A little way away the sister star, the less bright one, still sat and twinkled.

"What just happened?" asked Charlie in a curious voice.

"You tell me. You're always talking about it."

Charlie paused, his eyes suddenly alert and wide. Surely it couldn't be... no-one has ever seen... He cleared his throat. "A black hole?"

"Yep, that's right," replied the man, brushing it aside with a smile as if it was just one more everyday event in a mildly interesting day. Charlie couldn't believe it. No-one had ever managed to prove a black hole existed. And he had just seen one.

"Watch the less bright star," the man pointed.

Charlie watched. It seemed to be struggling too. "The gravitational pull?"

"That's right," the man smiled. "Look, give it a few more billion years..." he paused for a moment. "Yep, that'll do. Look it's collapsing, but it isn't as big as the other one, so the effect is slightly different."

Charlie watched as everything swirling around the star was sucked in, but this time there was no explosion, no blinding flash. Everything seemed to just crush together into the tiniest white spec. That was the White Dwarf.

"It's dead," the man concluded, but Charlie had the feeling it wasn't over yet.

There was a puff of smoke. Just a tiny puff like someone breathing out on a cold day.

"That's the hydrogen cloud given off from the dead star. Watch," said the man, excitedly, "This is the bit I love."

Charlie watched. There was a massive bang, like an explosion, which took Charlie by surprise. But there was no flash and nothing to see."

"That's an implosion, a nuclear reaction," the man commented. "It's making the hydrogen fuse together and that makes helium and then light, and then the other elements."

As Charlie watched, the cloud of gas contracted into a tight ball. Light began to spray out of the ball, green, blue, red, golden rays, scattered randomly as if flicked from a paint brush. Then glittery particles seemed to spread from it.

"A supernova!" muttered Charlie in utter astonishment. "No way!!... It's a supernova! The birth of a star! It's amazing." It was truly amazing. He was seeing the creation of something from nothing.

"Not just the birth of a star, Charlie, the birth of a whole world. Isn't it beautiful? This is life, Charlie. The universe moves on. One world dies and out of it another is born." Charlie had never seen anything so beautiful in his life. "Look, it's beginning to die again."

"So soon?"

"It has to, Charlie. It's only as it dies that life begins."

As Charlie watched the ball began to bubble hotter and hotter and expand. With a small pop the outer skin split off, fragmented and started to orbit the burning white core at the centre. It was just as the man had explained it a few minutes earlier.

"Wicked!" said Charlie.

"That's the birth of the planets, Charlie. The start of life."

Charlie looked around. He waved his hands and spun in the air excitedly. Then just as quickly as the excitement had hit him, all his questions returned to haunt him, as if forgotten for a fleeting moment in the excitement of it all. He frowned.

"Where do I fit into this? I'm gone in the blink of an eye. That's what you said." There were more thoughts spinning around in his head than stars and planets in the space around him. It just couldn't be. How could he live, think so many thoughts, be so complicated and have so many feelings and then just die? What about his dad? He had died, just like that, and Charlie would follow him, and that would be it... the end... no reason or purpose in either of them having lived. It just couldn't be. However beautiful it was, all he had just seen... there had to be more. A darkness spread through his mind again like a disease. It often happened. His breathing sped up and he was suddenly panicking. The thought that there was absolutely no purpose to his or his dad's lives was just so awful, and there was nothing he could do about it.

The man smiled. "You know Charlie, you are the only person on earth who has ever or will ever see what you have just seen. How does that make you feel?"

Charlie nodded to himself. "A bit bigger, I guess."

"Charlie, I made all that happen. I made this entire universe with its hundred trillion stars, each with its thousands of planets each with its own special environment and... life! And yet, between all that, I've come here to spend a bit of time with you." There was a pause. Charlie didn't know how to feel. "I know how much you loved your dad. He's well. Sends you his love. He's happy Charlie."

"But how... you know my dad?" Charlie's mind was reeling. "I don't know how to understand this."

"Do you know why I showed you all that?"

Charlie just stared.

"That's for you. My present. When you've finished your life down there on earth, it's not the end Charlie. I have a bigger job for you up here."

Charlie's mind was blank. "What?"

"That." The man pointed at the white hot star with its planets, dust and debris circling it. "I want you to help me with Centurion eighty eight. It doesn't do that all on its own, you know! We have a hundred thousand planets to design, millions of life forms, from moss that grows on the rocks to beings that roam the planets, to dream up and create. Sunsets to paint, mountains to build, oceans to discover, streams to carve out with our fingertips. I'd like to do that with you, Charlie, if you want to.   And of course... if..."

Chapter 14

Agnes's Vision...

Upstairs
Realm 3... Just Outside the Wall

The bright light seemed to hit the front of her head causing a deep throbbing pain resembling a really bad headache or that feeling when you've eaten ice cream that's just too cold. She fell back and smacked the back of her head on the wooden floor. Ouch! Her head hurt all over now. Well, that was just great wasn't it? She just lay there and kept her eyes shut tight, biting her lip against the pain. Then she realised she was rocking from the left to the right as if in time with the gentle waves of the sea. Strange, she thought. She opened one eye. Why didn't she recognise the walls and open roof of the Gathering Hut? She was lying in the hull of a small wooden boat, staring at a deep black sky with stars, which looked larger than usual. She sat up quickly and looked around her. She wasn't sure what shocked her most, the guy sitting in the boat with her or the fact that the boat seemed to be suspended in mid air hundreds of feet above the ground... correction, thousands of feet. She thought she'd start with the guy. He was a strange looking guy, dressed in white shirt and trousers, narrow, serious looking face, long hair pulled back in a ponytail. His body was folded up in the small rowing boat but he looked like he must be very tall when he stood up straight.

He had noticed her stare. "Rafe!" he shouted, as if announcing a new discovery to the world.

"Sorry?" Agnes replied.

"Rafe's the name, zippin's the game! Pleased to meet you." He beamed a rather over enthusiastic smile at her. It was a very cute smile but it didn't cut any ice with Agnes.

"Who are you?" Agnes demanded. "Where are we? And what am I doing here?"

"We're in Jerome's fishing boat," Rafe replied, as if that settled the matter and everything must now be clear. "He said I could borrow it." Agnes crinkled up her freckle-strewn nose in puzzlement. "I thought it'd be a good way to show you round," Rafe continued. "We zip here, we zip there... we zip everywhere!" And with that he heaved on the left hand oar and the little boat fell to the left, cascading down about fifty feet very fast... rather too fast for Agnes's liking... and finished with a neat swoon to bring it back level. Rafe beamed at her.

"Don't be stupid" Agnes shot back. "Fishing boats go on water. What are we doing up here?"

"Ah well, Jerome lives here you see. It's his mansion. He was a fisherman back when, well... you know." There was a long pause. Agnes stared. No, she didn't know. Rafe continued, undeterred. "Always said he feels more comfortable in a boat after spending his previous life out on the waters fishing. The Lord said he thought that it would be a real groovy idea. Said if Jerome wanted to swap it in a few million years when he felt more comfortable in the city, that's fine and dandy."

"What are you talking about?"

Rafe frowned and lowered his tone as if now explaining to a rather dim three year old. "Not much water out here you see. The Lord said he didn't see why he couldn't fly it. We nick named him Zippy! It's the only flying boat about these parts, you know."

"Are you stupid or something?" Agnes shot back.

"Err," Rafe's smile began to crack. He leant forward and lowered his voice in a conspiratorial tone. "I have to admit, it's my first time doing a tour. Columbus said you might be a difficult one and did I want to give it a miss, but I said It'd be really cool and thought I might try and arrange for the boat... try to impress you a bit. You won't give a bad report on me will you? Not that it matters really. I'm new in the Watchers. I'm just booked in for a short stint, a million years to start. They said it was best to stick to the golden wings and halo routine... you know, harps and songs stuff, big appearances, choirs and such, but I thought a more informal approach... try something new. Am I rambling? I'm rambling aren't I?"

Agnes nodded. She didn't have a clue what he was talking about. Was this guy speaking English? "A tour?" she asked. "You mentioned a tour?"

"Oh yes, we give tours now and again," Rafe replied, "Not very often though. You are very privileged."

"Really," Agnes replied doubtfully. "A tour of what exactly?"

"That." Rafe pointed back over her shoulder.

Agnes turned and stared. She nearly fell out of the boat. She was speechless. It was far away, maybe a mile or more. But it was gigantic. It was... what was it? It was shaped like a pyramid and colourful like a bright rainbow, tinged with gold. It looked like an island. Agnes had only ever been abroad once, and the sight before her reminded her of looking out of the airplane window and seeing the coast of France below her. It looked like an island, floating in the sea, except there was no sea. It was surrounded by space and stars. The Island was sitting on... well... nothing. Agnes banished the thought from her mind. That was ridiculous!

"Want a closer look?" Rafe put in. Agnes glanced back and Rafe could see the sparkle in her eyes. Maybe Columbus had been right. "You don't need to impress them," he had said. "Just show her the city!" Agnes nodded, and then clutched desperately onto the sides of the rowing boat as Rafe whistled and it zoomed down and right, almost leaving her sitting in mid-space. "Geronimo!" Rafe whooped as they arced around, then slowed and began to glide gently around the edge of the island. The island was so big that they appeared to be moving quite slowly but Agnes could feel the air (was it air?) blowing over her face at quite a pace.

They were now very close, maybe a few hundred feet off the island. Agnes could see a tall wall, like the walls of a castle, which surrounded the whole island. But the bricks shone like gold. The wall curved up and down, following the contours of the rolling hills and valleys, and yet outside the wall was just... well... space. There were magnificent gates in the wall at various points, made of glittering diamond. Over the top of the wall Agnes could see so many different sights her mind just couldn't take it in. There were modern roads and houses, tall skyscrapers, and yet as they moved around further that gave way to green meadows, forests and she could see a medieval castle. But there was something strange about everything. It all looked brighter and more colourful than anything she had ever seen, as if she had spent her life looking at everything through sunglasses and she had just taken them off. She was too far away to make out people, but she could definitely see movement and she could see a vast expanse of water and a large ship. She squinted. It looked like a really old fashioned Viking longboat.

Her mind was struggling to take it all in. Whilst one part of her was goggle eyed at all the sights in front of her, she was also aware of the pyramid shape. She was staring at the lower level of what appeared to be three platforms. The lower level was a whole city... bigger... a whole world, with land and oceans and everything, and yet above her she could see the underneath of the second level, just sort of hovering there. And in the distance she could see the very edge of the top level. The architect in her looked around for the columns supporting the upper levels but she could see none.

Rafe cleared his throat. "Do you like the City?"

Agnes didn't quite know how to answer. "Yeah," she mumbled. It seemed an inadequate answer. Everything she could see looked beautiful. Though there were so many diverse worlds here, it all seemed to flow, one into the next. She definitely got a warm feeling looking at it all.

"What is this place?"

The answer she received added yet another layer of confusion. "We call it the City. It's what you know as heaven."

"Heaven?" Agnes mumbled. Her anger and the sharpness of her thoughts and tongue seemed to have evaporated from her whilst she had looked on the City. "Heaven? That's not possible." But even as she whispered it she knew this was very real. It was more real, more alive, more colourful, and more exuberant than anything she had ever felt in her life. As she stared, it felt like colour was flooding into her soul.

"To be precise," Rafe went on, suddenly back into ramble mode, "you are looking at the third heaven. The mainly humanoid Realm. Well, humanoid and er... other. I'm not supposed to talk about the other bit. Anyway—"

"Where are the supports? How does the second level stand on top of the first?"

"It just does," Rafe shrugged. "No supports. The Lord supports everything. It's just there."

"Unbelievable!"

Something strange then happened. Their rowing boat was still speeding along, passing the scene below them. As Agnes was watching the tall and expansive medieval castle, her view of it passed behind a tall golden rod, which stood amongst (but much taller than) the trees in the forest. Suddenly it vanished. The whole scene vanished and was replaced with row upon row of town houses. "Where did it go? The castle! Where did it go?"

Rafe chuckled. "It's still there. It's just through the portal... the other side of the golden rod. The City is bigger than you think. It's even bigger on the inside than the outside."

"But that's impossible!"

"No it isn't. It's absolutely fabulous!" Rafe enthused. "You've just got to remember that it's not physical in the sense you know. This is heaven. It's spiritual. It's different. You don't need posts to support the Realms, you don't need roads to get from place to place..." At precisely that moment a group of three people laying on their backs relaxing, floated past the boat about twenty meters off towards the walls. Agnes's eyes almost fell out of her head and rolled around in the bottom of the boat. "... and you don't need to stay on the ground. Just think... the possibilities are endless!"

The boat rounded a corner. The skyscrapers faded from view and another side of the wall came into view. A pair of massive diamond gates were wide open. Light and music seemed to tumble out and hit them as it came into view. But what caught Agnes's eye was all the people. There were thousands of them. They were floating, swimming, falling, dancing. Some lay on beds, some floated on armchairs, others zipped around on what looked like surf boards. Some were old, some young, but most looked teenage. Why was that, she wondered? So many questions. An old guy who looked a hundred if he was a day zoomed past in a neat spiral as if he was superman.

"Oh, cool one! It's party time!" Rafe exclaimed. Agnes giggled.

The music was indescribable. It was so loud Agnes felt it might burst her ear drums. Was it loud or was it just so magnificent that it seemed to warm her soul. She suddenly found her heels clicking to the beat.

"Ahhhh… emmmmm. Feel that rhythm!" Rafe was off in another world.

Agnes focused in on one lad who couldn't have been much older than her and appeared to be riding a surfboard. He had blonde long hair. His face showed a mixture of avid concentration, excitement and pleasure. His knees lent forward and backwards making minor adjustments to his stance on the board. By this he threaded in and out of people and objects with amazing skill. He dropped a hundred feet, he looped, he swung around and gave off a happy salute to someone relaxing on a long black leather sofa, which like everything else, was just sort of hanging there.

"The light!" said Agnes, suddenly realising. "It comes from the city!"

"Well of course it does!" said Rafe. "Where else would it come from?!" Everything in the City gave off light. It didn't come down from the sky. There was no sun, just space out there. But the City gave off its own amazing spectrum of light and colour.

The music and the colours had done something to Agnes, something nice… something which she didn't want to lose. It was one of those lovely moments in life when you feel all warm and gooey inside, and you wish you could bottle it and take a swig every time you were having a "nuts" day. She just wanted to stay here for ever, to be a part of this place.

"Now, over here I wanted to show you…" but Rafe's voice had faded away and Agnes was floating.

"No… NO!" bellowed Rafe, but it was too late. Rafe reached out to grab Agnes but she was gone. Zoooom! She was off, arms outstretched.

"I'm flying," she murmured to herself. "I'M FLYING!" she bellowed to the world. Suddenly she was moving a hundred thousand miles an hour, through the people, over the guy on the surf board, under the sofa, within inches of the diamond gate, over the wall. There was a huge town square below her, thousands of people celebrating and partying. Streets which led off the square were full of music and colour and were lined with happy people. The place heaved with joy and brilliant sunshine. It was a whole city of streets which spread out from the square like rays from the sun. Everything led back to the town square where the party was happening. The colours almost blurred as she moved so fast over the scene. It shot past below her. Now she flew over quite, empty streets of houses. But the houses were strange, all different. No home was the same as the one next to it. One small, one large, some huddled close together, some in huge grounds all on their own. A town house sat next to a forest leading up to a deserted log cabin. Beyond that lay a football pitch and then there was a large mansion with big brass gates and inside the gates behind the finely cut lawn was a... was that a?... a skate board park? What a weird place! She spotted a field of strange statues, and a tall tower which was so tall it seemed to overlook the world. As she looked, it was as if she could see what was going on inside each home. She could see people talking, having meals together, sleeping. Someone was painting a picture. Another person was running on a running track. There were a group of people who seemed to be practicing something in a field. She flew over the medieval castle again. She could see a large building works on the far side with hundreds of people who looked like tiny ants crawling all over the building. She passed over fields of grass and then suddenly the ground level began to rise, she arched her back and aimed upwards. The grass gave way to snow and she was suddenly zipping hundreds of feet over the most beautiful mountain range. She could see where the tree line stopped and the ice caps on top of the mountains. They were totally desolate. They looked awesome. There was a low valley and in the centre of the valley a large lake glistened below her, reflecting the mountains.

She was moving so fast that she almost didn't see it in time. And it was so fast that she almost didn't believe her eyes as the large silver disc came over the mountain horizon towards her. It was so out of place against the snow capped mountains that she just blinked. It looked like something out of a Steven Spielberg film... it was a space craft. It shot into view and then zoomed towards her. She careered off to the left and the space ship also swerved off to the left and they must have missed each other by inches. As Agnes tried to regain her flight path a hand caught the scruff of her neck and heaved her back into the boat.

"What do you think you're doing?" Rafe looked positively terrified. "You can't just fly off like that! We're not in down town Tescos now, you know!"

"But I can," said Agnes. "I can! Did you see me? Wasn't that incredible?" She stopped and frowned for a second. "Was that a flying saucer, I just saw?"

"Er, yeah but don't tell, OK? I'm not supposed to mention the aliens. It's just Creevy. He's comfortable with it. Never got used to living on the ground. After being a space ranger, you can understand it. The Lord says that maybe—
"

"Let me guess," Agnes cut in. "Maybe in a couple of million years he'll fancy a change?"

"Yeah, how d'you know that?"

"I'm catching on," Agnes replied. "So let me guess. That castle is owned by some guy who was once King Arthur or something like that."

"No, actually that belongs to Brian. He was an accountant. Says he fancied a change. Never takes off his armour these days."

"All these people are happy, Rafe."

"Yes."

They sat in silence as they drifted back over the City. They passed a golden post and the mountains faded, giving way to a golden beach, an ocean shore and a coral reef which arced around the shoreline.

"It's beautiful."

"It is," Rafe smiled back at her.

"Why couldn't we manage that in my world, Rafe?" He didn't answer.

"Who lives on the other levels?"

"Mainly angels on the second Realm. And The Lord on the top Realm. As a rule that is. But then we all zip around all over."

"Are you an angel?" Agnes asked.

"Yeah, but I'm only a little one. Not one of the proper ones."

Agnes pulled her knees up to her chest and hugged them. "I think you're the biggest one of all, Rafe. Thanks for this. It's... just awesome." Her voice trailed off. Rafe's smile beamed like a spoiled school kid.

"All those people were building on the castle. Why? Doesn't God just zap it all into existence?"

"Oh no!" said Rafe. "It's all built by hand. Lots of hard work. The difference here is that everyone works together. Everyone can do something they enjoy. Everyone has a purpose."

"I'd like to build," said Agnes

"I know."

"We've got one more zip call to make," the angel announced. "This is a special one. The Lord said he'd thought about it for a long time and he thought you deserved it."

"He thinks about me? God thinks about me?"

"Of course he does! He's God."

"But, what I mean is… he actually takes the time to work things out for me?"

"This tour was his groove, kid! Wasn't my idea. Who knows what he's up to?"

"I never got the impression my life had much planning to it." She sniffed. For some reason she felt very emotional. She hugged her legs closer and clamped her mouth shut. She watched the ground zip away below their boat whilst Rafe whistled and rowed and the boat swooned left and right at his command. Below she could see the people like ants milling around the streets. What did they all do here? Was every single one of them happy? There was a flash of light as they passed under a golden rod. The scene changed below them. They were flying above a forest. All the buildings were gone.

"Portal," Rafe explained.

"How?"

"Well, technically a portal's just a switch over to a different dimension on the lumos loctus scale. Simple stuff," Rafe shrugged. "Angel's play, as they say." Agnes wished she had never asked.

Rafe brought the boat to a stop on a cliff top overlooking the forest. There was a huge but silent waterfall to their left. Ahead Agnes could see forest as far as the eye could see. Where the cliff fell away there was a drop which must have been a mile deep and far below Agnes could see the deep blue rock pools. She had never seen such a beautiful place in all her life. She felt safe in the forest. It reminded her of Ronnie.

They sat down on the edge of the cliff.

"Rafe! There's a sun. I thought the City had no sun?"

"The Lord made one here, just in this portal."

"Why here?"

"For you," Rafe answered simply. "He knew you'd like one. Watch, it's about to set."

They sat and watched together as the sun sank onto the horizon and the whole forest basin was flooded with orange.

"Rafe, God didn't make that just for me, did he?"

"Of course!" Rafe replied as if it was nothing special, just knocked together in a couple of nanoseconds.

Agnes smiled. Thank you God.

"Anyway, time is short so we have one more important thing to show you. We gotta hustle kid."

Agnes jumped to her feet and rubbed her hands. "OK, where to now?"

"Down there." Rafe pointed down the mile drop to the deep blue rock pools.

"What do I do? Fly there?"

Rafe nodded. "There's someone for you to meet down there. This is where I say goodbye."

Agnes looked down the rocks uneasily. "Who? Who's down there?"

Rafe smiled. "Only one way to find out."

It was the first time Agnes had noticed the angel standing at full height. She only reached just past his waist. He was huge. She hugged him anyway. Then she turned to the cliff and dived off. She let her body fall in a very smart diving action. As the water raced towards her she felt the exhilaration of the oxygen catching in her lungs and the air whipping past her face. She pulled out of the dive in a neat swooping arc and landed smoothly on the rocks. She looked around. Nothing. She let herself fall back into the water. Beautiful. Everything about this place was larger than life. She felt better than she had done in months... years. All the things she worried about seemed unimportant now. All the things which had hurt her, all the scars which had been left by the death of Ronnie and by her mother's hurt had vanished. It felt like all her life had been a black and white photo and someone had just breathed colour into it. She felt like she was a new person... maybe she was.

"Hi." The voice called from the edge of the forest. She looked up. She couldn't believe her eyes. It was her brother, Ronnie!

Chapter 15

Monty's Vision
A Day in the Life of God...

Upstairs
Realm 1... Map Room

O K, who turned the lights out?" For a horrible moment I thought I was back in the well, falling. I was definitely moving very fast. First it felt like darkness around me, then stars and space, and then some kind of spiral. Was it a dream? Where had Hash and the fire gone? It had to be another dream. I must have just drifted off, in the early hours in the warmth of the fire. I relaxed. After all I was experienced at this action man stuff now. I'd been in a bank raid, I'd fought my way through a castle. There was nothing they could chuck at me that would faze me anymore. I was rising up... up... up. There was a glimpse of a huge wall made of gold and a massive city but I was moving so fast, it was gone in a flash. I was still rising. There were bright white lights and I could see tall white... something... around me. Were they angels? Had I died? Then a large set of deep oak wooden doors were in front of me like the entrance to a mansion. I was still. I was about to look around and get my bearings but before I had a chance the doors began the swing open.

Wow! I was expecting to walk into a room. Instead I walked through the doors into a large field. Above me the stars shone in the night sky, and yet the scene before me seemed as bright as daylight. In front of me was a dusty path, which led over the brow of the hill. The first thing I noticed was the dust on the path, which seemed to sparkle like gold. Strange. On my right was a fence and beyond it another field, but the fence caught my eye because that was strange too. It was built, half of old flat stones, as a stone mason of years gone by would have built it, and then it appeared to be patched up and overlaid in places with what looked like plastic. It was a strange mixture of old and modern. I noticed the same golden sparkling in the stones of the fence, as if they had been mined in a gold region and had streaks of gold running through them.

I followed the path forward. I crested the top of the hill and met a very strange sight. There's this guy sitting on a red armchair. He's just sitting there. I stopped dead in my tracks. Should I disturb him?

Suddenly he looked around. A broad smile cracked his face and he jumped up. He was a slightly older guy, wrinkles on the face, losing his hair a bit, casual look. He seemed oddly familiar but I didn't think we had met before.

"Monty! I've been expecting you!"

I look from side to side. "Really?" I blurted. I guess he was talking to me.

"Come on." He glanced at his watch. "We'd better get going or we're gonna be late for the welcome party." He waved his right hand in some mysterious gesture and to my astonishment a square patch of grass, about a meter wide, dropped smoothly and silently down a couple of inches and seemed to just slide away, leaving a perfect square hole. Right in front of my feet! Unbelievable! There was a low buzzing noise and an elevator rose up through the hole. It was a very old fashioned one. The guy from the red seat beamed at me. He had obviously seen my jaw drop and was pleased with the effect of his magic tricks. It annoyed me and I immediately put on my indifferent, couldn't care less face.

The elevator was a curvy shape. Each of its top corners curved out like a balloon and then curled back into a neat point. It looked like an Indian turban.

"Shall we?" The red armchair guy pulled open the criss-cross wire door, which folded back neatly and he gestured to me.

"Show NO FEAR!" I told myself.

"Whatever," I said casually and sauntered leisurely into the elevator. Inside panic was beginning to set in. Where were we going? Was he gonna torture me? Would this be my last sight of the night sky, as I descended to my torturous death?

He pulled the gate closed and we both stood there for a moment.

"You gonna press a button?" I asked. I noticed three buttons marked 'Realms 1 - God', 'Realm 2 - Angels', 'Realm 3 - Beings'.

"No need," the guy replied. As he spoke the elevator lurched into motion and started going down. "But if you want me to, I can?"

"No, no. I'm cool," I replied, trying desperately to maintain my coolness. We stood side by side. I avoided looking at him. I could vaguely see dull colours speeding past the outside grate of the elevator. It seemed to be moving quite fast for such an old style lift.

"So where are we?" I asked as casually as I could.

"Heaven," the guy replied. I snorted. I couldn't help it. What sort of joker did this guy take me for?!

"I don't believe in heaven," I shot back.

"That's no surprise to me! You're in the majority," he replied. "It don't change how things are though."

Hmmm. OK, so he was a smart Alec.

"You know," he went on, "so many people don't believe in me, I sometimes wonder if I exist!" He laughed at his own joke. Oh great. This guy was a laugh a minute. Just what I need, someone who thinks they're a comedian!

"So, that makes you God then, does it?"

"I guess so. You know, this will be much more fun if you just relax a bit. Let go."

"Yeah right!" I said with as much sarcasm as I could muster. I wasn't going to give this joker the satisfaction. "So you're the geezer who died on a cross and all that jazz?"

He held out his left arm. I glanced down. I couldn't believe it. There was a hole in his wrist. Right the way through. Ahhhh yuck, that was gross! It had red tinges of bloodstains around the edge. I gulped and stayed silent. I'm only eleven. I'm not supposed to see stuff like that.

"So where are we going?" I asked after a couple of minutes.

"I thought I'd give you a tour. A day in the life of God. That'd make some red letter day, wouldn't it?!"

I was feeling a bit more subdued after the wrist episode. Was this for real?

"Why me?" I asked.

"Because I like you, Monty." He turned and smiled at me. It seemed oddly genuine. I narrowed my eyes and tried to maintain my composure as a smooth and logical investigator of dreams. I was, after all, quite an expert at this now.

Ding! The elevator stopped and God (giving him the benefit of the doubt here) opens the wire grill.

I stepped out onto white. No other way of describing it... everything was white.

Ding! My head shot around at the sound, just in time to see the elevator departing, and we were left on a planet of white. I felt like an ant standing on a mile wide white chocolate button. In all directions I could just see white disappearing over the horizon. Even above us there seemed to be a white ceiling, but everything was so white, I couldn't tell how far away it was. I squinted my eyes and could just make out what looked like the golden wall I had glimpsed when I arrived here in... heaven (I was finding it hard even to think the word!) The golden wall was behind and below us.

"Come on then!" and with that God marched off towards the white horizon.

"Is this it?" I asked, as I ran to keep up.

"Sorry. Is this what?"

"Well, is this... you know... heaven?" I blurted. "It's just. Well, I don't want to be rude. It's just a bit... white?"

He chuckled. "No, this isn't heaven. This is just the Landing Pad."

"So, was that field beyond the elevator heaven?" I persisted.

"Nope. That was the Map Room."

"So what exactly is heaven?" I have to admit that the question had never ever crossed my mind before.

"Difficult to explain," he replied. Was that it? Was that all the answer I was going to get?

"It's a bit like..." he went on. "It's a bit like trying to explain the Internet to an ant. Best if I show you. But first we have the welcome party."

He compared me to an ant!! I wasn't impressed!

We had been walking for about ten minutes. My brain felt like it had taken up residence in a Daz washing powder advert. I tried shutting my eyes but was disturbed to note that I could still see white... everywhere, white! If heaven was like this, I didn't wanna be here!

Then a black spot appeared on the horizon. It grew larger as we got closer to it. We continued walking right up to the edge of the white. It finished in a huge rectangular hole in the ground. Beyond the hole I could see space. There was an eternity of darkness with stars twinkling in the distance, all different shapes and sizes. It was a stunning sight. It felt like standing in the docking port of the death star in star wars. I just hoped that Darth Vader wasn't gonna pitch up from anywhere.

"Look down," God instructed. I looked down and I could see earth. It was beautiful. It was like looking back at earth from the moon. I could see the blue oceans, the green patches of land, all inter-speckled by patches of dense cloud. It was moving. It gave the strange feeling of standing on a space ship whilst it hovered and shifted into position in orbit. I fully expected Doctor Spock to appear any minute.

"Better move back. They're arriving." We walked back about a hundred yards from the hole and waited.

"So why all the space and the white wash treatment?" I asked.

"We had a couple of thousand in one go once. It can get a bit confusing till they understand what's going on. We have to let them adjust."

We waited.

"A couple of thousand... what exactly?"

He didn't answer. We watched.

I don't know quite what I expected, but it wasn't that.

Suddenly over the brink of the rectangular hole came some movement. Out climbed... what was it? As it got closer I noticed they were... Knights? Two of them. Knights in armour. What was this? What was going on? I felt like I was in the middle of a dress rehearsal for the local armature dramatics society. Both were dressed head to foot in chain mail. Over the top they wore red material coverings, drawn in at the waste by a thick belt, and with an unmistakable white cross on them.

One of them drew his sword, a look of wide-eyed fear on his face.

"Where are we?"

"My arm!" said the other one, touching his right arm gently as if it was hurt. "The wound... it's gone!"

"Peace," said the red armchair guy next to me.

"My Lord?" The knight with the drawn sword squinted. "Where did the battle go? Are we...? Columbert... Where's Columbert?"

"He chose badly," God replied. Suddenly both men kneeled down on one knee. The man with the sword laid it down in front of him on the white surface.

"My Lord!" he spoke. "We have fought and died in your name, for this purpose."

"We are here," said the other one.

It was a strange moment. These men had just died in battle and were now meeting their maker. My emotions were tugging but I wasn't going to give in.

God walked over, slapped both men on the back and stretched out a hand to pull them to their feet.

But then I was distracted again. A space man in full white space gear floated up out of the rectangular hole, looking like Bruce Willis out of Armageddon. I blinked and glanced across at God.

"Space walk went wrong," he replied by way of explanation. The spaceman hovered in mid-air for a moment and came to land on the white chocolate button.

"Come on," said God. "We'll leave them to the Welcome Party."

As we backed away, I could see a strange group of people walking up to the two knights and the spaceman. There were strange thin looking people who seemed really tall. They were all dressed in white. Then there were others; a small kid and a group of men and women dressed in old fashioned leather jerkins. A group of knights in armour and a woman just dressed normally, a bit like my mum would dress. A smile beamed across her face and she ran over to the spaceman. I turned and walked away. I didn't understand what I was seeing.

We walked back across the white chocolate button in silence.

"Hang on!" I stopped in sudden realisation. "The knights. White cross. They were fighting in the crusades?"

"That's right."

"But the crusades are generally considered to have been a mistake. To try to convert people by a holy war. Right?"

"Agreed," he replied. "Definitely not the right way to go about it."

"So how come they're here?"

"You never made a mistake, Monty?"

"Well yeah," I squirmed a little, "but there are small mistakes, and blooming great big ones."

"I like big mistakes," he replied. It took me by surprise.

He saw my confused expression. "You know what I get the biggest kick out of, Monty?"

I shook my head. I didn't have a clue what this guy was gonna say next.

"Forgiving people. People who are forgiven lots, love lots. Remember that, Monty. It's important."

"I don't understand. Two knights and a spaceman? They wouldn't have died at the same time."

"No," he replied. "But when you die down there doesn't necessarily determine when you arrive here. Difficult to explain. Different time streams."

"So what happened to Columbert?"

"We all make our own choices?" he replied solemnly.

We walked back towards the city and down what must have been a few hundred steps. My legs were killing me by the time we reached ground level again.

In front of me was a huge valley. There were farm houses, fields and a mill, and a variety of old and new style farming. To my left I could see a tractor being driven round. To my right someone walked the fields carrying a heavy scythe. Ducks and chickens wandered around outside a farm house. Next to them a huge lion lay down sleepily. People wandered past it but didn't seem scared at all. Mostly it was very young kids working the fields and some older teenagers, and a just a few older people. But the older people didn't always seem to be in charge. I could see what looked like a ten year old giving directions to another boy at least two foot taller. There was something very curious about this place. I couldn't quite put my finger on it.

There was a sudden question in my mind, prompted by what I had just seen in the white zone. "Am I dead?"

"Far from it," God replied. "You're probably more alive now than you have ever been."

"These people... They're working! Aren't we all supposed to just, like, have fun and party up here?"

"Look at them!" he replied. I looked. He was right. There was no getting away from the fact that they were happy. They were singing and whistling, taking their time, laughing and talking. Whilst the kids worked, I could see a couple of adults doing somersaults in the hay. It seemed oddly bizarre.

"There's something about this place," I muttered.

God smiled. "You noticed! That's a good sign."

"Sign of what?!" I shot back.

God held up his hand. "Be at peace, Monty," he said softly. "I'm not trying to trick you. That feeling. Describe it."

I stopped and leaned on the fence. I watched the action in the field and tried to pinpoint the difference in me. There was something missing that was normally there. Then it hit me.

"I'm not worried." God clapped me on the back and said nothing. He began to walk on. I was not worried. For the first time I realised that there had always been a list of concerns and problems in the back of my mind, like the residual noise of cars and aeroplanes which you could never get away from in a city, and so you just got used to it always being there. But I felt nothing like that here. I felt free. I was no longer waiting to be told off, put down, or told I was wrong. I had even given some verbal to this guy, God. And yet he hadn't zapped me with lightening and turned me to a cinder... yet! Maybe there was hope for me. There was something else too. The suspicion I had felt when I first arrived was beginning to evaporate. I felt like I had spent a life fighting the system, fighting a losing battle to do things right. Life had always been a difficult balancing act between keeping out of trouble but looking after number one... keeping ahead of people like my dad who wanted to doom my life forever. Worries... more worries. There were so many for a kid aged eleven. Getting through school, SATS and GCSE's, what to do when you grew up, getting hold of cash to buy football cards, people's expectations, keeping your nose out of trouble, steering clear of those who wanted to see you mushed into pulp, getting up in the mornings, and most worrying of all whether I'd ever get the Alan Smith card or I'd never have a full set. It was exhausting just thinking about it. But here, in this place, I didn't feel any of that. It was as if I could do anything... and what I wanted to do was to see this place and enjoy this feeling while it lasted.

"Hey, wait!" I ran to catch up.

I ran past tall golden posts on each side of me and felt a warm breeze on my face. My surroundings suddenly changed. In front of me was an African style plain. It was beautiful. Strange trees grew, alone and isolated, misshapen, disfigured. To one side of me were a group of grass huts. Outside them a small tribe of very short, dark-skinned people cooked something on a spit over a dusty desert fire.

"What just happened?" I blurted.

"It's a portal," he explained, as if I was expected to understand this. "Look," he continued. "Ordinary, simple things. A complex world isn't always a good thing. These people choose a life like this."

"They choose it?" I asked, to be sure about this.

"Yes, everyone up here chooses how they want to live."

"But I thought heaven was a strict place. No bad things allowed, and everyone is forced to worship God all the time?... no offence meant, but, you know... rather boring," I added.

"No offence taken," he grinned at me. He was enjoying this, teaching dumb old me a thing or two. I bristled slightly, annoyed.

"Heaven isn't strict. It's a place for people who have learnt, that's all. Your life down there on earth, Monty. It's a lesson. And what is worship, Monty? It means to bring pleasure to God." He raised his hands to indicate everything around him. "This brings me pleasure." Then he turned to me and pointed at me. "You bring me pleasure, Monty. That's why I made you," he smiled.

We walked through another portal. We were fighting our way through a crowd. In front of us was a massive stadium. I'd been to Wembley once, and I can tell you, this was really really huge.

"What is that?" I blurted.

"Oh, that," he replied casually. "We have a lot of football supporters here."

"Wow, cool," I said. This place was growing on me.

We finally reached our destination. We were in front of the gates of a mansion. It was huge. The gates opened automatically for us and we wandered in. There was a rather posh looking circular lake and fountain, around which the path to the front double doors went. As we walked through the gate I noticed a kid, about my age, baseball cap, holding onto a skateboard, which he had upright and was leaning on.

"You're late!" exclaimed the boy in a strong American accent.

God smiled. "This is Josh. Josh, I'd like you to meet Monty."

I nodded. So where were this kid's parents? Surely you don't have God come around to visit and just send your kid down to meet him!

"Hey dude," replied the kid with a smile and he threw me a skateboard. I missed it and it fell on my left foot.

"So, we skatin' or what, Mister Boss Man?" drooled the American accent.

"Er, I don't skate," I said firmly. No-one was listening. They were walking off in deep conversation. I followed. As we turned the corner I saw the skateboard park. The whole of one side of the mansion gardens had been carved away and there was a large concrete skateboard park, complete with jumps, tracks, loops and curves.

God turned to me and winked.

"The skateboard, one of my better inventions."

"Your inventions!" I exclaimed in surprise.

"Yeah, mine," he replied. "I invented everything good! Look, don't you just love this kid!" He pointed over to Josh, who was at that moment, ten feet off the ground in the midst of a somersault. And with that God took a red baseball cap out of his pocket and placed it on his head. He then stamped down on the back of the skateboard lying at his feet. It flipped neatly up into his hand, and he was away with a "whoop! Wait for me, Josh!"

I couldn't believe this. God on a skateboard??!! Get real!

God skidded to a halt. He dropped the board on the ground, looked up, and then popped the tail of the board hard with the toe of his left foot. As the board did a neat 360 turn he jumped, his feet met the board in mid-air and God and board landed together on the half-pipe tube.

"Way to go!" Josh shouted (accent in full flow), from where God was on the ramps. "What a Kick-flip! Hey, Mister Boss Man, take the Vert ramp."

With that, God built some pace on the half-pipe until he reached the very edge, which turned ninety degrees up... straight up. God did a perfectly controlled climb, slowed almost to a stand still and the board fell away from the ramp. He did a neat swivel of the hips as he was floating static in mid-air and then landed perfectly on the board as it hit the concrete ground.

Josh gave a whoop and a clap.

"Hey, dude M," shouted the kid. Was he talking to me? "Get you're butt on that board and get over here."

Huh! Snotty little kid. I was sure I was marginally older than he was. But still I had a burning desire to try it out... but at the same time I didn't want to embarrass myself.

"Come on!" urged God. "It's easier than it looks." I tentatively picked up my board and walked across to where Josh had stopped and flipped his skateboard. We started off.

"Ya gotta learn to Ollie it first, 'kay?"

"Er, what?" I didn't understand what on earth he was talking about.

"Just follow me, kay? It's not position of the feet that matters. Just pop the board hard with the ball of your foot. Watch." With that, Josh jumped on his board. It rolled along the ground with a rumbling sound. He popped the tail of the board with the ball of his foot and as if by magic the whole board jumped about six inches into the air, neatly up the curb and onto the ramp.

"Piece of pie, 'ey Dude M? Go on kid, pop it!"

I stepped on my board tentatively, pushed off with my left foot, wobbled slightly, wiggling my hips far too much to keep my balance and I felt stupid. I must look like a total buffoon! OK, here goes. I thumped my foot down hard on the tail and to my astonishment the board seemed to rise up with my feet and land neatly on the ramp.

"Unbelievable!" I mumbled.

"Way to go, Dude M!" exuded the American accent. He let me try out a few ramps and half-pipes before he suggested I try the kick-flip.

"You might want to start trying it with your front foot just above the middle of the board, with the back-half of your foot sort'a hanging off, and at about a forty-five degree angle."

I just blinked.

"The board should flip up to your feet. Then just ride it out. You'll need to develop your flick."

Was this kid speaking outer Mongolian or something? Everything he said just seemed to go straight over my head.

I got on the board and just went for it. My first attempt ended in a heap on the ground. But the second attempt was pretty decent. It seemed like just minutes and I had tried dropping off the Vert ramp and seemed to be ridding like a pro. It seemed so easy. The board just seemed to follow my feet.

"It really is that easy!" God called over, as if he had read my thoughts... which, I guess thinking about it, he probably had. He picked up his board. "You see, it's different here. Everything's working for you, here. It's not the same on earth. In your world, if you eat too much you get fat, if you run too fast you get tired, if you play computer games you normally lose for the first hundred and fifty goes. And of course, if you try to learn to skateboard, you fall off and look stupid for the first six months. Not here. None of that happens. This place is on your side.

Cool, I thought!

There was no doubt we had worked up a sweat. I was feeling very pleased with myself.

"Right, how about some dinner, Josh!"

Josh flipped his board and we made our way inside. We went through the mansion sized hall and into a small room edged with beanbags. In the middle were platters of steaming food. We all slouched into the beanbags and started to dig in. It was a cool way to eat. The food however was strange. I couldn't describe it. The chips looked like normal chips but the platters were laden with slices of something.

"Trusstles," said God.

"Sorry, what?"

"Trusstles," God repeated. "The food. It's Trusstles. We don't eat meat... obviously... but we grow all sorts of things that you wouldn't dream of. I took my first ever bite of Trusstles. My mouth exploded. It was spicy hot to begin with but then it soothed the throat. As I ate I was feeling healthier and more alive with each mouthful.

We all relaxed and munched for several minutes, filling and refilling our plates. Large gold goblets were filled brimming with some liquid which tasted fruity and colourful. I was desperate to find out more. I had so many questions.

"So you died when you were about ten, then?" I asked Josh in my most solemn voice. I wasn't sure how acceptable it was to talk about death. But to my surprise, both Josh and God suddenly broke down into uncontrollable laughter, rolling about on their beanbags.

"What!" I demanded, irritably. I didn't like being the brunt of their jokes. God just held up a hand to indicate for me to hold on a moment. He couldn't talk, he was laughing too much. In fact he laughed so much he fell off his beanbag.

"What!?" I repeated, now quite agitated.

"I'm sorry!" God said.

"It gets 'em every time, Boss!" Josh said through fits of giggles.

"Josh actually lived till he was quite old when he was on earth," God explained. "He was quite famous."

"Abraham Lincoln," put in Josh. The food in his mouth and the accent must be why I misheard. For a minute I thought he had said Abraham Lincoln!

"Well, that's the name I went by then, anyway. All a bit of a hazy memory now."

"Abraham Lincoln?" I repeated. No-one blinked. "Naaa! You're kiddin' me," I went on. "As in American President, forming a League of nations and all that?" I was shaking my head. "He's just a kid! No offence," I added to Josh.

"He morphed," said God.

"I morphed," repeated the American accent. "I chose to be ten. Ten is much more fun than sixty. Trust me, I know."

"Show him," gestured God. Josh crinkled up his nose.

"No… I don't want to." He looked reluctant. But God just gave him a pleading look. Josh stood up. I watched intently. What was about to happen? Then it happened. The kid began to change. It was indiscernible at first but there, three feet away from me, standing on a beanbag, the kid was getting taller. His face was wrinkling. His hair was thinning. His clothes were turning black. I shook my head and blinked. Where Josh had stood, there was now an old man in black suit and black top hat. He sat back down on the beanbag as easily as the ten year old. I didn't know what to say. Everything in this place was freaking me out. Young people were old people, Knights in shining armour lived next door to space men, and God did neat loops on a skateboard.

The whole place was totally crazy... Absolutely barking mad!!

I looked again and Josh was "morphing" back. The little kid smiled. I just kept my distance. They were both waiting for some sort of comment.

"That's disgusting!" I said. "If that had been on TV it would be rated eighteen. I feel sick."

God gave me a serious stare. "You know, Monty. There's a kid inside all of us, just dying to get out. Didn't you find that on the skateboard park? You desperately wanted to come on, but something held you back?" He could see I was struggling. I didn't want to just let go. But he was right. There was part of me just dying to let go. It seemed just unbelievably appetising to just let it all drift away and be me.

"Up here, Monty, we can just be ourselves." God smiled. Was it really that simple?

"Now," God continued. "Down to business."

Business? This did not sound like a good turn of events. The lights were low, the food had been mesmerising and I felt a million bucks. I didn't want to get down to business, I wanted to talk and explore this place more. This... God... was an amazing guy. Not like I had imagined at all.

There was pause. I waited for something to happen. The silence was now getting embarrassingly long. What was going on?

"I think you want to start?" God urged. Did I? It was news to me! "Remember Monty, let go." Let go?... OK, let go. What was the first thing in my mind, if I could say anything?

"Why am I here?" I asked. "You said it was 'cause you liked me, but why am I really here?"

God replied, "I was a carpenter once, you know?" I nodded. I knew the story.

"I loved it. I would take a block of wood and I would imagine what I wanted it to be. Then I would chip away at it until it began to look like I had imagined. But it was never exactly right. And so I would continue to work, and work at it, day and night sometimes, until it was perfect. Because that was my passion. Sometimes there was a knot in the wood or a piece would brake and I would have to begin from the start again. It was painstaking work, but extremely satisfying. You're a block of wood Monty and I have a vision for what you could be. It's a brilliant vision, Monty. You couldn't imagine the places you could go, the things you could do and be. And so I chip away at you with my chisel. But we have a saying up here. We chip away with the chisel, and every now and again we have to use the jackhammer. Today's a jackhammer day."

"You've certainly made an impression, Lord," I murmured. It was the first time I had called him Lord. That's what the knights had called him. It seemed appropriate to call God, "Lord."

Again, he waited.

"Why are all the bad things happening to me?" I couldn't help it. I had to know. I thought about my sleepless nights, bank raids, neck ache, and aliens.

God picked up a slice of Trusstles and played with it in his fingers. It was very sticky stuff.

"What's important in that world of yours, Monty? Friends are important, Monty. And truth is important. I've put you there to learn. Not to play, but to learn. You have difficult choices to make. I gave you a gift..." The chocolates came to my mind immediately. God had started this all off with the chocolates. "... but it is your choice how you use that gift. It has the potential to help a lot of people, including your friends, Monty. But there is a cost. You have to choose between yourself and your friends. You can choose the easy and painless life, or you can choose to join in and use what I have given you. But every time you use it, there is a cost for you. You have found that already, haven't you?"

"That doesn't seem fair," I muttered. Well, God had said to let go, so I was, well, letting go.

"Whoever said anything about fair? Life ain't fair, Monty. Is it fair that you're living in the comfort of England whilst others are born in starving Africa." OK, OK, I got the message… I was squirming.

God continued, "It's not about fair, it's about using the chisel on you, Monty. It's through hardships that we develop into the people we could be. I want you to develop. There is a battle waiting for you out there, Monty. But it's up to you."

"I've asked Josh here to pray for you." I stared at Josh. There was a serious, steely, very adult look on the ten year old face now. Our eyes met and for a brief second there was an unsaid agreement. I would battle, and Josh would pray. And between us we would get through.

"When am I going to die, Lord?" The question had been burning a hole in my mind. I had meant to find the right time to ask but there was no right time.

God smiled. "When you're ready." Ready for what, I thought?

"It's not unpleasant, you know. Dying," God continued. "People are afraid of it because they don't know what's beyond… they've never seen all this. But you have no need to be afraid of that, now. No, there are other things for you to worry about."

Josh glanced at his watch. "Oh no! I've gotta dash, Boss. I'll be late for work."

"It doesn't matter if you're a bit late, Josh!" God replied as Josh dashed from the table.

"I don't wanna be late! I love it too much!" and with that he was off. "See ya, dude M! Be cool!"

I glanced out the window. It was evening here. Where would a ten year old be going to work at night? I asked the question and then realised my mistake. He wasn't a ten year old, despite appearances.

"He's a Watcher," God replied.

"A watcher?" I asked.

"He watches your world. Deep in the depths of the second heaven is a place where very few are allowed to enter. It is a dangerous place, a place where your world meets our world here. It is the place of the Watchers. They're mostly angels. Angels are very cunning, very careful. They plan ahead and they never miss an attack."

"An attack?"

"It is a very dangerous place down in your world, Monty. The enemy is always attacking. It is more dangerous still between the worlds. We have planned your visit here for many years. Hundreds of thousands of angels have been involved at each step of the way. One of the largest protective details we have completed for a long time guarded you in the moments of your travel between the worlds."

I couldn't believe it. Everywhere I looked, and with everything I heard, new worlds were opening up.

"This was all planned?" I blurted.

"Of course!" God raised a finger in the air and appeared to write something. A calendar appeared in midair. I wasn't sure if it looked real or sort of projected, like a computer image. It was certainly tatty with use, covered in scribbles and finger marks. "Look." God pointed to the top left corner where my name was printed... "Monty Pilchard."

"This is your calendar." I looked over it. There were so many items written in, scribbled, crossed out. Arrows had been drawn from one box to another to show an item being moved around. I could see the word "Chocolate" written in block capitals. I scanned down to today's date. The word "Vision" was written. I had a sudden thought. My eyes glanced forward to tomorrow and beyond, but God obviously knew what I was thinking and the calendar vanished before I could read anything further.

"Doesn't do you well, to know what's coming." There was a twinkle in his eye.

"My life," I muttered. "It's all planned out?"

"Oh no, no!" God corrected. "Not at all. Why do you think there are so many crossings out? You and only you can make your choices, Monty. I just put in a little nudge now and again. It's the world's biggest game of chess, Monty."

"You call this a little nudge?"

God's face broke into a wide smile and he laughed, thumping his fist on the table. "Nice one, I like that."

"Now!" God announced, rubbing his hands and rising from the left over food strewn over the floor. "Come on then, dude M," God said mocking Josh's adopted title for me. "The night is still young."

I was intrigued.

God led me through to the back of the house. Then he paused, took something out of the back pocket of his jeans and handed it to me with a wink. I looked down. It was an Alan Smith football card. I couldn't believe my eyes. I looked up again to thank him but he had walked on ahead.

He opened a door and, yet again, I stood in stunned disbelief. The music hit me like a brick, it was so loud. There were thousands of kids dancing. God swivelled his baseball cap around so it was facing backwards and then boogied across to the DJ turntable. There was a cheer from the crowd.

"OK, dudes. Are we ready for some serious party time?" God called into the mic. Another cheer, and the music went up yet another notch in the volume. Unbelievable. There was God doing the funky chicken and scratching on an old vinyl record deck.

"I'd like to introduce ya'll to Dude M, in the corner there. He's just visiting with us for a while." His hands pointed in my direction and the spotlights seemed to follow. "Let's show him a real party!" The loudest cheer of all rose. I thought my ear drums were gonna burst.

Chapter 16
Zulu…

Downstairs
Galaxy ref: P5763EARTH
Grid: UK739~DXy94

T he light faded. I was back in the Gathering Hut. It seemed a long journey since I remembered sitting here last. How long had it been, I wondered? I looked across at the others. Buffy and Charlie both had stunned looks on their faces.

"If... what?" Charlie mumbled. "If what?... He didn't tell me what!" he said louder, almost shouting.

"Ronnie!" shouted Buffy. "He's alive! HE'S ALIVE!!" she screamed at me. She was now jumping round the hut like a maniac.

What had just happened here?

"If what?" Charlie repeated. "Centurion eighty eight... Yes I want to." He stood up and started bellowing through the open ceiling, "Yes I want to!"

They'd all gone mad. It was sort of reassuring to know there may be people more insane than I was.

Where was Hash? He was gone.

Had this been a dream? Or had I really been somewhere? If it had been a dream, had it really meant anything? I didn't feel half as confident now that God wasn't standing by my side.

There was a strange sound by my left ear a sort of whoosh, thud. I looked around. Nothing there.

There it was again... whoosh, thud. Whoosh, thud.

"Bloomin' heck!" said Charlie. "Look!"

I followed his gaze. There were three darts buried in the log wall opposite me. Each was about six inches of thin hand-carved wood with three or four coloured feathers hanging loosely off the end.

We stared at each other. Whoosh, thud. Buffy jumped back. Another dart twanged in the wall about an inch from where her head had just been.

"We're being attacked!" she shouted.

"No way!" shouted Charlie in disbelief.

"Hit the deck!" Buffy hissed.

We all crouched down on the floor of the hut. Buffy crawled round and closed all the window shutters. We were safe for a few minutes.

"What's going on?" whispered Charlie.

"Can they get us from above?" I said, glancing at the open roof. There weren't many climbable trees higher than the Gathering Hut.

"Who's they?" said Buffy. She had a good point. "We've gotta get out of here," she said, "or we're gonna be trapped."

Charlie had pulled a dart out. He was examining it. Then I noticed it. There was a skateboard in the corner, propped up against the wall. I blinked. It had been real. That was from my dream. Time stopped for a moment as I tried to work this out in my mind.

"Come on, Fish!" shouted Buffy. She was making for the door.

"Hold on," said Charlie, an ashen look on his face. He pointed at the wall. Where the darts had hit the wall, the wood of the logs had already turned black and was flaking off.

"What do they put on the darts?" he said.

"Poison on the tips probably," I replied.

"Looks more like acid," said Buffy.

"Great!" I said, "that's all we need."

"I don't get it!" Charlie said in a strained voice, tossing the dart away. It was one of his favourite phrases when he was in a low mood. He could bring an end to any conversation that way. "Why are these gits attacking—"

"It's just been a weird week, Charlie. Leave it at that," I interrupted. And it had been... a very strange week.

"Come on," said Buffy again. "Let's get out of here."

I grabbed the skateboard. "I got an idea."

Buffy crinkled up her nose. "Fish? You can't skateboard for toffee!"

"Cheers," I smiled sweetly and headed out the door.

"Stop!" she said in one of her stern voices, which you didn't disobey. "I know this place like the back of my hand. I'll go first."

I followed her out. I didn't feel any fear till I walked out of the hut. Then there was a whoosh, whoosh, whoosh very close by. I looked across the log walk to the steps down. My eyes met the eyes of a short black guy, loin cloth, war paint, piece of bone through his nose. He had a long blow pipe to his lips. I was petrified. This was definitely not good. What was he doing here? I'd been teleported to the middle of Zulu land, or something.

I saw the guy's cheeks move. Whoosh, thud. The dart was buried in the bottom of my skateboard, which I'd pulled up in front of me as a gut reaction.

"MOVE!" shrieked Charlie. "They're in the hut! Their coming in the hut!"

I threw the board on the bridge. It was made of wood planks. I figured the wheels would cope. I jumped on it and suddenly I was flying across the bridge.

Whoosh, whoosh, whoosh. I heard the darts clatter into the branches of the trees. I was across the bridge. A Zulu guy jumped out in front of me. OK, here goes. I crouched low and launched myself. At exactly the same time I popped the back of the board as hard as I could. The board did a neat 360 and my feet landed back, perfectly. I was about three feet off the platform, the board at a forty-five degree angle. I heard a thud, thud as darts hit the underside of the board in front of me.

This was lunacy! What was I doing?! My head was suddenly full of doubts, I couldn't do any of this. Why hadn't I just stayed in the spare room and kept myself to myself.

I was still sailing through the air in semi-crouch position. Then the wheels of my skateboard landed on Zulu man, with a rather louder thud, and he was toast.

"Nice one, Fish," shouted Buffy before she swung on the rope vine like something out of Tarzan and Jane.

Whoosh, whoosh... thud, thud. I looked around to see another Zulu man briefly, but then he was knocked out of the tree by... Hash. Hash was here. Cool! I saw him for a fleeting moment then he was gone.

I had a warm glow... I'm invincible! I pushed off for the log walk. OK, I admit it, it was a little too adventurous. I just felt on top of the world for a moment. The log was curved. The board slid to one side. My hip hit the log hard, the skateboard clattered into the trees below, and the last bit of warm glow evaporated.

My fingernails grasped desperately for a grip as I bounced off the log. My left hand caught hold. I dangled. My hip was throbbing and I could feel the pain coming back in my neck and shoulder. I could feel my left hand getting weaker.

"Help!" I shouted. Nothing. "Help!"

It was so annoying. Just when my day was starting to look up, as well! At least it couldn't get much worse!

Then I saw Zulu man across the trees, below me. He was standing on the spy deck. Oh great! Whoosh, thud. It buried in the wood three inches away from my left hand. I craned my neck to see what Zulu man was doing. He was reloading. I had to do something.

"Fish!" It was Charlie. "Hold on buddy."

Quick! I wanted to shout, but I concentrated on holding on.

Whoosh... I closed my eyes and prayed. Thud. Pain in my left hand. Wow... Unbelievable pain, like someone had just rammed a nail in my hand. But something strange... dizziness. The ground below me was spinning. I looked up... My hand! The back of my left hand had turned black. I couldn't feel my fingers. The whole hand was throbbing like a huge heartbeat... caboom... caboom... caboom.

I could see black shadows swirling around me.

"Get off!" I yelled at them. I waved my right fist. They were laughing at me. Caboom... caboom. I reached for them. My left hand... it had slipped. I was gonna fall. I looked down. It was hundreds of feet. I was gonna die. Caboom... caboom.

Something slapped against my hand. It held fast.

"Caught ya, buddy!" It was Charlie.

"Get him up... quick!" It was Agnes. Her voice sounded faint.

"Come on buddy. I need your help. Reach."

I couldn't feel my body. I was floating. I looked down, but I could only see grey.

"Reach!" It was Charlie.

Caboom... caboom.

"REACH!"

My hand was free. I was flying.

I was falling... again.

Chapter 17

Svenerion Xertox...

Upstairs
Realm 1... Map Room

Creevy walked a little nervously into the Map Room.

"I knew it was a bad idea," he muttered to himself. He sighed. How had he let Stex talk him into it? He felt like kicking himself. Stex had just seemed so desperate to see earth. And heaven was all about caring about the guy next to you, even if it was a Biops! No! No excuses, it had been a bad idea.

The red velvet armchair was in a different part of the Map Room today. In front of it, hovering in mid-air was a strange looking green and flat oblong disc. Svenerion Xertox was an unusual planet, located not that far away from earth. In its primitive time all the inhabitants had been convinced their planet was round like a ball. Then they had discovered space travel and realised that in fact Svenerion Xertox was flat. That's why so many explorers had died, when they had been exploring and fallen off the edge of the world.

It wasn't actually a very interesting planet (created before earth... God made further design improvements before he created earth), and that's why most of the inhabitants preferred space travel to staying on the bright green planet surface.

God was just turning the time dial on the underneath left corner of the disc as Creevy approached rather apprehensively. He was about to launch into his apology for the Stex earth visit incident, which he had to admit had not been one of his better days, when a broad smile spread across God's face. "Creevy! I just wanted to call you up here and thank you personally for helping me out with Stex."

"Yeah, I'm really sorr... Er..." Creevy paused. "You did?"

"Yep! Biops' like Stex have a lot they have to learn. This is all part of the learning. Remember, using the chisel."

"It is?" Creevy was confused, but he smiled anyway. He suddenly felt on top of the world. The Main Man always seemed to have a way of brightening things up and sorting things out.

"Hey," said Creevy just noticing the floating disc, "that's Svenerion Xertox!"

"That's right," God replied. "The question is, what do we do with it?"

Creevy looked lovingly at his planet... once his home long ago (before he got zapped in the red gas cloud, that is).

"They're not doing very well are they?" he replied.

God shook his head. "Not really. I made them with fifteen ears each, you know, but they're still not very good listeners!"

"A tough place, Pre-world," Creevy pondered.

"But important, in order for them to learn. How else would it work up here if we didn't learn?"

Creevy nodded and frowned at the small green oblong floating in front of him. So this was it, he thought. The Main Man was going to write them off because they didn't learn. They were both silent for a minute as they watched the zillions of small green aliens zipping around in their daily lives.

"How do you communicate with a colony of ants, Creevy?" The question came out of the blue.

"Sorry?" Creevy shook his head. He always seemed to have the strangest conversations with the Main Man.

"You could stamp on them, that'd get a message across," God went on, "or you could become an ant yourself... sit down and chat to them."

There was a long pause.

"What... you mean go down there, like you did with earth?"

"That's right," God replied. "What sort of God would I be if I wasn't willing to take part in what I created. I made a promise to your planet, Creevy, not to abandon it, and I keep my promises."

Creevy stared at God. He had a sombre look on his face. He knew it had been hard for God, being a human being on earth.

"Why's it so hard?" Creevy asked. "I mean, you can be in three billion places at once, anyway? What's so different about going down onto a planet?"

"It's not difficult to be God in a number of places. That's the easy bit. But to set aside who I am and become human, be a part of what I created is... It's difficult to explain." He smiled. "There is also a risk. It can always fail. But then if you care, you take risks, don't you Creevy. Just like you did with Stex."

God rubbed his hands together, shook himself out of his sombre mood and an energetic smile came back onto his face.

"I have a task for you Creevy," he said, changing the subject. "I'd like you to meet George."

Over the brow of the green meadow came a man Creevy had never met before. He looked about twenty years old, long blonde hair, but then looks and age meant very little up here.

"George is leading a special building project. I need you to set aside your space craft and help George. It's a mansion for someone very special."

"Of course." It was strange, thought Creevy, but he had been feeling a bit off the space travel since the Stex, earth visit thing. This was a welcome change. God always had a way of knowing these things.

Once Creevy and George had gone, the angels arrived and stood around silently in a semi-circle. They were the most senior of the angels.

Gabe watched intently, from his place in the very centre of the semi-circle. He had seen this only once before. It had been the most important protective detail he had ever been given in his long and prestigious career... to protect God, himself, when he had been born in a stable in that strange globular world, earth. And as a baby! Why a baby? It had been a monumental risk, but the Chief had insisted it had to be done. The secrecy and security over that one operation had been unbelievably complex. The diversionary tactics alone had kept a hundred thousand of the angel army busy. The Watchers had been on full alert. But he, Gabe, had been the angel there with the Chief, with the close hidden protection brief. And he had been there to strengthen the Chief when he had most needed it. He had watched the Chief as he sat in the olive garden and struggled with the idea of dying for a world. Yes, thought the angel, he and the Chief had been on many adventures together, and perhaps here was the start of another one. The angel's eyes snapped back. God was on the move again.

They watched as a strong wind blew through the Map Room. God reached forward and placed a finger onto that strange oblong disc of Svenerion Xertox. Just for a moment, God seemed to waver, looking thinner and gaunter than normal. When he turned back to the angels he had a determined but sad look on his face. And he'd left a part of himself behind in the strange oblong planet.

"Shall I accompany you again, Chief?"

"Not this time, Gabe. I need you for a different assignment."

Chapter 18

The Second Letter...

Downstairs
Galaxy ref: P5763EARTH
Grid: UK742~BCz87

And that's how I ended up in hospital for a second time. From here on in things were about to get very confusing. One thing, however, was for sure. I had felt like a million bucks during my heaven vision. It felt like I'd spent a month there, and I missed it. It felt more real to me than this real life did.

Anyway, back to hospital... I woke up. My left arm was in plaster, and I couldn't move my head because my neck was in one of those neck braces. I looked down at my feet. They were all strung up on pulleys. On the upside, I was back in my private room with Nurse Heartly as my personal nurse. On balance, it was worth it.

The TV was on and Nurse Heartly was pottering about when I first woke up. She said I'd had a nasty fall and muttered something about forest and middle of the night.

My first visitor was Mum. She hugged me. It was the most painful hug I'd ever had in my life. She kept wittering on about how much she loved me. I asked if she loved me enough to buy me a personal stereo with headphones, and she said she did, so I suggested she stopped hugging me and went and bought one now. Why didn't nurse Heartly hug me like that? I'm sure it wouldn't hurt as much.

Next visitor was Rupert, worst luck, armed with bible verses. I told him that if he turned up again in the yellow scarf, I'd set Charlie on him. Don't worry, I was very subtle about it.

Next was Dad, with his normal, "Hey kiddo!" He had brought me a scrap book. Said I could use it to collect news clippings from the papers about all his interviews and TV appearances.

"Look," he said excitedly. "I've already started it for you. That's me on CNN. That's me waving to the crowd from the aeroplane. Look! Me in the cruiser. Me advertising washing powder."

"Er... Thanks, Dad." He didn't ask about my injuries.

Next was Jacob. Said he'd brought me some Cuban cigars, but the nurse had confiscated them. "Borin' places these 'ospitals, ain't they Monty?"

I gave him the scrap book and asked him to bin it on the way out.

Nurse Heartly fed me tasteless mush for lunch. I didn't care. I could just stare into her eyes forever.

"Oh," she said as she was leaving the room. "I almost forgot. We found this in your trouser pocket." She handed me the Alan Smith football card. I'd almost forgotten about it. I stared at it for a few minutes and then hid it somewhere safe.

Mid-afternoon Buffy sneaked around the bedroom door.

"Fish... Fish," she hissed. "I'm not supposed to be here..." Then she stopped, and stared at me. "Heck Fish! What have they done to you?"

"It's worse than it looks," I reassured her. "Neck brace is temporary, leg broken in two places... Arm they're still working on."

She was still staring. "Er... Yes?" I prompted.

"We really thought you were a goner when you fell." Her voice was a little shaky.

Yes, that was right. I'd fallen. It was as if I'd blocked it out, but now it was all coming back.

"Zulu's with blow pipes?" I shook my head. "I mean, where did they come from?"

"And it gets weirder too," she went on. "I had the weirdest dream... you know, when the fire blew."

My eyes went wide. "So did I!"

There were footsteps outside the door.

"No time now," said Buffy. "Anyone asked you any questions yet?"

I shook my head.

"My mum's been quizzing me all afternoon. What we were doing out at night, and all that. We had to drag you to the hospital, you see. I haven't told them about the treetops or the Zulu's, OK? So don't mention it. Charlie and Hash were never there either. OK?"

She paused. I was waiting to hear what outrageous story she'd dreamed up."

"And...?" I prompted.

She had turned red.

"I'm your girlfriend. We'd sneaked out. We'd done some climbing. I told them we sneak out sometimes to see each other."

"What?!" I blurted.

"It was the best I could do on the spur of the moment, OK!" she hissed angrily, before bolting for the door. "Just stick to it!"

I hid underneath the covers. This was awful. What if the guys at school found out!

It was then that Mum and Dad arrived again and now they were over the initial shock of almost losing their beloved son (that's me) it was serious chat time. Mum was very upset about the lying and sneaking out of the house stuff. She made me promise I'd never do it again before she let me have the personal stereo she'd bought me. But Dad was even worse. He kept saying things like, "Monty, you little rascal. Agnes, ay? She does have rather a lot of freckles."

Mum said, "Why didn't you just tell us, Monty? Of course you can have her round at any time."

Oh good grief. I was gonna puke. Give me a bucket!

I had to make some excuse about Buffy's friends and promising to keep it quiet. I couldn't believe the drivel I was hearing from my own lips.

"So what happened to the hand?" said Dad. "The doctor says it's infected with some sort of fast working poison. Their going to do some more tests on it tomorrow."

I shrugged. "Got bitten by something in the forest, I guess."

Eventually the nurse (not Honey Heartly... I was heartbroken to find she had clocked off duty) ushered them out.

Mum kissed me on the cheek.

"Take care Kiddo," said Dad, giving me a light punch on the chin, which was actually agony. Couldn't he see I was wearing a neck brace?

Sleep, as usual, never came. And it was unbearable not being able to move. I longed for the treetops, for the space, the stars. That night seemed to last so long. Why couldn't I sleep, just for one flipin' night! I was unbelievably bored. Then I remembered and I flicked on the light.

With new found interest I grabbed my rather shinny clean, not read very much, bible. I shut my eyes, held it spine down and let it fall open. How strange. It was that same bit again, about a guy called Balaam and a talking donkey. I remembered that last time I'd read it I had really thought it was stupid. But now I read the whole passage through with interest. You see, the story goes that God didn't want Balaam to go where he was going. So God sent an angel to block the narrow pass. Now, our guy Balaam, riding his donkey, couldn't see the angel, but his donkey could (interesting, I thought. You hear lots of stories of animals who seem to sense things which people don't). Anyway, the donkey refuses to walk through the pass, so Balaam beats the donkey with a stick (nice guy!) Eventually God gives the donkey a voice and it says, "why 're you beating me you great stupid git? It's the angel with the sword you gotta be careful of," or words to that effect. And I knew now, why God had given me that page of my bible to read (twice!). He speaks to stubborn people in unusual ways sometimes. For Balaam it was a donkey, for me a box of chocolates. Hey, who was I to call Balaam a freak? "Using the chisel," that's what God had called it.

I grabbed my Alan Smith football card and decided that would make a suitable bookmark for my bible.

I had one more thing I wanted to do and, since I still had a lot of night left, I decided to start writing a diary now. I would go back to Christmas and record all the strange events which had taken place. I cast my mind back to Christmas lunch and began to write.

The next day three interesting things happened. The first was an embarrassingly stupid conversation with Nurse Heartly. I awoke to Nurse Heartly who needed to change the dressing on my arm. I was alarmed to see, as they broke the plaster off, how black the hand was.

"Don't worry," she said, "It's improving. More blood tests and then MRI scan at eleven. The doctor wants to run more tests today, check nothing else is broken and work out what infected your hand." She smiled at me and suddenly I didn't care anymore if the hand dropped off or not.

I found myself saying, "Have you got a boyfriend?"

She gave me a quizzical look. "No," she replied, "but your girlfriend said she'd visit you again today. She's very cute, with the freckles." She raised her eyebrows in a sort of, "caught you out on that one, didn't I," look before she left. I couldn't believe it. I was gonna kill Buffy!

Charlie was my first visitor of the day. He was in one of his morose, glum moods.

"Fish," he launched straight into it. "I've got a problem."

Hey, I'm the one strung up in bed, mister! No "sorry I dropped you, Fish," or "sorry 'bout the neck, legs, arm and everything else." Thanks mate! I thought. He hadn't even brought me anything.

"... well three problems actually. 'If'... everything was dependent on an 'If'. And then there was Centurion eighty-eight. It doesn't exist."

"Charlie," I replied, "you're rambling. I ain't got the first clue what you're talking about, mate. And, if you don't mind me saying so, I got some problems too!" I pointed at the bed with my one remaining good arm. "You dropped me, you idiot!"

There was a long silence. Charlie went red and squirmed uncomfortably. I was being a bit harsh. I relented.

"Thanks for trying to save me, though. I really appreciate it."

Then Charlie told me the whole story, his vision, the worlds dying and being born, and most importantly Centurion eighty-eight, the star God wanted Charlie to work on with him. I told him my one and we compared notes. I was gob-smacked that he'd had one too. It had never crossed my mind until Buffy had briefly mentioned she had had a strange dream yesterday.

"Problem is," said Charlie, "I'm not sure if I believe it. I've checked all the star charts. There are no Centurion stars logged. Not eighty-six, seven or eight."

"Well I don't know, Charlie, maybe you gotta discover it or maybe it's too far away or happens in the future. There are loads of possible reasons."

I showed him my Alan Smith footie card and explained how sure of it all I was. But this was a real problem for Charlie. "Nope, he definitely said they were logged on our charts. And what about the 'If'," he went on. When he'd met God, God had finished by saying Charlie could have all this, help with the planet building... "If..." and then the vision had ended. "If... what? I gotta know!" he said desperately.

"That one's easy," I said. "If you trust, Charlie. This is your test, Charlie. You can't see Centurion now, but you have to trust."

Charlie was up and pacing the room now. It was making my neck ache, trying to follow him with my eyes.

"Trust?" he said, "I'm not sure I can, Fish, not sure I can."

Another silence.

"Great thought though, isn't it," I said. "Heaven... creating your own world, Charlie. Just imagine it." We couldn't.

"What was the third thing?" I asked.

"What?"

"You said, three problems."

"Oh yeah. Hash has gone."

I was still puzzled after Charlie had left. How could Hash have vanished... gone? It made no sense. I'd visit his home once I was out of here and sort out that mystery.

Charlie's visit was the second strange event of the day but the third one was the strangest of all. Mum and Dad visited again and insisted on staying with me all through the tests. They brought me a bag of stuff including my football card collection and after rummaging at the bottom of my rucksack I found my box of chocolates. Strange, I thought. Mum wouldn't have packed that. And how did it get there. Last time I'd seen it, it had been in the tree top huts.

"Oh," said Dad, rummaging around in his pocket. "Some post came for you as well." He handed me an envelope. I noticed a foreign post mark and pocketed it straight away.

My tests were all "A1," as the Doc called it, the neck brace was off, as was the left arm (plaster I mean, not the arm itself). I was only left to hobble along on crutches for six weeks. The Doc was still puzzled about the black hand, but they had pumped me with antibi-whatsits and all sorts of other drugs (I was higher than on Jacob's stout) and the blackness was receding.

They were going to let me out tomorrow and I was in for a more comfortable night since I wasn't all strung up.

That night I waited till it was late, visitors had departed and the hospital seemed calm and peaceful. I climbed out of bed and tottered to the window, from where I could see all sorts of activity four floors below me. A car screeched to a halt where a heavily pregnant woman was helped out and ushered through the front doors of the hospital. Far over to the right was the ambulance station and I could see the flashing blue light as one departed into the night. Twice I'd been brought in here, apparently, in a flashing blue light ambulance, but I hadn't known anything about it. It would have been quite cool had I been able to actually enjoy it!

I sat there for a bit watching the comings and goings whilst I updated my diary for today's events. Then I picked up my bible again, shut my eyes and opened at random. It was a tiny little story Jesus told about a mustard seed. The gist of it was that a small seed grows into a large plant. OK, I'm still with it so far... that's easy. As I watched the tiny people moving about in the streets far below, it seemed to me that the heaven I'd visited was like a mustard seed. To many people it seemed small and they missed it altogether... never even realised it was there as they went about their busy lives. But I knew it was out there, and I'd seen it... it was really mega-huge. All you had to do is look. I marked the place with my Alan Smith football card.

Then I remembered the letter. Of course! How could I have forgotten? I pulled the crinkled envelope out of my pocket and tore it open.

It read:

"Monsieur Monty,

Monsieur Cogan said I must write. I thank you for your prayers. We were caught by the floods. They destroy much of the herds, but then they fell back and we escape.

My tribe was attacked on our travels to high land. Dark warriors from the Dackoney tribe attacked us by night. They attack with deathly poison blowpipes. I had a vision of you kneeling to pray, Monsieur Monty, and the warriors vanished.

I know your prayers saved us. We are in debt to you always.

Keep using the gift given to you and not to be afraid.

From Senia."

I read it through again and then sellotaped it into my diary. Well that explained my Zulu warriors, maybe. Was it possible that things I did here would effect what happens to a remote tribe in Africa? I wasn't sure anymore if I should be surprised by these things. Time and time again, weird things were just, sort of, happening. It was like I'd suddenly shifted lane on the space highway and been caught up into a spiritual slip stream. The only puzzling thing was the fact that I hadn't actually prayed for her. I'd never prayed... didn't know how. I felt a pang of guilt. There they were heaping thankyous onto me and I hadn't lifted a finger.

I knew what I had to do now though. I pulled out the box of chocolates. It was a rather battered looking box now (a bit like me!). There was only one chocolate left. It was the gold foil wrapped important looking rectangular one, that you always find right in the middle of the box. I grabbed the golden leaflet. It was called, *"The President"*. The title fitted; it looked an important one. I unwrapped it. The smell of rich chocolate wafted up to my nostrils.

I wasn't scared to eat it. I was working the mystery out. This was a gift from the man upstairs and I'd got to know him a bit now. It was a gift with which I could help people. But there was a cost. It hurt me. I wasn't scared anymore. There was nothing to be scared of. I'd become a stronger person. I'd seen a glimpse of what this life was really all about. A few days back I'd been confused and hopeless. Now I looked forward to the place I'd be going one day... The Boss was getting it ready for me.

As usual I turned it over to read yet another strange inscription on the back.

"You will never know the full effect of the things you do, but history waits to write them."

I took my first bite.

The next day Mum and Dad picked me up from the hospital. I practiced on my crutches, and I then had two visits to make. I waited till Mum had popped out and then persuaded Dad to drive me around to Hash's house.

I knocked on the door and waited. It was your standard suburban semi, the other side of town from us. Hash lived with foster parents. He'd lived in a home for a while, but had been here with his new family for years now. I'd spent time here with Hash... we played computer games together when it was just the two of us. Between us we were really good at them. But when we met with Charlie as well, then we generally met up at Charlie's house since he had a massive bedroom (with a balcony, which held all his telescope stuff). And as for me, I had always ended up stuck in the tiny spare room at our's, so that had never been any good for meeting up. That was all before the Night Owls of course.

The door opened. It was Missus Watson.

"Oh, hello Monty," she said, smiling sweetly at me. "Very sorry to hear about the accident. How is the leg?"

"It'll mend, thanks, Missus Watson. Is Hash, I mean Arnold, in at all?"

"Oh no, dear," she answered. "Didn't you know? He's moved onto another family." I was stunned.

"Oh. Why's that?" I blurted. "How can I get in contact with him?" It all came tumbling out at random.

"I'm afraid I'm not allowed to talk about it or give out details. You'd have to contact the adoption agency." The sweet smile never left her face, but she was as tight as a clam when it came to giving out any information. You would have thought Hash was grassing up the Mafia and on a secret witness relocation programme or something like that. So that was it. Hash had vanished from the face of the planet. Maybe he'd been adopted? Good on ya, Hash! I hoped so. Anyway, I was sure he would get in contact with Charlie and me when he'd got settled.

I was using Dad a bit like a taxi... next stop was Jacob. I told Dad I'd hobble back, the exercise would do me good.

Jacob seemed very relieved that I was on the mend.

"Worried for ya, Monty, I was."

I sat down on the ugly sofa and stared at the ducks on the out of date wall paper. I showed Jacob the second letter and asked him about the prayer stuff. Jacob seemed to have some simple and straightforward beliefs in God without all the churchy, religious stuff. I respected that. He was also the only adult I knew who treated me like an equal, giving me straight answers, not like a kid.

Jacob rubbed his bristly chin thoughtfully.

"Ya see, I dun' know much 'bout this prayer lark. But I recon, Monty, that prayer ain't 'bout talk, tis 'bout action, 'bout showin' ya commitment. Maybe that's what we did with the chocolates? Ol' God, 'e respects people who put their money where their mouth is. All this churchy talk stuff don' cut no ice wit' 'im."

Maybe he was right. Our courage in using the chocolates was like a prayer which God had then acted on. We'd eaten the African Elephant chocolate and he'd answered the prayer. Wow! That was cool.

Chapter 19

Puzzles...

Downstairs
Galaxy ref: P5763EARTH
Grid: UK739~DXy94

O uch! That hurt," I hissed. "Get off. It's no use. I can't do this."

They were trying to get me up to the tree tops for a Night Owl's meeting. It was very nice of them, and all that. But let's face it. It was a really dumb thing to do when I had a broken leg, in plaster. I was in pain. I had one arm over Charlie's shoulder and the other over Donny's.

"Come on, we shouldn't do this," I said. "What if my mum checks up on me." I was a bit concerned about that, since she now knew I'd been sneaking out at nights.

"Don't be a wuss!" said Buffy. "No, Charlie. Put his leg over the branch... over there!" She was directing the "Move Monty" project.

"It's gonna be really dangerous for me up there," I persisted, almost pleading. "What if I fall?"

"You fell without the plaster, remember?" she retorted. "You'll be safer with it. You won't be able to move as much."

Oh, that was nice, wasn't it! She really had a way with words.

Half an hour later I was safely settled in the Gathering Hut. Everyone was wiping the sweat from there brow and huffing and blowing with the exhaustion of carrying me up. I had to admit, looking round, that it really was nice to be back. This place had a homely sort of feel to it. Donny tossed out packets of crinkle crisps and cheese strings and we began. Each of us, Charlie, Buffy and me, told our stories. I saw Charlie and Buffy both gazing longingly out of the open roof, as if they might just catch a glimpse of heaven between a couple of stars. Then we explained to Jacob and Donny about the Zulus and I showed them the second letter. Donny just sat in wide-eyed astonishment.

"It's just like Argentina in eighty-nine," he started. "I heard about this guy—"

"Can it, Donny!" interrupted Charlie. "I think perhaps we're just, like..." He paused, not wanting to be the one to say it. "Imagining some of this stuff." We began to protest but he held his hand up to stop us. "Seriously, bozzos, we had a shock from the fire and our brains blew a bit of a fuse, that's all."

I shook my head. "The football card! The skateboard!"

"Big deal! You got hundreds of football cards—"

"Not Smithy!" I interrupted.

"You didn't think you did. Then you found it. So what?"

"The skateboard?"

"There's a tonne of junk up here!" He had a point. In one corner of the hut were the remains of Charlie's telescope. There were books, gameboys, tennis rackets, empty cups, sweet wrappers, even for some reason a bike just outside the door. I frowned.

"The Zulus!" Buffy persisted. "And the letters."

Charlie went despondently quiet. "I just don't know, bozzos."

"I think it sounds brilliant!" announced Jacob. "Let's not knock it for the mo. Let's enjoy it for a while." It was a good plan.

We all laid flat on our backs on the platform.

"So which one would you like to be Centurion eighty-eight, then Charlie?" I asked.

He gazed for a few moments. "That one."

"Maybe one of those stars, is 'eaven?" said Jacob.

We all pondered the idea for a minute. I fixed my eyes on one particular star.

"So what about Hash?" said Donny. "He might have seen something too!"

He had a good point.

That night, when I got home, I opened my bible at random again. I read about this geezer called Jacob. Now the interesting thing about old Jake was that when he went on a camping trip he laid down in the desert and he saw a flight of stairs which ran from the desert floor, right up into heaven. And when old Jake looked at it, he could see angels going up and down, going about their work. I was reminded of what God had told me... you know, Boss Man God in the red baseball cap... when I'd met him. He'd said Josh worked for the Watchers, a special bit of heaven where they moved between heaven and earth. He'd called it a dangerous place.

I stared out my window at the night sky. Somewhere up there was Josh. He'd said he would pray for me. It made me feel good... I felt in good hands. Thank you Josh... Thank you Mister Boss Man!

A couple more weeks passed. I was bored. I didn't try going back to the treetops with my plaster on; it was just too difficult. Mum had taken me to the hospital yesterday and it had finally come off - at last!! It felt like I'd suddenly grown a new pair of legs, it had seemed so long without them. And so it was finally back to school tomorrow. I was slightly dreading it. Dad was still around, which was so good. We felt like a normal family for the first time in years. Still no word from Hash, I hadn't seen Nurse Heartly at all since I'd been in hospital, and my vision of heaven was beginning to fade slightly in my memory. It was as if there was something missing. I had eaten the last chocolate but nothing had yet happened. The excitement had gone... I'd fallen back out of my spiritual roller coaster. I sighed and crawled over to the desk.

On the desk sat my computer. Since I wasn't treetoping tonight, I would have a go at Hash and my latest computer game. I wouldn't normally do this without Hash but he wasn't here so, why not! I flicked on the computer, rubbed the sweat off my hands on my jersey and glanced at my watch. Two am. Plenty of time. I never slept a single wink, anyway. Hash and I had played computer games together for years. We weren't that into the shoot 'em up games, more the long term strategy games. And we were really good at them. We'd completed all the Tombraiders, done the latest Hitman, breezed through Final Fantasy, managed our way through Championship Manager, and done Red Force One, the war game. We were the best. We had also had a go at the Sims, but that had no end, nothing to aim at. Our latest game was much better. The screen turned blue, then the American flag came up, fluttering in the background. A man appeared at a desk and pointed at me. *"Your country needs you!"* it said.

"Yeah, yeah. Get on with it," I muttered. The game was called Oval Office. I was the President and I just had the little job of running America. There were a number of different parts to the game... you had to run the US economy, money and stuff, and the Secret Service who guarded you... one slip up there and an assassin would drop you. National Security, or the NS module, as it was called, was cool. As well as running CIA and sending out spies, and stuff like that, you could choose to go to war and there was a whole module, Pentagon, where you ran the war from. Hash and I were good at the war and spy stuff but rubbish at the money stuff, which was why our poll rating was so bad and it was looking like we weren't gonna get re-elected as President.

I had to admit, I wouldn't like to do this for real. Running a country was scary stuff. People lived and died on the decisions you made. The maid burns your eggs in the morning and you have a bad hair day and that was Iraq blown to smithereens.

I clicked on my Poll rating. 47 percent. It wasn't brilliant. I clicked start. Decisions and meetings began to flip up on the screen in front of me... raise taxes? NO... cut spending? YES, but only in bits people wouldn't notice... Bomb Cuba? Erm, yeah, why not. It flipped into the Pentagon module and I spent ten minutes planning my Cuba invasion. This was a cool game.

I was interrupted by a flashing message. It happened sometimes. Being President meant things happened quickly.

"New Module Loading" flashed up on the screen.

Then... *"Modem... Loading to main frame..."* started to blink on the screen and I heard the sound of the dialup on the phone.

Neat! I thought. It must have been downloading some new software or something. It had never done that before.

The bedroom door creaked behind me. It was Dad in a dressing gown, rubbing the sleepy bits out of his eyes.

"Hey, Kiddo. What's happening?"

"Oh, hi Dad." I glanced back at the computer. "Er... I couldn't sleep."

"It's the early hours, Mont! You're back to school tomorrow."

"Yeah, I know. Sorry."

"You worried about it?" he asked.

"I guess, a little," I replied. I was. It's like, when you haven't done something for a long time, you get worried about going back to it.

Dad smiled. "Hey, I got tickets to the town match tomorrow night. You coming?"

"Oh yeah!" I said, suddenly excited.

"Well get some sleep, and don't tell your mother you're up so late, or she won't let you go."

Dad winked at me.

"I'm glad you're home, Dad."

"Love you, Kiddo."

Dad left and I turned back to switch off the machine. But I paused.

"Tapping Oval office..." it was flashing at me as a loading bar filled from left to right across the screen. Then the screen changed.

I read the new module, title screen. *"Sleaze module..."* I read the narrative on the title screen. OK, I got the idea. My Poll rating was dropping, so the game had set me a new objective. *"Accumulate personal wealth in case you don't get re-elected"* it read. I got the drift. This was a game of cover your backside.

Messages started scrolling up the screen.

"Senator Roberts offers you $5 million to scrap pollution laws, to boost his car industry."

"James Stean, your biggest fund raiser asks a personal favour... reduce laws on worker rights to allow cheaper super market goods."

"The Head of CIA has informed you that he has a dirt file on you. He wants to meet."

Geezz! What was I supposed to do with this lot? Did these guys really operate like this? I'd already learned not to mess with worker rights, or your Poll rating went down the toilet. I stared at the rest of the list of bribes and dodgy decisions.

Did Presidents really have to face these kinds of problems and decisions? "Come on, Fish, you jerk. It's a game."

The screen started blinking, black and white at me. It read:

"THIS IS NOT A SIMULATION, MONTY."

"Senator requests immediate answer."

Nah, I preferred the war simulator. This was too hard. There were no obvious right or wrongs.

I reached down to switch off the computer. It was then that I noticed it. I blinked. It wasn't plugged in. The plug was lying on the floor. But that was impossible. I tried to flick the on/off... the screen just stared at me.

"THIS IS NOT A SIMULATION, MONTY."

Hang on, it had used my name!

I came too with a start. I must have dozed off. *"But I never sleep!"* was my first reaction. I had actually slept!! This was progress.

I stared at the computer screen. It was beeping at me, but other than that, it was blank. Had it spoken to me? Nah, I must have just dreamt it... but then, I wasn't sure I believed in coincidences any more. No, this wasn't a coincidence, it was starting again. Fish was back in the slipstream.

And it had given me an idea for finding Hash.

"Hey, Fish!" called Mowbray, across the recreation field ("the rec," as we called it). It was the next morning and I was walking ever so slowly into school. It wasn't the leg that was slowing me down, just a feeling of dread. I had enjoyed being off school, even if I had been plastered up like a concrete block. I didn't want to be back into the routine of lessons. I wanted to keep my freedom a bit.

Mowbray was running over to me.

"Fish! Heard about the fall," he said, wide-eyed. "Roy said you're lucky to be alive!"

Well the shoulder and back of my neck were giving me more jip than usual and there was the odd twinge, but I was OK.

"Anyway, I swapped desks with Agnes." He smiled at me. I stared back.

"Er... So?" What did I care.

Mowbray ploughed on, undaunted by my lack of interest. "You know, so you two can be next to each other. And she can help you... you know, if you need a hand to get around... You know, since you two are going out and all."

He stared at me again with the same gormless smile. I couldn't believe it. I hated him! How could he do that? I had a great urge to thump that smile right down the back of his throat. Safe to say, I didn't reply. I just pushed past him and went to hunt out Buffy and remove all her limbs one by one, like when you pull the legs off those large daddy longlegs spiders.

"What were you thinking?!" I hissed at her under my breath during ITC.

"I couldn't help it," she pleaded. "My mum was standing there. I couldn't say no!"

"Scuz bucket!"

She narrowed her eyes and huffed at me.

After school me and Charlie went to the arcade. I shared my plan to find Hash as we played on the slot machines. Charlie thought it was cool so the next day we bunked off school.

First stop, the bank. I needed the escape fund. Charlie waited outside. He didn't want Charlene to see he was out of school or it would get back to his mum.

I queued up. It was kind'a strange looking round at this place where we'd been in the bank raid. This had been where it had all began.

Ding!

"Hi love," said Charlene, disinterestedly.

"I want to make a withdrawal from my account," I said.

"How much, dear?" I really didn't see what Charlie's brother saw in her. Straggly greasy hair, thick as a plank and never showed the slightest interest in anything in life... including Charlie's brother. Just being within ten yards of her seemed to bring on a depressed, gloomy feeling.

"Er..." I wasn't quite sure how much. "All of it," I replied. I handed over my account details.

She clicked on a computer screen. I waited.

"But, Monty love. You've got over a thousand pounds in there. Does your dad know you're taking it all out." She spoke very slowly and smiled at me as if I was three.

Nosy cow!

"It's my account. Just give me the money!" I replied.

She pursed her lips. I could see the cogs of brain ticking over. She was thinking. It was a slow process for Charlene. She didn't do it very often.

"How do ya want it, love?"

"Fifties and twenties," I replied.

"So how come you got so much money, dear? What you saving for?"

"Nothing!" I replied a little too hastily. She eyed me suspiciously, as she counted it out. Why couldn't she mind her own business?

"You got it?" asked Charlie, as I got outside. "Can I see it? I've never seen that much cash before."

Neither had I. It was impressive.

"You gotta get your brother to ditch Charlene, Charlie. She's a disaster."

Next stop was the local government office. I'd never been in here before. We walked into a wide, virtually empty space. The walls were all a drab brown and peeling, the brown occasionally broken by posters advertising giving up smoking and filling in tax returns.

We walked up to the counter, where a woman, chewing gum, was reading a paperback. She hadn't noticed us. I cleared my throat. No reaction. Unbelievable! Was she real or just a waxworks model? Maybe if I danced on the counter?

"Yessss...?" She didn't look up from her book.

"Er. We're trying to find out about Hash."

"Arnold Bleacher," Charlie corrected me, with Hash's proper name.

"He was adopted," I continued, "by—"

"Level three, room 101," replied the book woman.

"Sorry," I blurted.

She finally looked up with a very pained expression, which said, "bog off, can't you see I'm reading my book?"

"Stairs?... Floor three. Room 101." She pointed over to the stairs.

"Thank you," I squeaked, and we made for the stairs.

Typical. Room 101 was the only place in the building with a queue. There must have been about twenty people in front of us, all looking bored to tears. What was it with people and queues? Grownups just seemed to love standing in queues looking bored, as if it was their duty and by doing it the world might be saved. I thought back to heaven. There hadn't been a single queue. And I hadn't seen that bored expression on anyone's face. The people there had looked alive. The people here looked dead. There was a flicker of something inside me. Although my vision had grown dim, it was still there. There was a longing for something more than all this.

I turned to Charlie. "So, you found your star yet?"

He shook his head in a sort of, "I don't wanna talk about it," look.

I shrugged. "It's out there, Charlie."

We waited silently. Then it was our turn.

We were faced with a male version of Charlene. I repeated my speech about Hash. He handed me a form.

"Fill this out in triplicate."

I stared at it. It was a huge form. "Have you got a pen?" I asked.

He pointed me over to a bank of desks.

We seated ourselves at a desk and I started down the form. It was headed *"Adoption and Fostering Trace - Form XT947"*. Name, address and so it went on...

"NI number?" I asked Charlie. "What's one of them?"

"Just stick anything down."

We filled in Hash's details, and tried to go back up to the counter.

"Hey," shouted a large man with bulging eyes, standing in the line. "There's a queue here, you know. You blind or somink?"

He smiled bravely and gained admiring looks from those standing around him in the queue. He was their hero, obviously standing all day in queues, just waiting for that blissful opportunity to throw out some young whippersnapper like me. The Boss Man hadn't been like that. I'd got the district impression he had been determined to make me into something special... "Using the chisel, Monty..." not trying desperately to kick me out. Charlie and me took up our position at the back of the queue. Twenty minutes later we were back in front of the male version of Charlene. There was a yellow line on the floor. Everyone was supposed to queue behind it. We stepped over the line and up to the counter.

"Form?"

"Er, yeah." I shoved it under the glass.

"Are you a relative?"

I glanced at Charlie. He shrugged.

"Er, no," I replied.

"Sorry, we can only release information to relatives."

"But we queued up twice for—"

"Only relatives." The guy had no expression. I tried smiling sweetly. The guy just stared through me.

"Next!" he called.

"Hold on!" I said. Me and Charlie stepped back to consult.

"Shall we?" I whispered.

"Yeah," Charlie replied. "You do it."

"No," I hissed. "You do it. I can't!"

"No, you!" Charlie insisted.

"How much?" I asked. Charlie just shrugged.

The people in the queue were all jostling for position, restlessly, like the starting grid for a formula one Grand Prix.

"What's going on?" bulging eyes demanded from half-way back down the queue. It was now or never.

Me and Charlie had a plan. We knew this wouldn't be easy. But we'd seen people do it on TV.

I approached the desk again. Could I do this? Male Charlene was staring through me again. I was beginning to think he wasn't actually real. Maybe he was just a robot.

"Look," I whispered, in a conspiratorial tone, "fifty quid if you can tell me where we'll find him." I was suddenly scared. I'd stepped over the line. I could get arrested and thrown in prison for this!

But it was wasted on this guy! Male Charlene just stared. His eyebrows drew close together in a sort of confused frown. The robot programming had gone into meltdown... This does not compute!

"OK, OK. A hundred."

"But you're not a relative?" he replied, confused.

Unbelievable! They must give these sorts of people gormless lessons... How to be a total moron in three easy steps.

"Yeah, you could do with the cash though, yeah?" I encouraged. The guy stared down at the form, back up at me, back at the form.

"You haven't filled you're NI number in correctly."

"What?" I replied. I reached in my pocket and laid some cash on the desk.

He was totally lost now. "No fee," he replied. "But you're NI number is incorrect."

And that was it. A fat woman with a large handbag, which was bigger than me, muscled in and me and Charlie were left looking on. We'd missed our only chance to find Hash. I felt drained and miserable after our wasted day queuing.

So we spent some of the escape fund down the local chippie. The day wasn't totally wasted.

That evening, back at home, I had a surprise coming. The doorbell went during Emmerdale. Dad pretended not to hear it and Mum tutted and huffed, but neither of them moved. It rang again. I glanced at them. No reaction, so I dragged myself out of my chair as slowly and noisily and with as much pain and effort as I could, as if it was a major strain. I needn't have bothered, it was wasted. I opened the door and did an immediate double-take. It was Nurse Heartly! My heart skipped a beat. She was in her nurse's uniform, with a long overcoat over the top. She fluttered her eye-lids at me. I did my best not to stare at her legs but I failed miserably. Then I suddenly realised we were both just standing there like stuffed chickens. Say something, Fish, you moron, I told myself. Why does this sort of thing always happen just at that very moment when you want to impress someone? Suddenly it was as if my brain had popped out to lunch and my throat was dry.

"You're looking better, Monty," she said. I just smiled gormlessly.

"Can I come in? I need to talk to you." This was it! She was going to tell me she couldn't live without me.

"I'm nearly twelve, you know." Why had I said that? I was so stupid. She was still standing on the doorstep.

"Can I come in?"

"Yes." YES... YES... Course you can come in... Stay forever!!

I guided her into the kitchen, about as far away from Mum and Dad as I could.

"You can call me Honey now we're out of the hospital." She looked around the kitchen. "You look older than twelve. I'm sixteen."

I knew. I had found out everything I could about her, but I couldn't tell her that. She thought I looked older!! If only Charlie could see this. He was never gonna believe this in a million years.

I poured her a coke. My hands were shaking so much she asked if I needed some help. I cursed myself.

"The trouble is," she started, "I have a problem. Strange things have been happening to me, and I can trace it back to when..." She paused and stared at her feet. Suddenly the tables had turned. She looked all flushed and embarrassed and I felt strong and confident. "I can trace it back to when... You see, I ate one of the chocolates out of that box someone brought you."

I was stunned. I hadn't even noticed that one had gone missing. How was I gonna explain this to her?

"I know I shouldn't have—" she continued.

"Let's go for a walk." I grabbed my coat.

We walked up to the park. I didn't think I wanted to take her to the treetops yet, but I'd probably have to in order to prove my story.

The park was empty. We lay down on the grass and stared up at the stars, which were just beginning to come out though it was only early evening.

"Did you know that the light from a star takes twenty billion years to get from there to here? So when you look at those stars, you are actually seeing what happened twenty billion years ago." I was reciting that from Charlie's vision, he'd told me, but it made for a good chat-up line.

"Gosh," she replied. I must admit, I thought it deserved a bit more than a, "gosh." I'd worked hard on that one.

She told me about her problems. It had started with sleepless nights, then some strange dreams about a pink piano. It all sounded familiar territory... but why a pink piano?

"I always wanted to be a musician, a professional pianist," she said, dreamily. "Anyway..."

Then one day she had been staring at an elderly patient's heart monitor and the line was no longer showing the peaks and troughs of a heartbeat, it spelt my name, *"Monty"*. When she shook her head it was all back to normal. Then it had happened again on a patient's records. Then the final straw had been when she'd received a letter postmarked from Africa. She'd opened it up and it had told her to *"talk to Monty"*.

"Look, I know this all sound really stupid, but I'm worried."

I took a deep breath. "It's not stupid," I said.

I told her about the chocolates, the treetops, the visions, the letters... everything. She listened in rapt attention.

"Can I see the treetops, Monty?" she asked.

"Sure," I replied. "My friends call me Fish by the way."

"OK, Fish."

"Can I kis... ki... Carry your coat for you?" We were clambering up to the platform. What was I thinking?! My brain had just turned into jelly. This was just a dream come true. The treetops were deserted. It was too early for the rest of the gang to arrive. We sat on the spy deck and chatted. She talked about nursing college and boyfriend troubles. I told her about Hash going missing and my and Charlie's quest to find him. It was then that she had a brainwave.

"I could find out for you," she announced. "I'm a nurse. I can contact any of the adoption agencies and ask questions. It's easy."

Bingo! It was a good idea. We arranged to meet up the next day to make the calls.

Honey narrowed her eyes and pulled her knees up to her chest. She was thinking about something.

"It's all so strange, though, Fish. Stuff like this just doesn't happen."

"Yes it does," I replied. "I reckon it happens all the time. We just don't notice." A picture of Charlene and the gormless moron in room 101 fluttered through my mind. "We're either too busy or too bored, or we've just switched off from life. But in actual fact, weird things are happening everywhere. No day is the same as the last."

She giggled at me. "What's this then, Wordsworth?"

We laughed and then she had to go.

"It's been nice, Fish. Thank you." She lingered a moment. I was desperate to kiss her. And then she was gone and my light faded.

This had been such a strange day. I decided to write up my diary before I made my way up to the treetops. I sat in the alcove by my window and stared out over the world... "Pre-world," the Boss Man had called it. A time for us to learn. All of this built, just as the introduction... just as the first line on the first page of a life that would last for eternity.

I finished bringing my diary up to date and I fished around in my rucksack for my bible. I flicked my thumb down one corner of the pages and opened at random; my normal technique. This was a story about Joe... Joseph to be precise... Now, I was immediately interested in this Joe guy for one special reason. It said he had dreams, and not just any old dreams, but ones with a meaning, ones that told the future. Wow, that was wicked! I, of course now an expert dream investigator, was keen to see what it had to say. Now Joe didn't understand the first dreams he had and he got into trouble with his brothers, who being a nice sort of bunch, beat him up, stuffed him in a hole and then sold him as a slave. I was kind'a glad I was an only child. He ended up in prison, and would have stayed there save for one important thing... he listened to other peoples dreams and had the guts to speak out and tell them what they meant. That saved him. He explained a dream which the king had... something about storing up food now because a famine was coming... and suddenly he is in charge of the country. Then he... There was a thump as the bible slipped off my lap onto the floor.

I'm dreaming again, which is so good because it means that at last I'm able to sleep again.

But where am I? I'm in a very smart looking room. At one end is a large oak desk. I'm in America, since there is a large stars and stripes flag behind the desk. Books line the shelves of a large bookcase, and a pile of papers sit on the desk. In the centre of the room are a couple of easy chairs and a large coffee table. It definitely looks like the kind'a room I wouldn't be allowed to play in back home.

So what sort of dream is this? Is it one with a meaning? Am I watching something real? It's just a dream, I tell myself. They always seem so real when you're in them. Was my vision of heaven just a dream as well? No, it seemed different. It just can't have been, and then there was the Alan Smith card and the skateboard. Charlie was wrong. I'd definitely never set eyes on a Smithy card before.

There's a noise and my head snaps round automatically. Smart guy, suit, greased back greying hair walks in. I'm suddenly panicking... he'll see me! I'm about to dive for cover. Too late.

"Mister President, sir, Mike Mayer, CIA Director is here to see you. Shall I send him in?" asks the suit.

OK, I say gingerly to myself. So I'm the American President. I glance down at myself. Come off it, I'm eleven! I can't run a country!

"Mister President, sir?" asks the suit again.

I've learnt how to do this now. You just go with the flow. It's a dream, Fish, don't worry about it.

"Er, yeah, send him in."

The suit frowns. "You alright, Sir? You're looking a bit peaky."

"You ever wanna forget all this?" I ponder out loud, "and just be eleven again?"

"Every other day, Sir! I know, Sir. It's a tough job."

"Yeah well, just remember, eleven was tough too."

"Coffee, Sir?"

"Yeah... NO! Can I just have a coke?"

"Coke?" repeats the suit in astonishment. "We don't have coke, Sir."

"Isn't there just a coke machine somewhere?"

"The Whitehouse doesn't have coke machines, Sir."

Great! I'm the most important man in the world and I can't get a coke! In walks something that resembles an overweight baboon. This must be the CIA guy... CHANGE... The room is swirling. I feel sick.

I'm in a field, forest in the distance. I recognise this place! I'm back in my first castle dream again.

"Right you are, squire!" comes the gruff voice again, from behind. I turn to see the same short guy, old-fashioned leather tunic. I'm suddenly a bit nervous. I don't want that same dream again. It hurt last time. Attacking castles just ain't my thing really.

"Choice of weapons to take with you, sir?" he says. I realise immediately, this is different. He'd never said that before. OK, let's see where we go from here. I look around for the swords and spears. There's nothing nearby.

"We have tanks?" he says.

Tanks? Tanks of what? Suddenly in the middle of the vast plain of rambling meadows and hills a long line of army tanks appear. Each one is huge, like a monster about to pounce. Well I had to admit, it'd be much easier to take the castle with this lot. I imagined myself driving over the ridge in my tank and seeing the look on the faces of the knight on the castle turrets as I blasted them. They wouldn't look so smug this time.

"Or jump jets?" There is a sudden ear-piercing roar from above. It is louder than anything I've ever heard before. My ears feel like they've been ripped off my head, they're hurting so much. I collapse to my knees and look up. The sky is full of fighter jets, circling slowly like vultures waiting for the kill.

The jet flames point downward so they can hover in mid-air. The noise gets even louder as the giant dinosaurs come down to land, burning up the grass and cutting deep furrows in the ground as they do.

"Or the star wars defence system?" continues the old-fashioned leather tunic man. I look up. Green flashing dots appear across the blue sky. They spoil the naturalness of the sunny day. Green laser beams shoot out to join them all together, and finally, what looks like, large steel shields begin to appear within the laser framework, blinking into existence and blocking out the sun. It casts a dark shadow over all the metal monsters on the ground. There is something very disturbing about it all. The once beautiful rambling meadow is now a steel jungle... the grass burnt away, the sun blocked out. It's horrible.

Hey! It'd be fun to ride one of them, though!

"Go on then, Squire. Your mission awaits you."

I look down. I'm dressed in a jump suit. I have a helmet in my hand. Ahead of me, on one of the aircraft, the cockpit opens. I gulp.

"Er... I can't drive that!" I blurt.

I look around. Leather tunic man has vanished. So I walk up to the plane. I seem to know where to place my hands and feet to climb in. I plug my helmet lead into a slot on the dashboard. Immediately words and numbers light up in front of my eyes, on the inside of my visor, which has closed by itself.

My hands move expertly over the dash. With a buzz, the cockpit cover closes and seals shut. My left hand rests on the launch lever, my right hand on the flight stick. I slowly pull the lever up. Unbelievable! This huge monster rises into the sky at my command. Stick forward, and suddenly my head is thrown back against the headrest as if it's been superglued there. Inside my visor the reading says we're travelling at mach 1... the speed of sound.

"Target acquisition in thirty seconds," says an electronic voice. Cool! This was like my Oval Office game. Capow! I can blast things to smithereens. I press the information button. A line drawing of a city with tall buildings rotates inside my visor.

"Caracas. Capital city of Venezuela. Population, five million."

I gulp. This was a city... normal people going about their daily lives. Why bomb them?

"Target acquisition in ten seconds,"

The cover flicks off the red fire button on top of the stick.

"Nine."

I can't do this!

"Eight."

It's just a dream, Fish. Go with the flow.

"Seven."

No! My hand reaches out and my index finger hits the abort button.

"Voice comms on one," says the electronic voice. Then suddenly there's a human voice there.

"Captain Pilchard. What's going on?"

"Six."

I ignore the voice. Something is wrong. The plane isn't aborting.

"Five. Missiles armed."

"Captain Pilchard. Why are you trying to abort?"

"Four." The number rings loudly in my brain. Four seconds and I am about to annihilate a city of five million people, and there's nothing I can do to stop it. Nice. I preferred the castle dream. That had been about helping someone.

"Three. Launch code activated."

"This is a direct order from the President!" comes the human voice again. It sounds tense. Why would it sound tense?

"Two. Weapons Autopilot enabled."

There must be a way to stop it, or he wouldn't be so worried. But what?

"This sucks!" I yell at the snotty guy at the other end.

"This is your orders!" he yells back.

Then I see it. The self-destruct button. Time stops. My plane is just hanging there in mid-air. I'm feeling a little uncomfortable here. I don't want my brain to come to the inevitable conclusion... press the self-destruct button and you're dead. I don't want to die! But logic tells me it's better for me to die than for five million people to. Humm... This is just a dream, right? You can't really die when you're dreaming. Can you? It just seems so real. I can't believe I'd survive.

"ONE!"

I close my eyes and reach out for the self-destruct button. It sinks into the dash with a click.

BLACK... Everything is black... I can't feel a thing... I'm dead. Oh pig snot!

Chapter 20
The Dark Stranger...

Downstairs
Galaxy ref: P5763EARTH
Grid: UK775~YxD101

The dark cloak was pulled over his head so that no-one could see his face. The dark stranger walked swiftly down the alleyway to the upstream. He reached the end of the alleyway. It was a dead end. Ahead were the backs of the run down apartments. He glanced in all directions. A cat squealed and there was a smash as a dustbin lid fell to the ground, but other than that all was silent and no eyes watched. Midnight approached and the night sky was dark. The dark stranger looked at his watch. Thirty seconds. This was probably the most dangerous part of his mission. The return. Twenty-five seconds. He glanced again at the dark sky, trying to make out what if any enemies might be lurking. He could see nothing. His return was no random event, thought up on the spur of the moment. It had been carefully planned. Ten seconds.

The cloak swirled around in a tight spiral. It shot upwards, there was a flash of light and it was gone. The cat squealed and ran.

Chapter 21

Finding Hash...

Downstairs
Galaxy ref: P5763EARTH
Grid: UK729~Ami16

N o Way!" said Charlie, when I told him about Nurse Heartly, the next day. It was after school. Mum and Dad were out and we were in front of the TV with the PS2 plugged in.

"Yeah, really. She'll be round any minute."

Charlie was gawking at me, his eyes as large as saucers. "She's gonna make the call for us?"

"Yep."

"And you reckon she fancies you?"

"Well, er...maybe," I mused. I shrugged. She was a girl. Who had a clue how they thought? They never made any sense. Just look at old Buffy for instance. Mad as a hatter.

The doorbell rang. Nurse Heartly came in. She was in jeans and a t-shirt, hair down. She looked younger. Charlie just gaped at her with his mouth open. He looked like a loony on drugs.

She smiled at him.

I said, "Shut your mouth, Charlie."

"Right! Shall I make the call?" asked Honey.

We nodded. We all sat round the kitchen table. Honey was taking ages on the phone. My mind wandered back to my dream of the night before. I'd never made the treetops. But at least I was still alive. I'd woken up the next morning with that lovely sleepy feeling which I hadn't felt for months.

"Name, Arnold Bleacher. Yeah, a full search. Thanks," I heard Honey saying into the phone.

She winked at me in a sort of, "leave it to me, it's a piece of cake" look.

So, the dream. Had it just been a crazy, random dream, or did it really mean something? I'd thought the well and castle dream had been stupid, but that had had a meaning. Old Joe, in the bible... his dreams had been really really stupid... a bale of hay waltzing across the stage of his dream and taking a bow... stupid or what? Yet, he'd discovered it had a meaning. In a funny way it had come true. The Boss Man definitely had a sense of humour!

"That's funny. Can you do some more traces. Somerset House, births, adoption records and all that? Thanks Trish, I'm grateful. It's important." Honey was jabbering like women did.

Charlie had wandered back to the PS2. I stared at Honey. She was absorbed in her conversation on the phone. She had nice ears.

So, now I had another mystery to solve. Venezuela? Caracus? Population, five million. I had to look it up and work out the link. Why there? Was the place in danger perhaps? And what was going to happen to me? Every time these things happened they had a bad side effect for me. Hmmm. I had made a choice in the dream. I'd refused to carry out my mission. Was that good or bad? Was that just a dream or would that have some effect in real life, like an answered prayer?... A bit like my well and castle dream. I'd saved Missus Agnes in the dream and it had also saved her in real life. Had I just saved Venezuela? I frowned. That was stupid... I was eleven, for goodness sake!! Added to which, I'd blown myself up in the dream... I'm not sure I wanted it to be real.

"He must exist!" said Honey. "That makes no sense. OK. Thanks Trish." She put down the phone. Charlie looked up from the PS2.

"Well?" I asked.

Honey frowned. "You're Arnold Bleacher. He doesn't exist."

"What?"

"No record. He was never fostered. I checked adoption records, children's homes. Nothing."

"He must exist," I replied with a nervous laugh. "What about the last address; the place he lived here?"

"It's not a foster house, Fish. I even checked the birth records. Arnold Bleacher was never born. I'm telling you he doesn't exist."

Me and Charlie looked at each other.

"What does that mean?" asked Charlie.

I was blowed if I knew! We ran round to Hash's old house. There was one more possibility. We could challenge his, so called, foster parents. Maybe they had kidnapped him at birth or something like that. But as we rounded the corner I saw, and for the first time it dawned on me that something very weird was going on here and I wasn't ever going to see Hash again. Outside his house was a "For Sale" sign. All the windows were boarded up. It was obvious that the place was vacant. The evil kidnapping foster parents had obviously moved on.

Chapter 22

The Return...

Upstairs
Realm 2... The Watchers Restricted Section, Portal 9742ab

The dark cloak rose slowly up into the giant circular atrium. Around its edge was the balcony where many of the Watchers often stood to receive the arrivals and to watch the world below. But today it was empty apart from one solitary figure waiting and watching for his friend's return. The white domed ceiling arched above him. The dark cloaked stranger breathed in deeply and smelt the air, as he landed nimbly on the balcony. It had been eleven years since he had last been here. It felt good to be back. There were many atriums similar to this one. All were within the special area of the second heaven... the Watchers. They were the Portals, the places from where the Watchers kept their watch on earth; the dangerous places where angels travelled between the worlds. Of course, in physical terms, the earth itself was light years away in deep space, but each portal opened a door, a bit like a secret passageway.

The dark figure landed on the balcony and embraced the other figure who had been waiting for him.

"Columbus! It is good to be back."

"Stephanos! We have missed you." He gave his friend a hearty slap on the back. "I am sorry that the welcome was not more... appropriate. But the Chief wants you to go to him and report directly."

The dark stranger nodded and departed. He walked swiftly along a deserted corridor. He walked through a door and out onto an open platform, outside. He didn't pause to gaze over the sight of middle heaven. He would have time enough to familiarise himself. Again he spiralled upwards and this time, when he stopped, he stood before the large double doors to the Map Room. As the doors opened he pulled down his hood.

The face and features looked older, however it was unmistakably the same face. For the last eleven years he had been known as Hash, but that was not his real name. Neither was Arnold Bleacher, the name given him by his first foster family. In actual fact he had never been born on earth. His records had been smuggled into the birth register at Somerset House and into the Government foster care records, and from there he had been allocated his first foster home. It was a highly secret and organised operation, to insert an agent. His real name was Stephanos. He was a Watcher, an angel of the Watchers. In fact, a senior Captain in the armies of heaven. His speciality? He was a sleeper. He had been inserted onto earth, unknown to the enemy. His task? To watch and protect, and not to be detected. For whilst he was down there, he was alone. It had been tough work. He had grown weary and tired over the past weeks as he'd tried to keep guard over the group of friends who were so important to the plan. And finally he'd had to break cover to protect them and fight the enemy. He had only just escaped with his life. He glanced down to the wound on his side, which still hurt. But he was back now. Eleven years! It seemed a long time, but then Hash, or Stephanos, was actually three hundred and seventy billion years old. He was an experienced Watcher. And so eleven years was but a second.

The double doors opened and Stephanos entered. He walked the familiar path over the brow of the hill and knelt before the Chief.

God smiled. "Rise up... please, Stephanos. You have done well." The two old friends embraced.

They chatted for a while and then gazed into the colourful blue and green ball, hanging in front of them, which was the earth, or if not the earth, the map of it. God reached down into the ocean and adjusted the time dial. The globe turned gently and they both leaned into it. As they got closer, the area just in front of their eyes grew larger as if placed under a magnifying glass.

Hash chuckled as he watched his friend, Charlie, on his balcony. "Charlie and his telescope, ay."

God raised his eyebrows slightly in mock surprise (he was just pretending though... being God meant you generally didn't get surprised by much).

"Not growing a sense of humour are you, Stephanos? I believe these humans might be rubbing off on you at last."

"I might be mistaken, Chief, for believing you planned that all along," the angel shot back.

"Angels with a sense of humour. Never allowed!" God joked.

"Really... Is that so?"

God smiled. "How many is it now, Stephanos?"

"I'm a sleeper. That was my four hundred and seventy five thousand and fifty first sleeper mission, Chief. Anyone would think you were trying to make a point."

"Just using the chisel," God replied.

Hash stared intently at Charlie, sitting despondently next to his second best telescope (Agnes having destroyed his super-duper one).

"You really liked them, didn't you?" said God.

"They were my friends," Hash replied. "You know, Chief, the more time I spend down there on earth, the more I feel. And sometimes feeling hurts. I'm not sure how much I like it, Chief."

"The chisel, Stephanos."

Stephanos nodded thoughtfully.

"So, will Charlie make it?" asked Hash.

"He has a struggle ahead," God replied. "Some of the things around him he cannot understand or explain. It doesn't all make sense and so he doesn't believe."

Charlie sat alone on his balcony, the dark evening lit only by his torch. Spread over the table were his books and star charts.

"He's still searching for his star," said Stephanos. "It's the one thing which will prove it's all true."

"He needs to step off the cliff," said God. "He needs to trust."

God adjusted the globe a hundredth of a millimetre to the left. Now under the spotlight was Agnes.

"Watch," said God. "This is a very important moment."

Agnes knelt by her bed and pulled out a rusty old tin soap box. She opened the lid and pulled out a pile of letters. They were her fake Ronnie letters. She looked at them with mixed feelings. She still felt so angry at being found out. She wasn't so much angry at Monty for reading them, but at herself for being stupid enough to leave them lying around and the embarrassment of being found out. Of course she had always known they weren't real, but then you can make yourself believe anything if you try hard enough. She had so much wanted them to be real... so much wanted to know her brother, to talk to him. And now she had done just that, during her tour of heaven, and so she didn't need these letters anymore. She walked them down to the kitchen and dropped them in the green paper bin.

It was strange, she thought. None of her family had ever been religious. The idea of religion scared her, but the idea of someone upstairs watching over her, taking care of her... the idea of a whole new world up there excited her. Ronnie had believed in something... Ronnie had got it right all along. Thank you God.

Chapter 23
A Spy in Our Midst...

Downstairs
Galaxy ref: P5763EARTH
Grid: UK739~DXy94

C aracas is the capital city of Venezuela. Its population is exactly five million. I'd looked it up. It spooked me. I hadn't known it, yet my dream had been deadly accurate. Maybe I'd heard the fact once and it was stuck in the back of my brain somewhere.

We were in the treetops. It was a cold night and we huddled around the fire of the gathering hut as it spat and crackled. I still didn't have a clue why Venezuela. But just at the moment the subject of our discussion was Hash.

"So, he was a spy in our midst all along!" said Jacob.

We all pondered this for a moment.

"I don't know how I feel about that," said Buffy. "I mean... he lied to us all that time about who he was."

Buffy was snuggled up in a Cinderella duvet she now kept permanently in the treetops. It was looking a bit ropy these days. Rats had nibbled one corner and it had been left out in the rain at numerous times. The colours had run.

"It may not be the answer," said Charlie. Mister moody git was in a happier frame of mind today, but ever since he couldn't find his Centurion eighty eight star he refused to believe. He doubted everything, made excuses for every event that happened. And all it took was for someone the mention the star and Charlie plunged into one of his black moods again.

"It's there in the book, Charlie," I replied. Last night I'd opened my bible and I'd been totally astonished at the words my eyes had fallen on. *"Do not forget to entertain strangers, for by so doing some people have entertained angels without even knowing it."* What a curious little sentence. Had people really spoken to strangers in the street to ask directions or chatted to someone on a train and they'd been an angel in disguise? The book sat open in the middle of the floor. We all stared at it.

"It just seems so unreal!" said Charlie. Yeah, he was right there!

"But Hash was always strange, wasn't he?" said Buffy. "I mean, which of us really knew him?"

"I never really knew him," I said.

"He was a traitor to the Night Owls!" announced Donny.

"No," I said. "A protector." Everyone nodded their agreement.

"Maybe he's watching us?" said Donny in a spooky voice, "right now."

We all stared around us. The little hut was silent, except for the pop and crackle of the flames from the fire we huddled around. I strained my senses trying to sense a glimpse of Hash. I liked the idea of him standing next to me... my protector.

Buffy broke the moment. "Agghh, yuck! I don't want him watching me when I get undressed!" We all burst out laughing. It echoed through the otherwise empty forest. My watch told me it was half past three in the morning. The world was asleep but we were sitting here pondering some of the deepest, most important questions in life.

"So, any of us," Donny continued in his spooky voice. He was really milking this one. "Any of us could be angels in disguise too."

"I don't think so," Buffy replied confidently. "We know each other too well. It was the thing we should have realised about Hash. We didn't know him. I'll tell you what though... it makes you wonder what else he's got planned. If God—"

"The Boss Man," I corrected. We had decided on the title we were gonna give him in the treetops.

"Yep, the Boss Man," Buffy rolled on like an unstoppable tidal wave hitting the beach. "If he went to the lengths of planning an angel to come down and protect us. Well, it makes you wonder what else he might have planned. He could be organising all sorts of things."

It was a thought. I remembered the calendar in my vision. There were all sorts of crossings out on it as God planned and adapted around all the choices I made. What had the Boss Man called it? One gigantic chess match.

Jacob leaned conspiratorially in towards the fire. His face glowed red through the flames.

"'Tis a battle!" he whispered. "A battle 'tween good an' evil down 'ere an' 'e's been takin' care of us. I reckon, if ya think 'bout all we've seen, an' 'ow old Fish 'ere 'as got 'urt. This is a dangerous place, this world."

Jacob suddenly looked down. We were all staring at him and he looked as if he was almost embarrassed, trying to work out whether to say something or not.

"I wish I'd been 'ere," he said with a note of regret in his voice. I glanced at Buffy. She shrugged.

"You are here," I replied, confused.

"No! When ya had ya dreams. Wish I could 'ave seen 'eaven, like ya did." The fire lit up his face. I could see all the wrinkles and lines. I bet they all told a story. The deep eyes were glassy, looking somewhere else, a different place, examining a million memories.

"I'm ready ta go. I'd like to see that place, see my Annie again."

Then there was a whimper, followed by a sudden wail as if we'd put a cat's tail through a mincing machine, and Buffy burst out in tears. Charlie looked totally bewildered and was edging away as if Buffy had just caught some deadly disease. He had that sort of, "Yuck, girls!" look on his face.

I was grasping for something to say, but could catch nothing but thin air. My mind was blank.

"I just feel so guilty and useless," Buffy blurted, tearfully, between sobs. We all gaped at her. Out of all of us she was, by some distance, definitely, the most not-useless, the most sensible and capable of the lot of us. And the most confident. What was she talking about?

"But Buffy," I said. "You built all this. What you've done is amazing."

Her breathing was uneven, as she tried to stifle her sobbing. She pulled her Cinderella duvet up round her face angrily as if trying to hide away the fact that she was crying.

"What if I get to heaven and God says I'm horrible 'cause I didn't try to save Ronnie?" Suddenly felt hot and clammy, thinking of all the people I'd blown out over the years when I should have helped them. Sorry Mister Boss Man. But an apology like that just seemed too easy. What did the Boss think of me? Then I remembered, I'd asked him, "why me?" and he'd said, "because I like you, Monty."

"Why didn't I meet the Boss Man?" she asked. "Fish and Charlie met him, but I only met an angel. Maybe he doesn't like me?"

I didn't think that was true, but what could you say?

"I was only a foot away when he fell. Sitting right next to him." Her eyes were still watery but she had a fixed, stony expression, like she had thought about this question so many times over the years that she had learned to blank out the feelings.

"Well," said Jacob, "I jus' said a silent prayer for ya, so I reckon y'll be 'll right now, 'kay?"

"Thanks Jacob," Buffy smiled weakly.

"I ate the last chocolate," I blurted suddenly. Well it had to be said, and this seemed to be an evening for confessions.

"After what happened last time?" said Charlie with an air of scepticism. "You ended up in hospital after skateboarding the tree, remember?"

Everyone fell about laughing. But there was something serious worrying me.

"Shut up, Charlie! Well, it just felt like the right thing to do. I felt like you, Jacob, ready to go. Didn't care about anything... and even better, thought I could make a difference, you know, do something important, help someone, by eating the chocolates." There was another long pause.

"And?" prompted Buffy, back to her normal steamroller fashion.

"But now my dad's back and there's Nurse Heartly!" Interrupted at this point by a roar from the boys. "And the vision I had... it's fading. All of a sudden, I'm beginning to dread what's gonna happen next. I don't want anything to change now. But something always happens, you know, when I eat the chocs."

"Nah!" said Donny, suddenly loud and animated. "You're like a real superhero, Spiderman or something. In the films they always have to make a choice between the girl and the job, don't they? Yeah, but they always get both in the end though."

I felt nine feet tall after being put in the same superhero bracket with Spiderman. Couldn't quite see myself in tights though, somehow. "Thanks Donny."

"Any more dreams?" asked Buffy.

"Yeah, what happened!" they all wanted to know. I told them the Venezuela dream, but that I didn't understand it.

"Oh, that's easy," said Donny. "Venezuela has vast oil reserves. If America needed oil or cash the easiest way would be to invade Venezuela."

My jaw dropped.

"How do you know all that... stuff?" asked Charlie.

Donny looked blankly at us. "What, that? Everyone knows that?"

Charlie and I exchanged bewildered looks. We didn't know it.

"Anyway, I've got a second cousin's brother who lives in Venezuela," Donny went on.

"Your second cousin's brother IS your second cousin, Donny," said Buffy.

"No," said Donny. "Don't be dim! It's his brother."

"What I mean is—"

"America would never invade Venezuela!" I said.

"There's more than one way to skin a cat," replied Donny. "That's what my second cousin's brother says."

"Don't call me dim!" shouted Buffy, throwing a pine cone over the fire, which caught Donny dead centre forehead. "There's no such thing as a second cousin's brother!"

"Derrrr! I have a second cousin. He has a brother. Yeahhh? OK? Got it now?"

Buffy had gone a deep red colour. Sort of like a nuclear bomb just before the mushroom cloud rises and all life forms within ninety miles get vaporised.

"He would also be your second cousin, you illiterate moron!" she hissed back, very menacingly. I have to admit, I'm a coward; I'd have backed down by now, regardless of how many brothers my second cousin had.

But something else was bugging me now. Had my dream been about America invading another country? Even if they did, what was I supposed to do about it?

"Anything else you haven't told us, Fish?" asked Charlie, trying to change the subject from second cousins.

I had a sudden pang of guilt. There was one thing I had never told a soul. I'd kept it all to myself, because... well... I wasn't quite sure if I was going mad or not. I took a deep breath.

"I met an alien." There was a long pause. "You know... green thing, nano nano, space ship." Another long pause. I ploughed on regardless. "I think it might have kidnapped someone too. There was a person speaking English and I could just see him inside the door."

"Door?"

"Of the space ship," I explained.

"Er, Fish?"

Chapter 24
The Giant Chess Match...

Upstairs
Realm 2... The Watchers Restricted Section, Portal 9742ab

God stood with Gabe, Columbus and Hash on the balcony of the Atrium. The look on the face of Columbus was grim. He was a large, flamboyant and outspoken angel. The leader of the Watchers, he was, like Gabe, a senior General in the ranks of heaven. He rubbed his chin and took a deep breath.

"I have to say, I don't like it."

"We need a crossover," God replied. "We need a link."

"Monty?" replied the big angel. "He is not ready yet."

Hash remained silent during the exchange. He was the most junior of the three. Gabe had a grin on his face. He was familiar with these exchanges between Columbus and the Chief. The Chief always wanted to push on, press the battle. He cared about these human beings so much, he would take risks to save them. Columbus had a mind the size of a planet. He organised and planned a thousand million moves a day in this war... this giant chess match. He was the best and everyone looked to his opinion. But Gabe knew that despite his reservations, whatever the Chief said, Columbus would do. And Gabe was the warrior. He would lead the army.

"Ready?" pressed God. "Was Mary ready? Daniel, when he was carted off to Babylon? Gideon, Joseph?"

Columbus drove on like a battering ram, undeterred. "But if the enemy gets a whiff of this they will kill him!"

"Then we must protect him." There was a moment's silence.

"Yes, Chief, we will," Columbus replied. God could see the crease in his brow. This Watcher carried a million burdens on his shoulders, and this was one more for him. This angel was very dear to his heart. God nodded and gave him a slap on the back.

"I know you will, Columbus. Thank you."

Chapter 25

Sweet Dreams...

Downstairs
Galaxy ref: P5763EARTH
Grid: UK729~Ami16

Telling them about the alien had definitely been a bad idea, I mused as I munched on a Jaffa cake I'd raided from the kitchen. They didn't believe me. I could hardly blame them. I wasn't sure if I believed me! I could still see the outline of a face... someone who had been very clearly human, waving frantically at me from the door. I hadn't really noticed him at the time, just heard the voice, but when I concentrated and recalled the events of that night, his outline was definitely there in the doorway. Could he really have been kidnapped? It worried me. I could go to the police... that would be a joke wouldn't it! "Yes sir, can you give me a description of the said Alien?" "Yes officer. Green, splodgy, lots of arms, and driving a silver spacecraft."

But the Fish Dreams Detective Agency had solved yet another mystery... The Venezuela dream mystery. So Venezuela was rich with oil fields, America needed the oil money and so it was possible, it could plan an invasion. My dreams may have a meaning, after all. But how could it be that I could dream about things which were gonna happen the other side of the ocean? It was impossible! And even if it were true, what could I do about it?

It was midnight and I was sitting on my stall by the open window. Ever since we started the treetops meetings, I'd loved the night sky, the breeze and the quiet open air of night time. All of a sudden I sensed something. I felt a prickling on the back of my neck, as if... what was it? As if I could sense danger, as if someone was in the room with me. My eyes searched round the room. Nothing. I noticed a crumpled sheet of paper fall from my desk. It was one of the Senia letters. I read through it again. *"Keep on using the gifts,"* it said.

Well, I had, hadn't I? I'd eaten the chocolates and look where that had got me! But what to do about my latest dream...

What would stop me writing letters too? If I wrote to the President of America my letter would never get through, would it? But then that was the Boss Man's problem. I just had to write the letter. I grabbed a pen and headed down stairs. In Dad's study I found some writing paper and I sat on the step outside the back door to write my letter. I could just see well enough by the light from the kitchen.

"Dear Mr President..."

When I'd finished I tucked it into one of Dad's smart embossed envelopes and addressed it to the White House, Washington, USA. I guessed that would get there.

I placed the letter carefully in the posting pile on Dad's desk. Dad always had a heap of fan mail and conference invitations to reply to. Then I wandered back upstairs. I looked in on Mum and Dad. Everything was peaceful and quiet. They were sound asleep. Dad looked content. I was glad he was home. I thought of Buffy and Missus Agnes, next door. Were they now sleeping soundly too? In an odd sort of way the chocolates had helped lots of people.

"You do work in odd ways though," I whispered. Then I lay on the bed and in seconds I was fast asleep. I slept so well and I didn't dream at all!! I count that as an extra special major triumph!

Chapter 26
The Warning...

Upstairs
Realm 2... The Watchers Restricted Section, Portal 9742ab

It was all about to commence. The watchers stood around the edge of the portal. There was little left for God to say.

"It is time… watch him well… don't let the enemy hurt him."

Chapter 27

The Rest of Your Life Starts Now...

Downstairs
Galaxy ref: P5763EARTH
Grid: UK729~Ami16

I died on a Tuesday. One minute you're there and the next... Whoosh!... you're off. No time for sorting things out or putting things right.

I was watching TV... The Simpsons, when things started going weird again. I'd got in from school dodged a kiss from Mum and raided the chocolate mountain in the kitchen cupboard above the dishwasher without being caught and then dived for my favourite arm chair and the TV remote. It was a slick and successfully implemented military operation.

It's always strange how things seem different the next day. What had seemed a great idea last night, of writing to the President and telling him not to invade Venezuela, now in the cold light of day, was a real turkey brained plan. I would retrieve my letter from Dad's fan mail pile and strike the entry from my diary when the Simpsons finished. I shook my head. I couldn't believe I was so dumb sometimes. It was strange. Every night, up there in the treetops, it all seemed so real... the whole heaven, Boss Man thing... all our plans and dreams. But down here, with school and home and Mum and Dad, it all seemed like stupid kids stuff. And I was sleeping again now, so I wasn't getting up to the treetops as much. The vision was fading again and life was returning to normal. All except for my latest dream, the jet fighter one. Maybe that's all it was, just a dream. And there was Nurse Heartly to think about. Would she date me?

Dad rolled in and made a grab for the remote, flicking it across to the news.

"Daaaad!!"

"Just wanna catch the headlines."

"Dad, I'm watching something!"

"You've been raiding the kitchen again."

"So!" I rolled my eyes in my best attempt to make Dad feel like he was being picky.

Why do parents have to be such morons sometimes?

"Hey, Paps is coming round this evening. Thought we could splash out, go out for a bite to eat. Sort'a celebrate you getting better and my new found success. What d'ya reckon Kiddo?"

I perked up a bit. "Hey, that'd be cool." It would be nicer than Christmas. Gramps would lay off the "crawling through the jungles of Burma" stories if Dad didn't encourage him, and it'd just be family. I sort'a liked Missus Agnes and Buffy but it was nice to just be us.

"Look!" said Dad, as his face came up on the news.

"And Ronnie Pilchard, our very own national hero," the TV presenter announced, "will be attending Buckingham Palace this week to receive the George Cross medal, which he was awarded earlier this year for..."

They started to reshow the CCTV footage. I knew it off by heart by now. But had I heard right?

I turned to Dad. "Buckingham Palace?"

He grinned. "That's right."

"To meet the Queen!?"

"Uh-huh. And you're coming too. Apparently she wants to meet you."

"Really?"

"Uh-huh."

Wow! I was gonna meet the Queen! Today was suddenly looking up. And I had a cunning plan. That'd be a good chat up line for Nurse Heartly, wouldn't it... "Hey, fancy coming to meet the Queen with me?" Bit more impressive than taking her to the flicks.

Then it happened, just as I turned back to the TV, feeling rather smug with myself.

"In other news," the TV droned on, "scientists have made what they have called a startling new discovery. A new solar system on the outskirts of the known universe has now come within range of the most powerful of the world's telescopes, which is based at the NASA observatory in Colorado. The new star has been named by John Irvin, the man who first saw it, as Centurion eighty eight."

My jaw dropped. Charlie!

I jumped up from my seat and raced past Dad, just catching the next piece of news as I went... "In more local news, police have rounded up a group of fifteen Zulu warriors, who have been living in Vitenbury forest for the last month."

I paused at the door and glanced back at the TV news.

"Don't know where they get all this sort of rubbish from!" snorted Dad.

I didn't answer. I raced out the front door. I had to go and tell Charlie. This was it! This was what he had been waiting for. The vision was back with a vengeance, blazing in my mind. It was real, all of it was real!

I sprinted down the road and around the corner into Staunton Road. There was a newsagent across the road a couple of hundred yards ahead and outside I could see a group of older kids, bikes lying on the pavement. They were larking around and tossing sweet papers on the ground.

I can still remember that moment, like time had gone into slow motion. Charlene came around the corner up ahead, in all her smart bank gear. She'd obviously just got off work. She never looked that smart the rest of the time. She was generally a slob. On the other side of the road I spotted Jacob, as he rounded a bend. He was taking his usual stroll up to the newsagents to get his Evening Standard, and a microwave dinner from the small fridge section they kept since the supermarket was a way away. He was staring down at the palm of his hand, counting his change as he walked. That's why he never saw me.

I shouted his name across the street and swerved my run out into the road, to head him off. The kids outside the shop looked up at me when I shouted. So did Jacob. The coins dropped from his hand, spinning in the air and bouncing off the pavement with a ching, ching, ching. His hand stretched out towards me and he started to run, a contorted look on his face. But why?

I was staring at his face when the car hit me. It came from nowhere. Actually, it wasn't the driver's fault. Truth is, I hadn't been looking.

Jacob's face spiralled round and round as I flew over the windscreen and roof of the car. I didn't actually feel much. Then it was all black.

And that's how I ended up in hospital for the third time. It was all rather unexpected, really. And Charlie... I hadn't told Charlie!

I vaguely remembered the flashing blue lights and the jolts and swaying of the ambulance. Then the white walls of the hospital. They were swaying too. Different faces swam in and out of my vision, Mum, Dad, Nurse Heartly and Missus Agnes. They mouthed words but I couldn't hear them. And I didn't feel any pain. I wished they'd stop swaying though. I was beginning to feel seasick.

Strange thoughts kept leaping into my mind. I couldn't remember where I'd left my Alan Smith football card, and that worried me. I mustn't forget to feed the rabbit. It suddenly seemed very important. And I'd forgotten to switch the TV off and I was really worried the house was gonna blow up. Hang on... we didn't have a rabbit!? Everything was jumbled up in my mind like someone was trying to make scrambled eggs out of my brain.

I could see a kid sitting on the edge of a well. He was young; about six or seven. He was very close to the edge. It made me feel uncomfortable. Where was I? There was a farm house. I was standing on the front path leading up to an old oak front door, which was open. No-one else was around. I was surrounded by luscious deep green fields of grass. I was about to walk over to the kid by the well when there was a call from the doorway. I looked round. It was Nurse Heartly.

"Monty," she called. "Come on." She beckoned me over. She looked drop-dead gorgeous, as ever. "Quickly!" she called, and I began to walk towards her as she moved back inside the door.

But something wasn't right. The back of my neck felt sweaty and prickly. I glanced back at the kid by the well. He was climbing up onto the circular stone wall, which surrounded the well.

"Don't worry about him," called Honey. "He's fine." I hesitated. It wasn't right to let him do that. He might fall.

"Now Monty!" called Honey. Her voice sounded cross. "It's now or never. What's it to be?" She was standing there, hands on hips, in that way girls do, while you're still trying to work out what you did wrong. I didn't want to upset or lose her. And if the kid fell, it was just a dream wasn't it? But something held me there. I didn't want to choose. Choices like this sucked! It was like having to choose between homework (which you knew you had to get done) or going out with your mates, or like choosing your options at school when you still didn't have a clue what you wanted to be one day. All those sort of decisions sucked!

I turned and started back towards the well.

"Suit yourself," the voice behind me said, tartly. "I'm off now."

I hesitated again, my pace slowed. I felt annoyed and stupid now. I had lost her just because of this stupid kid, who'd probably be fine. I could feel my face flushing red, because I felt stupid.

"You're a turkey, Fish!" I muttered to myself.

I looked up. The kid was tottering right on the edge.

"Hey!" I shouted. He looked up and then, to my horror, he started to fall. I raced towards the well. It seemed to take a lifetime and with each step the kid was falling, desperately flapping his hands as if that might stop him. I was within arms length when he disappeared within the wall of the well with a scream. I thought, for a minute, I'd lost him, I'd been too slow, but one hand clung onto the top of the wall. I grabbed it and pulled him up with all my might.

Then the other hand reached up and clasped hold of me and he clambered back over the wall. But to my astonishment it was no longer the kid. My eyes went wide with surprise. What was going on? It was the Boss Man. I was so pleased to see him again. Then I felt a bit hot under the collar thinking that I had hesitated to help him.

"Monty!" he called enthusiastically as a broad grin spread across his face. "Thank you!"

"I don't understand," I said. "How come you..." My voice trailed off as I pointed back at the well.

"It was a test. There's always a test, Monty. Always a judgement."

I still didn't understand.

"You chose to believe in me, Monty."

"I did?" All I had done was help a kid who was falling. And anyway, I was sure Rupert, back at youth group, didn't think I was churchified enough to believe in anything yet. He was always giving me those looks, as if I was some lost puppy dog he'd like to sort out or if that fails then drown in the river. Hey, but this guy I was talking to was God, so I guessed he knew a little bit more about it than Rupert. I'd give him the benefit of the doubt... just this once.

The Boss Man burst into loud howls of laughter.

"That's what I like about you, Monty. You've got a great sense of humour." Then I remembered, he always knew what I was thinking. He went on with the explanation. "When you came up here to visit. That's when you called me "Lord" for the very first time. Do you remember? But there's always a test."

I crinkled up my nose. "I still don't get it."

"How do you prove what you believe and what you're committed to?"

I wasn't sure if this was a question I was supposed to answer or one of those ones he'd answer for me.

I thought about it. The answer was obvious. "By what you do, I guess."

"Exactly!" His eyes sparked at my answer. "It's that thing which goes on in our dreams, Monty, in the deepest part of our soul, where no-one sees and where we can't organise it and control it and pretend to be something we're not.

That tells us who we are, what the deepest desires of our heart are, Monty. You chose well. When I was in need, you helped me."

"But I didn't know it was you," I blurted.

"Whenever you helped anyone, you helped me, Monty."

My shoulders suddenly sagged. Who had I ever helped? I remembered when Buffy had burst into tears in the treetops because she hadn't saved her brother. I had suddenly thought of all the people I had blown out and not cared about over the years.

"Monty, the gift I gave you was courage. You used that gift. I set a rule that for every chocolate you ate, you would help others, but it'd pain you. But even when you knew it would cause you pain, you carried on, because you knew it would help people. And you've helped more people than you could ever know. That's courage. That's what using the chisel is all about!" he said with a grin. "That's what Pre-world is about. Preparing for the main event, before you go on to somewhere better. What's the difference between heaven and here, Monty?"

There was a distinct difference. But exactly what it was, was difficult to put into words.

"Up there, people have learned to live with each other," he continued, "not to compete with each other. That's what this life is about, learning that. It's a simple lesson. You know, Monty, this is where your life really starts. Right here, right now." He slapped me on the back. "You've done so well. But you've got one more important decision to make, and only you can make it."

I remembered the car accident. "Am I dead?"

"That's up to you, Monty."

"Er, sorry?" What did that mean?

Everything changed. The lights in the hospital room seemed to be flashing brighter and then dimmer again. It was doing my head in. Blurred faces kept flashing across my vision. I was feeling dreamy, floating up on the clouds. The blur cleared and I looked down. To my astonishment, I could see me, down on the bed. Mum and Dad were either side of the bed, Buffy and Missus Agnes a little further back. I could see the top of the wardrobe in the corner. It was covered in dust and someone had stuffed an old plate of food up there with a mouldy chicken leg on it. That was disgusting! What was going on? Why was I floating up here? Nurses and doctors were suddenly streaming into the room. The nurses were pushing trolleys of equipment. My dad was shouting, mum crying. Nurses pulled them away from the bed. Missus Agnes was rushing Buffy out the door. There was Nurse Heartly. She was backing away towards the wall, a hand up, covering her face. There were tears running down her cheeks. The doctors were plastering all sorts of wires and stuff all over me. One of them was punching my body. Why was he doing that? This was it, I must be dieing.

Then I felt a hand on my shoulder.

"So, Monty, I finally get to meet you. The boy all this fuss is about."

My head jerked around. It was a strange looking guy, white, long face. I recognised the type immediately from my heaven vision. It was an angel.

"Who the blazes are you?" I asked.

"You can call me Gabe."

"What's going on?" My heart was beating fast in my chest. I had a bad feeling about all this.

"What do you think is happening, Monty?" Gabe replied calmly.

"Am I dead?"

"Very nearly. Look." Gabe pointed down to the bed, where I... er, the other me, that is... lay, covered it tubes and wires, nurses and doctors still huddled round, panicking. "We don't have long."

"Long for what?"

"We have an important mission for you, but I have to ask you, do you want to go? You have a choice to make, Monty. You can still go back there." He pointed back at the bed. "There is time. Or you can go forward," he stared up towards heaven. "Start the rest of your life."

"But my friends..." All sorts of thoughts were flashing through my mind... my friends, parents, how could I leave them?... I had a life here; I felt suddenly robbed. But then I remembered. The place of the vision, a place with no pain, no hardship, no voices in the back of my mind tempting me to do the wrong thing... evenings spent with Josh and the Boss Man, not to mention, no school! It was a place I longed to go. The angel had mentioned a mission.

"What mission?"

"There is a long journey ahead. It will not be easy. It is all part of the plan. And as for your friends, Monty, this is for them. If you choose to go on, your friends will be safe."

I stared down. Dad was holding Mum. She was crying. Outside the room sat Agnes, ashen-faced. I suddenly missed them.

"How?"

"I cannot explain," the angel replied. Suddenly he looked away. He was mouthing words and put his hand to his ear as if he was listening on an ear piece. "The window is closing. If we're gonna go, we must go now."

"I'm only eleven," I said. "This isn't fair. I can't make that choice."

"Life doesn't end here, Monty," Gabe replied softly. "It gets better. And you will see your friends again."

"You say this is for them, will help them?"

"Yes. This will make all the difference."

"Then I'll go."

The angel smiled. "He said you were a brave one. He was not wrong."

"You will sleep now for a while. As I said, we have a long journey ahead."

I took one last look down. I saw the room. They were all so upset. They couldn't see it... couldn't see that there was so much more. I wasn't gone, I was just going onto something better. I was rising higher now. As I looked down, I could see beyond the hospital room. Millions of people wandered the streets, going about their lives. None of them saw it, none of them had a clue just how big it all was outside their tiny world.

Then it began to fade, I yawned sleepily and my eyes closed. In the blackness I saw the faint reflection of stars whizzing by in my eye-lids, I felt myself swung one way and then the other. And I felt a strange black chill running down my spine, as if something dark and horrible was lurking nearby. Gabe had said it would be a dangerous trip. What did that mean? Were there enemies out there waiting to attack us? Was this why I felt this chill?

Chapter 28
The Landing Pad...

Upstairs
Realm 3... The Landing Pad

My eyes flicked open and here I was, standing in a familiar place. I was back on top of the mile wide white chocolate button, The Landing Pad, as the Boss Man had called it. In all directions it was white, going as far as I could see into the distance, where the white floor curved away, like the camber of the earth, and met the white ceiling on the horizon. As I squinted I could just make out the golden wall, way off in the distance.

I'd been here before, but at that time I'd just been visiting. It felt a bit more nerve-tingling actually being the dead guy. I was alone. I wasn't sure what to do. And I didn't know how I felt about this. Visiting was fun, coming on a one way ticket was a bit spooky.

I looked down at myself. There was nothing remarkable. I was wearing the same clothes that I'd been walking down Staunton Road in, barely... what was it? It couldn't have been more than an hour ago, but now it felt like a million light years ago!

OK, let's do it. I started to walk. I knew the chocolate button treatment was just part of "getting used to heaven"... orientation, the Boss Man had called it. Eventually they'd find me.

I walked... and walked... and walked. And a strange thing was happening. The more I walked, the less nervous I felt. The crash and the hospital seemed to be dimming to a distant memory. I felt... excited. Josh!... would I see Josh again? I began to run. Then I began to realise just how different I felt. I wasn't getting out of breath running. I felt super-fit, not an ache or pain in the world. I sprinted over the milk white surface. And my mind... that felt different too. It was difficult to describe, but all those thoughts which made me worry, or sad, all those guilty feelings I'd carried around, always in the back of my mind. They were gone. The memories were all still there, they just seemed as if they belonged in another world or to another person. I felt absolutely incredible. I gave out a loud whoop, and laughed. I had arrived. I jumped into the air and... I didn't come back down. Err? Wow! I was swimming in the white sky.

"Monty? Is that you?"

I swam round to where the voice had come from.

"Jacob!" I shouted. I landed and ran towards him.

"What are you doing here?" Then it hit me. He'd been trying to save me. He must have been caught by the car too.

He gave me a grin and his eyes seemed to sparkle. I hugged him.

"I've been waitin' for this 'ere momen' for a long time, Fish, I 'ave." He looked around. "We're 'ome, Fish. We're 'ome!!" he yelled.

We walked together. It felt good. And then in the distance we could see dots on the horizon. The dots grew into people. Jacob stopped.

"Annie?" he said.

"Jacob? My Jacob?" My eyes were drawn to a girl at the front of the crowd, about eighteen, nineteen years old, dressed in a skirt and crop top. She was wide-eyed with excitement. But surely she was a bit young for this old codger! And when I looked around at Jacob, my jaw dropped in astonishment. Before my eyes, he was changing. The skin was tightening over the face, the hair thickening into a dark brown mop of hair, the muscles strengthening.

The girl let out a little yelp and ran to him. The, now teenage kid Jacob, scooped her up and swung her around.

I looked back at the crowd. There were loads of people milling around now. A crowd of young and old, none of which I recognised, crammed in around Jacob. I guess he had known a lot of people in his time.

I scanned the remaining crowd for any face I recognised. The crowd seemed to be an even mix of angels and people, mostly young people. Then I stopped, glanced back. There he was.

"Hash!" A smile beamed across his face. He'd just been waiting to see if I recognised him. I ran and hugged him. It was the same face, the same Hash, but he was older, and so tall! I had been right all along. He was an angel.

"Fish! You made it." he shouted with more feeling than I had ever heard from him before.

"Why didn't you tell us?" I punched him on the arm in jest. I had so many questions to ask him.

He held something out to me in his hand. I looked down. It was a brown leather-bound book.

"My diary! How did that get here?"

"They brought it," Hash replied. Out of the crowd stepped a human, an angel and an... I did a double-take. I couldn't believe it.

"You?" I said.

The green alien-looking thing shrugged.

"I know you!" I repeated in astonishment. It was my alien, who'd landed in a spaceship. And the human had been the kid at the door who I'd thought had been kidnapped.

"This is Creevy, Stex and Rafe," Hash introduced them. "They risked life and limb to get your diary. Now you have a final job to do."

I took the diary. "What do you want me to do with it?"

"Complete the story, of course," replied Hash. "Then they're gonna take it back again."

"But I'm dead?" I said, rather confused.

"So? Write about it."

"What... everything?" I glanced around the landing pad and then down again at the diary.

"Yes," Hash replied, "write everything."

Chapter 29
The Diary...

Upstairs
Realm 2... The Wall

I had to admit, heaven was such a cool place. I'd only been here a few days and, what with writing up the diary and all, I hadn't had much of a chance to look around yet. I was just itching to explore it. Everyone kept telling me to slow down. "You've got a few billion years here, kid," they'd say, and of course they were right. Eternity gave you a bit of time to relax, chill out and soak up the heat. But I couldn't help it, I was too excited. I loved the portals. I'd learnt a new trick. When you passed the golden rods, which were the portal entrances, and you felt the hot breeze on your face, you could grab the rod and swing round. It was amazing. You'd see the different worlds each side of the portal flashing back and forth like a strobe light.

And, not to mention morphing. It was a strange thing to get used to, that however young or old people looked, it bore no relation to how old they actually were in heaven years. On the earth, older people had always been in charge, but in heaven it was all different. You'd come across little five year olds who were billions of years old and had visited the outer planets of heaven! And that was because outward appearance meant very little up here. You could choose what you looked like. Watch... there you go, see? I was showing off. I'd just turned into a twenty-something. Morphing was cool.

Anyway, I had just run up Main Street and was climbing the stairs of the golden wall to the look out point where I knew Creevy's ship was. It was being readied for the return journey, the special mission to take back the diary. I didn't want to miss it.

"Hey, Creevy!" I called. "You're not going without me!"

Stex was standing on the side looking on.

"Too late," he said. "They're just launching. And anyway, Creevy and Rafe, they're Watchers now, but we're not. They'll not allow us through, especially after last time," he added, rolling his eyes. I'd heard all about Stex's first escape attempt, and of course, I'd seen it from the other end.

The strange rubbery silver disc of a spacecraft bobbed slightly in the dock, as the drives started up to move it out into deep space.

"I'm not missing this one," I said to Stex. I grabbed his collar in one hand and made a lunge for the end of the docking rope with the other. "Got it!"

We were whipped up and off the wall, and we trailed behind the ship as it swerved neatly left. The space portal opened, a bright white rectangle against the blackness of deep space, and Creevy steered neatly into it, dead centre. And with a glint and a sparkle we vanished and were gone.

And that's how I found myself crouching in the bush, just outside the kitchen window of my house... my old house, that is. Rafe was sweating and huffing, a worried look on his face.

"I don't like this at all," he said.

"Shh," Creevy waved him to be quiet.

"You're not supposed to be here!" he hissed at Stex and me.

"So what exactly is a window for?" asked Stex.

"Can it, Stex!" Creevy gave a short reply. "Right, you know your way around, Fish, so you and me go in. Rafe, you watch for sight-seers. Everybody got it."

There were mumbles of, "yep," "OK Creevy,"

"Er, so what do I do?" asked Stex.

"Absolutely nothing. Comprende? Don't even breath, Stex."

It was evening. Creevy held my leather diary. It seemed rather odd to be breaking back into my bedroom. It was strange, no longer to belong in this place.

"Fish! Stop daydreaming. Snap to it. Rafe?"

Rafe's eagle eyes swept the doors and windows down the street for any sign of humans. He was an angel. His eyes missed nothing. Every movement, every stray leaf blowing in the breeze.

Fish was my new heaven name... till a better name came up, at least. At last I had got rid of the name I'd hated for the last eleven years.

"Clear," Rafe whispered.

"Clear what?" asked Stex.

"Follow me," I said, making for the drainpipe.

"What you doing?!" hissed Creevy, "Come on!"

And with that he started to float up to the bedroom window.

Cool! I pushed off and followed. Creevy waved his hand and the window clicked open. We stepped inside.

"What a mess!" said the alien. "It's been turned over."

"Er, no. This is how I like it," I replied. Creevy shot me a worried look. I stared around and smiled. All my stuff... football cards, computer games, last week's clothes lying on the floor. But then it wasn't my stuff any more, was it?

"So where does the diary go, kid?"

"Er, over—"

Just then, there was movement outside the bedroom door. I froze. We stood and watched in horror as the brass door knob began to turn.

"Quick, hide!" Creevy hissed. He pushed me down to the floor, behind the bed and he bolted for the wardrobe, tossing the diary as he went.

I scrambled under the bed, and stared back longingly at the window, wanting to get out. Mum and Dad just couldn't find me here! It would be just impossible to explain. Imagine it... how do you explain that? "Oh, hi Mum, Dad, yeah, I know I'm dead and all that, but you know how it is. We were just out in the space ship and we thought we'd drop in. Oh, and this is Creevy. He's an alien, and... er... yes, he's dead too." No, they couldn't find me here. But that wasn't all of it. I wasn't sure if I wanted to see them again. It was too soon, too raw. I guess that's why they didn't allow new people in the Watchers.

The door opened, and from under the bed, I saw two pairs of feet walk into the room.

Chapter 30
A Close Shave...

Downstairs
Galaxy ref: P5763EARTH
Grid: UK739~DXy94

Monty's dad twisted the handle and opened the bedroom door. He paused before entering, taking a sharp breath. He hadn't been in here since... it happened. He paused in the doorway and looked around. His wife, standing behind him, squeezed his hand encouragingly.

The problem for Monty's dad was that he kept seeing glimpses of Monty. He'd walk into a room and just for a fleeting moment he'd glimpse Monty, then he'd look back and... nothing. It was just his memory playing tricks on him.

"You got the boxes, Mol?"

She held them up. "Where d'ya wanna start?"

They were going to start packing up some of Monty's things. Dad walked over to the chest of drawers, stepping on a squeaky dog bone on the way over.

"This is a tip!" he said. "What did he need this stuff for? A dog bone?"

His wife shrugged. "He hit teenage early, I think."

Dad started loading the contents of the drawers into boxes, but he kept coming across things... an old birthday card, a programme from the Town football match, an old photo from a holiday in Devon when Monty had won a goldfish at the fairground. The room even smelt of memories. It was as if he was right in there with them.

Dad opened the wardrobe and was immediately hit by a cascade of toys, books, a punch bag and a life-size green rubber alien with fourteen or so arms.

"A green rubber alien?" he shook his head. He gave it a kick with his foot and it squeaked. "What's the point in that? Where did he get all this stuff?"

Molly shrugged.

Dad sat down on the bed. "OK, what junk's he stuffed under here. Dad knelt down and glanced under the bed. Not too bad, he thought. Just two pairs of trainers, a school bag and Monty. Bed side cabinet?... Football cards, brush. He looked up... Monty... Monty? He looked back at the bed, in two minds as to whether to check underneath again. His shoulders sagged.

"I can't do this, Mol. I saw him again. This is so... It hasn't sunk in yet that he's gone."

Dad picked up a brown leather book off the bed and opened it up. As he leafed through it he suddenly became more interested.

"Hey, Mol. Come and look at this."

"What is it?"

"It's a diary. He must have kept a diary," Dad said. "Did you know about that?"

Molly shook her head. "No idea."

"What he's written... it's is incredible," Dad said, whipping through the pages quickly. "But that's impossible, Mol!" Dad lingered, unable to pull his eyes away from one particular page. It was the diary entry for the final hospital visit. He read his son's description of looking down on his body, seeing the abandoned chicken leg on top of the wardrobe, the angel. He flicked over the page and read the white chocolate button page. He flicked it over again... Main Street, the Wall. "How could he write this?"

It was actually a good thing that they were engrossed in the diary or they might have noticed the strange sight of a head bobbing up and down at the bedroom window. It was Stex, making excited gestures through the glass. Then he decided to come in. The only problem was, he hadn't quite worked out the idea of glass yet.

Monty's mum and dad suddenly jumped as they heard the thump and crack of something slamming into the window pane very hard. It rattled the woodwork, and glass splinters fell all over the carpet.

"What on earth?!"

Whatever it was slid down the window pane and fell away with a yelp.

"Blasted pigeons!" snapped Dad.

Chapter 31

The Final Meeting and the Pact...

Upstairs
Realm 3... Moweoran Quadrant
Main Street, Floogier House

O K, I get it," said Stex as he swigged a large gulp of floogier juice. "It's to catch the rain, so you can save some for later... right, Fish?"

"No!" I screamed in mock anger and frustration, thumping my hand on the wooden table. I was trying to explain the use of an umbrella.

Creevy arrived with seven more floogier juices. We always sent him to the bar. Having three dozen arms helped carrying the drinks.

"Cheers, Boris!" he called over his shoulder.

"Stex," I continued patiently to explain, "it keeps the rain off you."

"But why would you want to do that?"

Everyone round the table laughed. "Give it up, kid," said Creevy. "It's a lost cause." It was understandable of course. It did rain in heaven, but it wasn't like on earth, cold, damp, and making your clothes all uncomfortable. Up here it was refreshing and everyone actually went out to be in the rain. Can you believe that?

"So, Stex, you've been to earth now. What did you think?" asked Rafe. Next to him sat Hash. It was great having Hash and Jacob here. I looked over at teenage Jacob and his Annie in animated discussion. I guess they had a few million years to catch up on.

Stex gazed into the air for a moment. His nose crinkled as he thought. "It's not what I thought it'd be like. I don't think I'll go back. To be honest, I don't know what you guys make all the fuss about really! It's nothing special."

Creevy thumped the table with three hands and rolled his eyes in frustration. "He's cured!" he announced.

"Tell us about another one of your missions, Stephanos," Josh called.

"Hash!" I corrected. I was determined to stick to the name I knew. I still couldn't believe this was my best mate who, all along, had been a secret agent.

Hash gave a sly smile. "Well," he started. "In my fifth millennium, I was sent on a very special sleeper mission. I slept thirty-seven years, all for one very important moment. I was sent to guard a stone."

"A stone?" queried Creevy, scratching his head with his fifth hand.

"Yep, a stone, believe it or not. I was in Northern Britain. There was this young nobleman who was crowned king. King Arthur he was called." He paused, keeping the suspense going.

"Yes, and?" prompted Rafe, excitedly. He loved the mission stories.

"Well," Hash continued, "there was a test which had to be passed by anyone who would rule all Britain. They had to pull the king's sword from the stone." Hash took a swig of floogier juice and wiped the froth from his lips, before he continued.

I stared out the porch of the floogier house, onto Main Street. It was a glorious day, and I was suddenly keen to do something.

"I gotta run, guys!" I said suddenly. "I'll catch you at the match." And I was off, despite protests from my friends. I ran down Main, through the fifth east portal, past the stadium and back under the golden arch. It was a short cut Josh had shown me. I passed the gates of Josh's mansion and glanced in at the skateboard park. I was keen to develop my kickflip a bit.

My new home was next door to Josh's. I loved it. It was just perfect. It was small, but it was mine. No more getting kicked out 'cause Missus Agnes needed a room. That reminded me of the task, I was keen to do. I rushed past the raised treetop garden. That was so nice of George, Stex and Creevy to add. (They had built my home... they'd done well.) It had walkways and tree houses. It was cool. In my living room was a bible. The Boss Man said I didn't need it anymore but I liked it. On my shelf was the first thirty volumes of the Heaven Chronicles. They were discs I could put in the halo-imager. They were so cool. I could see all the adventures and missions and history of heaven. I'd seen Hash on there.

The Boss Man was coming over later for a skate in Josh's park before the match.

The Boss Man had given me a portal. It was very cool of him. It was a small room on the top floor of my mansion. I walked through the door into the portal room. It was a very plain room, with no furniture or windows. A menu of portal options blinked into existence and then hung in mid-air, in front of me, like a hologram. I knew exactly where and when I wanted to be. I turned the dial and pressed the button... oh, the wonders of modern heaven technology. The blue and white colour on the walls began to fade and then to swirl. And then they reformed into deep browns and greens. A branch hung down and I smelt the damp smell of early morning foliage.

And I was there, with my friends. The quarter-moon was high above, watching down through the open roof of the Gathering Hut. An eerie silence surrounded a glum looking Charlie and Donny, both sitting there in silence, avoiding each other's stare. Charlie had his head in his hand, a desperately unhappy look on his face. As for me, I had to admit I was ecstatic, just to be here! They couldn't see me, of course. This was what they called a dormant portal. You could see but not take part, a bit like a 3D TV. A bit safer than my last portal adventure, I guess. But I could watch what was to be the final meeting of the Night Owls. I felt privileged. I whispered a "Thanks" to the Boss Man. My heart swelled, beating fast as I watched, waiting to see what they would do. I could begin to understand some of the excitement the Boss Man felt as he watched his world.

And so I slid down the log wall and sat quietly in the corner and watched.

There was a cracking of branches and the thud of feet outside the door, and then Buffy burst in. She was dressed in jeans, green sweater and heavy DM boots, which she always said were good for climbing. The frizzy red hair was tied back. It was a bad move. It always emphasised the front teeth, I thought, which stuck out like the gun barrel on a tank. She slouched down on a bean bag and climbed into her Cinderella duvet.

"Sorry I'm late. Mum was faffing about downstairs and just wouldn't go to bed."

Then she noticed the glum faces of the others and frowned. I had to admit, even the fire looked like a rather poor effort from Charlie tonight. He normally took pride in making it as fierce as possible, till it overheated the hut and looked like it was going to set the whole forest alight. No, tonight there was a blackness in the air and it was spreading through the hut like an infectious disease. Not even the memories, now ingrained in the very walls of the Gathering Hut, could brighten the mood.

Charlie tossed a stick hard at the fire. It bounced off. "This is pointless!"

No-one answered. Charlie got to his feet and started pacing around irritably. He swung his leg and booted the fire, angrily, as hard as he could.

"Watch it!" Buffy screamed as red-hot branches and cinders cascaded down on top of her. "What you doing, you great ape!" She quickly brushed glowing sparks off her duvet. "Idiot!"

Charlie glowered back at her. Donny hadn't moved, like he hadn't even registered the incident.

"Well, what's the point?" Charlie spat the words out angrily. "It's all rubbish isn't it. It's been good for a laugh and all that. But everything we've done... everything we've believed! None of it's actually true! That's the point, isn't it?"

Buffy shook her head, defiantly, but I could tell she was lost for words.

"It is rubbish!" Charlie insisted. "It has to be! Or why would Fish be gone?" Charlie glared across at Buffy. The question hung in the air. It was Charlie's challenge to the world. I wasn't sure I liked how this was shaping up. I'd never seen Charlie quite this angry and morose.

"Ay? Go on, tell me?" Charlie pushed. "See! You have no answer, do you? And that's because there's no other explanation!" Everything had to be clear cut to Charlie. It was black or it was white. If it wasn't true then it was all rubbish. It was just like his moods. He was either high as a kite or clinically depressed.

"But you found your star," Buffy replied hopefully, but rather lamely. "You must believe it."

Charlie weakened for a brief moment. His shoulders slumped. I could see the confusion in his eyes. He wanted, so much, to understand. It was so strange. Here I was, sitting three feet away and I knew all the answers... yet I was really another world away. I couldn't help them now.

"I won't believe it!" snarled Charlie, gaining momentum again after his temporary lapse. He snorted loudly. "Why do I want to believe in a God who kills people? I HATE YOU!!" he yelled up at the quarter-moon. "I - HATE - YOU!!"

It echoed across the empty forest, like a challenge to God. They all stared up, as if to see if God would answer the accusation, or perhaps strike Charlie down with a bolt of lightning. The moment passed.

"The chess match," Donny muttered suddenly, still sitting quietly, staring at the remains of the fire, his knees pulled up to his chest.

"What?" replied Charlie, angrily.

"Fish called it a giant chess match. What if there was a reason for it all?" Donny pondered. He had a perplexed look on his face, as if he was struggling on the very last answer in a crossword.

"Like what?" Charlie retorted.

"I dunno. But there could be... maybe something."

"Maybe we'll never know," said Buffy. "Would the Boss Man tell us? Why should he? We're just the little people, aren't we? Is he gonna explain to us all the things he does?"

"Jacob said we were in a battle," said Donny. "Maybe there's more to this. Maybe it's part of something much bigger?"

Charlie collapsed in a heap, exhausted. "I just miss him." He wrapped his arms round his legs and buried his head in them.

"So do I," whispered Buffy. I could see the tears rolling down her cheeks.

A sudden idea surged through me... I wanted them to see me, I wanted them to know I was there, so much!

"Do you think Fish is watching us?" asked Donny, suddenly perking up a bit.

"I hope so," said Buffy, glancing up, out of the open roof, at the stars.

"YES!" I shouted. "I CAN see you!" I was suddenly so excited.

Charlie and Buffy's heads both snapped around at the same instant.

I froze.

"What was that?" asked Buffy, her eyes narrowing.

"What?" Donny replied.

"Yeah, I felt something too," whispered Charlie. "It was like..." His eyes scanned the airwaves, suddenly alert and alive, as if trying to search something out, which was just out of his reach. He paused, still as a statue, listening intently, then shook his head. "No, nothing."

And that was it... it was just a moment when I almost touched them from my place, a billion light years away, to their place, right there in the treetops. It felt good. And then it was gone again, just like a wisp of smoke from the fire, lost in the breeze.

"Come on guys," I whispered to them, a bit out of desperation. "You can do this. Help them, Lord, please." They just couldn't give up on it all. Not now, not after everything that had happened.

"So what's next?" asked Buffy. They all stared down, despondently at the dead fire. "I say we either pack it all in now, or..." she paused, "we make a decision, right now, that we're gonna believe it, and stick with it. You remember your vision, Charlie? Remember the Zulus, the letters from Africa, the bank raid. It wasn't just a coincidence. Something weird but important has been going on here. And whatever we decide," she stared around at the others, "we all do it together. We owe that much to Fish."

They all nodded.

"Well," Charlie sighed, "you're right. My star does exist. It definitely all happened."

"Which means Fish is up there," said Buffy.

"And Jacob," added Donny.

"And Jacob," Buffy repeated. "And we'll see them again. So the only question is, do we want to? I do. Ronnie's up there too."

There was a long pause.

"What's he like, Charlie?" Donny asked. "The Boss Man. I never got to see him."

Charlie thought about it for a moment, remembering his adventure spinning in space. "He's cool. He made me feel important. And, you know, everyone thinks he's trying to catch you out or something, but he's not... it's like... he's on your side."

"I'm in," said Donny, making his decision. They both stared at Charlie.

"You said you hated him," Donny challenged.

"It's just... Aghh, how do... Why did he take Fish?"

"To a better place," said Buffy.

"Do you really believe that?" snapped Charlie.

"Absolutely! I saw it, remember?"

They all nodded. There was a long silence.

"It doesn't seem the same up here without Fish. He was always here."

"I don't think we should come up here again without him," Buffy announced. "I say we make a new pact."

"What sort of pact?" asked Donny, uncomfortably.

Buffy went on. "Hands in!" They both slapped a hand down on top of Buffy's in the centre of the hut. "We agree, solemnly, on pain of death..." All eyes were on Buffy now. She was giving them one of her "You better do this or I'll duff you up" looks. What were they going to do, I wondered? The sun was just beginning to peep over the top of the forest canopy. A faint orange glow began to flood into the Gathering Hut again, replacing the embers of the fire which Charlie had kicked into oblivion.

"...that we're gonna live our lives for that place," she pointed up out of the open roof, "up there, not for down here. When I went there, there was something about it... I can't describe it. But I wanna be there." Her mind drifted back to her whirlwind tour. "And, you know, if our task here is to be part of some giant cosmic chess match, then let's do it in style. For me, I wanna be a part of whatever the Boss Man's got planned. I think he has a purpose for me... something special. There's a reason why I'm here. Think how exciting it would be! It'd be like living Fish's box of chocolates every day of our lives. Think about it—"

"What does that actually mean though?" asked Donny. "What do we actually have to do?"

"Don't be a dunce, Donny! It means that whatever decisions we make in our lives from right now, this moment on, we always ask ourselves, what would the Boss Man do? We live heaven, down here, right now. We'll be part of something huge and exciting. And this is a pact for life! It's all or nothing. So, what do you say?" She looked from Donny to Charlie.

"I say we seal the pact," Charlie added.

"How?" asked Donny, a very worried look on his face. Whenever Charlie mentioned weird ideas like this it generally ended up being very unpleasant.

"Well, we are the Night Owls. This is the Night Owl Pact, right? You know what owls do?"

Donny and Buffy stared blankly, Donny's eyebrows getting closer and closer together in concern. "Er, no?" he almost whispered.

"They eat worms!" Charlie announced. The others looked at each other, confused.

"What, you want us to eat worms?!" Donny stammered with a nervous laugh. "You're kidding, right?"

"No!" said Buffy with a grin. "This is absolutely perfect. To seal such an important pact, it has to be something really difficult."

"And anyone who ever dares to break the pact, will be buried alive and their flesh will be slowly peeled off and it'll be food for worms, forever," said Charlie.

"What!?" Donny objected. "This is stupid. I'm not—"

"Don't be a wuss, Donny!" snapped Buffy. "Three worms please, Charlie."

At this point I was very glad I wasn't actually in the room with them.

"And," added Buffy. "I say we make this our last meeting of the Night Owls... BUT, we vow to return here in twenty years, to the day, and we see if we have kept the Pact and we see what the Boss Man has done in our lives."

"What would you wanna do with your life, Buf?" Charlie asked.

Buffy thought for a moment. "Build things. Maybe, for people who need them more than we do."

"Tree villages in Africa!" said Donny.

"What about you?"

Charlie shook his head. "No idea. But it's nice to think there's something out there for me."

Then he dodged out of the hut and returned a few moments later with the worms. He placed them in a polystyrene chip tray, left over from one of the many all night fish and chip shop runs.

"OK," said Buffy.

"Er. Do we actually have to, er, you know?" Donny's voice trailed off.

Buffy leaned down and picked up the first worm. She held it up so it dangled above her mouth. It was revolting! It must have been a full ten inches long. Donny's eyes went wide. He looked like he was gonna keel over just watching. Buffy had a look of stern determination on her face as she bit it clean in half.

No way! That was truly disgusting! I was grinding my fist into the floor now without realising it. It made me squirm.

Charlie ate his with no fuss or hesitation. Then it was Donny' turn. A sudden look of comprehension came onto his face as he realised his mistake. He had let it go too far. Buffy wasn't gonna let him out alive now, till he'd completed the pact. His face had turned a very pale green colour. He stared down at the last worm, then glanced at the door. I thought for a second he might make a run for it. The thought was obviously going through his mind.

I couldn't help smiling. This was a classic. This was better than the Simpsons!

"Are we gonna have to force feed you or what?" snapped Buffy, hands on hips and front teeth taking aim to fire.

Then I had an idea. Could they hear me? Maybe I could help them.

I walked round and stood right beside Donny. I leaned in towards his ear.

"Go on, Donny. You can do it," I whispered. I noticed a tuft of hair by the side of his ear move with the force of my breath. Strange. "Go on," I urged.

Donny slowly picked up the worm. It wriggled across his palm as he frowned at it.

"I can't do—"

Buffy raised her eyebrows. It was enough to cut him off mid-sentence.

"You can," I whispered. He closed his eyes, picked up the worm and took a bite.

"Well done!" squealed Buffy. "No going back." Charlie slapped him on the back. It wasn't the best thing to do in the circumstances... Donny puked all over the floor.

Let's get out of here!" said Charlie as they escaped the Gathering Hut. "How about our last ever game of treetop tag?"

"Cool!" Buffy thumped him in the chest and leaped down onto the spy deck. "You're it!"

I'd seen enough. I backed out of the portal room. And I knew they'd be OK. Just maybe this would make all the difference in the world to them.

As I backed away, the wooden walls of the Gathering Hut dimmed and blurred. Blank blue and white re-emerged onto the walls of the portal room, and I turned and stepped out, back into my house. I was surprised to see the Boss Man standing there, the normal broad grin spread across his face. He had an infectious smile.

"You OK?" he asked.

I nodded, but immediately a question bubbled to the surface.

"Ask away!" said the Boss Man. I was beginning to get used to the fact that he always knew what was going through your mind before you asked it.

"What was that all about, Lord?" I asked. "You know…" I opened my arms wide trying to capture the size of my question and put it into some words (Not that the Boss Man needed the words. He knew what I was trying to say.) "…everything… the chocolates, the dreams, alien space ships, the car crash… Why?" The question sort of hung for a few seconds. The Boss Man made no reply. "I spent eleven years down there. What was the point? What was my reason for being there? Was it to do with helping Missus Agnes?... or was it for them." I looked back at the portal room where my friends had been. "Or what? I just wanna know it achieved something."

The Boss Man shrugged at me. "Missus Agnes, your friends… maybe. Or perhaps there was something much bigger too. Maybe there are things you did which will cause ripples right across the world. What a thought ay, Monty! You just don't know."

"Really?" I blurted. It sounded a bit farfetched.

"Well, maybe, or maybe not. That will all depend on the thousands of millions of thoughts and decisions and outcomes which take place every second in earth time. It's a complex world out there, Monty. The giant chess match."

We stared at each other for a few moments. I shook my head. It was all far too complicated to get my brain round.

"Or maybe it was all just for you, Monty, to give you a glimpse of heaven. Just 'cause I like you a lot." He smiled. "Or think about this… perhaps your reason for living is still to come. Up here there is still an eternity for you to live."

"But if you ask my opinion," the Boss Man went on, "I think you made a big difference. I think it's time we shut that portal now. What do you think?"

"Will they be OK?" I asked.

"I'll watch over them for you. You'll be seeing them again soon."

I nodded. "Yeah. Let's shut it down."

Chapter 32
The Oval Office…

The Oval Office in the White House was… well, sort of, oval. It was the most important room in the White House, which was, itself, the home of the most important man in the world. The President was doing his early morning briefings. All his key advisors would give him an update on events going on around the world… the war in the Middle East, the effect of sanctions on Iran, the latest figures from the US economy. The President leaned back in his rather comfortable black leather, reclining, desk chair. He considered it to be the driving seat of the world. After all he had achieved a great deal from this very chair... he was a king. What he said went. He was, he thought to himself, with a sigh of satisfaction, BIGGER THAN GOD!

He pulled himself out of his trance and listened further to the man taking him through yet another list of statistics. Yes, he knew that his country, the great US of A was running out of money and had debts coming out of its ears. But he had a plan, he smiled to himself.

"Thanks, Tim," he said as the man left.

The President was a tall man, slicked back slightly greying hair and strong chin. He looked good on TV and he spoke strong words to the nation… to the world. Now he had to back it up with actions. But he had a plan… a plan that would see the cash rolling back into America and that meant a lot of happy Americans and an easy life for him. And what was his plan? Project Ven Tanker, as they called it.

His personal assistant entered the room. She was slim, tall and very professional and efficient. "The CIA director's ready for you, Mister President. To discuss Project Ven Tanker, the Venezuela situation."

"Thanks Gina, send him in." She paused.

"Before I do, sir, I need to give you an update. Something important in your mail this morning, sir."

"Go on. Make it quick, Gina."

She placed a letter on the desk in front of him. He scanned it.

"So what? I get a hundred thousand of these a day, Gina."

"But he knows the Venezuela plan, sir. That was supposed to be top secret."

"So? It's just a lucky guess," the President glanced back at the letter and read the name. "Monty Pilchard. He's a nobody. No-one would ever listen to him anyway. What do we know about him?"

"He's eleven. Lives in England."

"Oh, for goodness sake, Gina. He's a kid! I really couldn't care less what he writes! He's a nobody!!"

"Not anymore," the PA went on. "Apparently he is headline news in England. He was just killed in a freak car accident, yesterday."

"So were a hundred other kids, so the stats say. So what? I really don't care. Get Mike in here. Take this rubbish away."

"There's more. He wrote a diary. His dad says he's gonna sell it to the papers. Why would his Dad want to do that, unless there's something damaging in there? It could have a copy of this letter in it."

The President huffed. "So?" He raised his eyebrows in an annoyed gesture.

"His father is a national hero. He received the George Cross from the Queen last week."

There was a long pause. The President began to frown for the first time. Gina went on. "The Pilchard family is famous. National hero plus son killed in car accident." She said it very slowly so it'd sink in. "It's all over the papers. They have the public sympathy vote. Now add in this letter and the father publishing the diary. I don't know how he knew but if this hits the press, it will hit the press hard. We'll be crucified. We'll be dead and buried and out of this office quicker than you can say Jack Robinson."

The President glanced back at the Pilchard letter. Then back up at his PA. Then back at the letter. "Blast it!" he shouted. "How did the kid know?" He thumped the desk hard with his fist. Hmmmm... he fumed. Ok, he wasn't quite bigger than God yet... but he was getting there.

"OK, thanks Gina. Send Mike in."

The CIA Director, Mike Mayer, entered the office and the President's PA left. The President didn't rise or shake hands. "What have you got for me, Mike?"

"Stage one of the Venezuelan take over. We're ready to roll on it, sir. The oil fields will be our within the month. I just need the go ahead from you."

The President looked down once more at the Pilchard letter. How did this sort of thing manage to hit the English press?

"We cancel it, Mike,"

"What? But—"

"Project Ven Tanker is cancelled."

Chapter 33

The First Step...

Downstairs
Galaxy ref: P5763EARTH
Grid: UK789~TTui865

When Donny arrived at church on Sunday morning he felt downhearted. He'd made the pact... in fact, he could still taste the worm, he grimaced in disgust. He still felt a wave of nausea every time he thought about it. But now he had to take his first step to live up to the pact he had made.

He found Rupert in the upstairs corridor, pining up posters of Argentina.

Donny stuffed his hands as far down in his pockets as he could.

"I'm not coming anymore," he said awkwardly. There, he'd said it. He turned to leave. He wanted to get out of the church as quickly as he could. "I need to be goin—"

"Is it because of Monty?"

Donny didn't want to have this discussion. Everyone had been sad to hear about Fish.

"No," Donny replied. "Not exactly. It's just made me think about things a bit more and... well... I just don't think this," he gestured to the church around him, "is what it's all about. There's more to God than this." And that was the crux of it. This place sucked! He had come here since he was four and he'd never met God here, not like he'd done in the treetops. This was just a bunch of guys meeting up to compare good deeds and argue about what colour to paint the church hall. There was so much more. He knew there was. He'd seen it.

He waited uncomfortably for Rupert to object. He just wanted to get the conversation over and get out of here.

But to his surprise Rupert said, "You're right."

"Sorry?" Donny blurted looking up.

"You're right," Rupert repeated. "So don't leave. Do something about it. Change it!"

"Change it? I can't change it!" Donny shot back. "I'm twelve! I'm not allowed to do anything useful round here."

"Have you tried?"

No, thought Donny, he hadn't tried had he. As he was walking down the church steps a thought struck him. What if he was the only one who could change it? What if this was the task God had given him?

Donny's mouth twitched in annoyance. Rupert could be so irritating sometimes.

Sunday evening was the perfect opportunity for Charlie. With no more visits to the treetops planned he settled down on his balcony and put his eye to the telescope lens. He swept the sky, past Orion. He glanced down at the star chart, noting the grid reference of the new star. His eye went back to the lens. He adjusted it millimetre by millimetre. There it was… Centurion eighty-eight. His very own star. How could it be? It was on the outer-rim of the known universe and so what he was seeing now was actually distant past history, billions of years gone. What was it the Boss Man had said… "time's, rather rubbery really," or something like that. So was he actually seeing the Centurion galaxy after he'd worked on it… after he'd created it?

"No way," he muttered to himself. It was too much to think about. It made his brain ache. He stared up at the stars, flickering in the night sky, and let his mind wander for a moment. It all seemed so still and quiet up there, yet he knew different. What would it be like zipping around in space? All that room to fly around. Being able to go anywhere, see everything.

There was some talking in the road far below him. He swivelled the telescope round and adjusted the focus. The blurry mass came into focus. It was his older brother and Charlene. They were larking around and kissing on the corner of the street. Ughh, that was gross. Charlie focused back in on his star and ignored the loud footsteps of his brother, in the otherwise silent evening, as he ran up to the house.

So what was he, Charlie, gonna do with his life? It wasn't something he'd ever thought about much, but then after their last treetop meeting the question had stuck in his mind, like a splinter that gets lodged in your thumb and you can't shift it, but it continues to give you a dull ache. He could always start off on Centurion eighty-eight now. Why not? What would stop him? He could study science and—

His thoughts were interrupted when his bedroom door burst open.

"Charlie, guess what!!" his brother stammered nervously but excitedly at the door. Charlie looked round.

"Thought you could do with some good news, what with Monty and all." He couldn't get the grin off his face. What was he up to, thought Charlie?

"I know you'll be pleased. Me and Charlene. We're engaged. We're getting married!"

"What?!" Charlie blurted. "Charlene??"

"Yeah. You'll have to be my best man!"

Oh no, Charlie groaned.

Agnes was all alone, sweat dripping off her brow. She sat quietly on the spy deck, watching as the sun rose over the canopy of trees. It reminded her of heaven. She wondered just for a moment if Fish was also watching a sunrise, up there in heaven. She had been working hard all night. She had decided to complete the job. It was hard, long and painstakingly slow, but she was going to complete the treetops just as her and Ronnie had designed it. And she was going to do it all on her own. Each morning she would watch the sunrise and remember. And that way she would never forget… she would never take her eyes off heaven. Then she would wait and see what would happen. And one day, in many years time, they would all meet up here again. It was a good plan she thought.

Chapter 34
The Headlines...

The Heaven Diary Uncovered

The Sun, 8 August 2007,

Millions all over the world are showing unprecedented interest in the Heaven Diary, the unbelievable last weeks of the young boy, Montgomery Pilchard, recorded in his own diary before his tragic death, earlier this year.

About his visions he wrote: *"You know, the heaven I visited is like a mustard seed. To many people it seems small and they miss it, but it is out there, and it is huge. All you have to do is look."*

The boy's father, Ronald Pilchard, who has published the Diary, himself a well known celebrity after being awarded the George Cross earlier this year, has allowed the Sun exclusive rights to publish extracts from the diary.

Ronald Pilchard was today quoted as saying, "I'M RICH!"

Pilchard Fever hits America!

USA Today, August 29, 2007

US President Pays His Respects to Pilchard Boy

USA Today, September 23, 2007

The US President today paid his respects to Montgomery Pilchard, as an outstanding example of how citizens of today's world should be, and, he added, "a very special boy."

US President under Fire

The Sunday Mirror, 11 January, 2008

The US President is coming under greater pressure to explain his part in the Venezuela crisis, after fresh evidence was released to Congress yesterday regarding a formal CIA project, Project Ven Tanker. The CIA Director confirmed this project, planning the takeover of oil fields in Venezuela, was fully endorsed by the White House. It is believed this could be the downfall of the President.

And of course this has caused fresh speculation about the Heaven Diaries, published last year, as more facts revealed in the diaries have been proved true.

UFO Sighting!! Little Green Man Spotted by Local Farmer

The Sunday Sport, 23 April, 2008

Claims of a UFO sighting over the village of Little Hamlet! Farmer, Brian Savage claims to have seen the craft descend onto his mustard field in the early hours of Saturday morning. "I was out checkin' the tractors, like," said Savage, explaining the incident, "when the thing just came out a nowhere and landed right on top of me bloomin' mustard crop. Big spongy, rubbery silver thing, it was. Then, would you credit it, this green thing comes out, all sorts of hands and heads, he 'ad. And some kid… normal kid, like… follows 'im out. Then he opens his mouth and says 'Excuse me. Which way's Charlie's house?'"

Savage claims the craft left crop circles all over the mustard seed. Experts have interviewed Mister Savage, and committed him to a very nice hospital, white padded cells etc.

Pilchard Fortune!

Daily Mail, 21 October, 2009

Ronald Pilchard, Father of the Heaven Diary boy, was today announced in the top fifty richest people in Britain, valued at an estimated seventy five million pounds. He is currently reclining in his private yacht in Jamaica. He declined to comment.

Heaven's Lottery Winner!

Daily Express, 29 December, 2014

The final National Lottery winner of 2014 is 18 year old Charlie Peaterson, one of the famous children from the Heaven Diary seven years ago. In a strange quirk of fate, for the children who pledged to live their lives for heaven, maybe heaven has given something back! Peaterson said yesterday that he was donating the whole £12.8 million to cancer research.

Dame Agnes Brithwhistle, is awarded the Nobel Prize

The Daily Telegraph, 17 June 2034,

Dame Agnes Brithwhistle is awarded the Nobel Prize for her building works projects which are bringing hope and much needed funds to Africa. After speaking today at the United Nations summit, Dame Agnes, known for her tough talking, called on all countries to make a contribution to the effort. All the major G8 countries have committed to wiping third world debts and working towards the revival of the third world countries. This is an unprecedented achievement by Dame Agnes.

New Cure for Cancer Discovered

Financial Times, 5 May 2043

Sir Charles Peaterson, the renowned scientist, reputed for his proofs of Hawkins's Black hole theories, today announced a breakthrough in the fight against cancer. The discovery was made in the hospital research centre founded and funded by Sir Charles.

Sir Charles has stated that the care will be supplied free of charge to all patients, a move widely criticised by the drugs companies. Sir Charles was quoted as saying, "It's about taking care of people, that's all. Money doesn't come into it. I'll get my reward in another place, at another time."

Some years back Sir Charles was linked to the Heavenly Diary phenomenon.

Secret Meetings UNCOVERED!!

Private Eye, 15 June 2047

It has been discovered that celebrities are descending on Vitenbury Forest for secret meetings. Our reporter photographed Sir Charles Peaterson, Dame Agnes Brithwhistle, and Bishop of Kensington, The Right Rev Donald Osmond, all arriving in low profile, unmarked vehicles. He followed them into the forest but all three of them mysteriously disappeared from sight. When questioned, all three declined to comment. Private Eye is now investigating to see if this is part of some secret society or cult. Watch this space!

New Church Boss Appointed

The Daily Mirror, 23 April 2052,

The General Synod has made a surprise appointment of the Right Rev Donald Osmond as the new Arch Bishop of Canterbury, the most important post in the Church of England. The Daily Mirror religious correspondent, Edmond Vine, commented on the appointment as likely to lead to radical change in the church.

When questioned about the changes Arch Bishop Osmond said, "Yes, it has to change! It's about having a church which listens to God and that helps people. A little of God's Kingdom at the centre of every community. We've lost that, but I had a friend once who showed me that this is what life is all about."

"You know, the Kingdom of God is like a mustard seed. To many people it seems small and they miss it, but it is out there, and it is huge. All you have to do is look."

This is a quote from the once famous Heaven Dairy published in 2007. It is alleged that Right Rev Osmond was one of those children involved in the Heaven Diary episode. He refused to comment.

The end of an Era... Sir Charles Peaterson dies at age 94

The Guardian, 14 December 2085,

Sir Charles Peaterson, the world famous cosmologist and founder of the Xzenedonia cure for cancer, which has saved billions of lives, died today at age ninety-four.

His final words before he died were: "Dying? Course I'm not frightened of dying! It is life's biggest adventure. I'm looking forward to working on Centurion eighty eight. But most of all I'm looking forward to meeting up with my old friend, Monty, and sharing a bottle of stout together."

THE END

A note from the Author

My aim in this book has not been to try and give a picture of what heaven is really like... it will most definitely be very different to what I have written here... neither is it to put words into God's mouth which he never said. It is simply to spark the imagination a bit, to think about what heaven might really be like. It is so important to do this. You see, if all you think on is life down here, then you will, inevitably, be sidetracked on the mundane things in life, unhappy, depressed and, it must be said, tempted to be very disappointed in God. But if you look at heaven, then you are looking at the place which will one day be your home for eternity... that is exciting. When an athlete runs in the Olympics, they don't focus on the starting blocks, they focus on the finishing tape, the podium, the gold medal being around their neck... this spurs them on to reach that place.

I have really enjoyed writing this book, and I have learnt a great deal. Heaven is humungous! When you get there, you are going to find it is so much bigger than you ever imagined, and so much more interesting. Has it really sunk in yet? This is a real place with real people we are going to meet, real places to go and things to do. We are really going to meet and sit and chat with God.

Awesome!

Printed in the United Kingdom
by Lightning Source UK Ltd.
123907UK00001B/188/A

9 781847 999573